# RIDING NERDY

We Are Legion Book 1

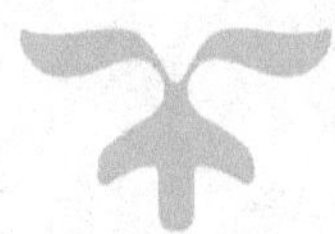

*To my Husband*

*I sleep to dream of you, my jaded
Morpheus, King undying. I lay before
you stripped bare – girl bone reduced to
ashes and fairy dust. Like dandelion
seeds, I am set free by the restless
whispers of that nightmare's child,
"Undying, undying, undone."*

*He's more myself than I am.*

*Whatever our souls are made of,*

*His and mine are the same.*

*— Emily Bronte, Wuthering Heights*

# Prologue

*Dusty for Short*

Like most nightmares, this one was born in the dark. Swaddled in shadows, it suckled moonlight as if it were mother's milk. Its cries were a raven's song, mocking and lonely, and its laughter was all revving motors and secrets tucked away and kept still.

Adele had never met a nightmare she couldn't wake from.

Until now.

Until loose gravel digs into the tender soles of her bare feet, and breathing is a punishment instead of a right. As she limps down the street, ears ringing, she curses her own foolishness. She should have taken the time to grab a pair of shoes on her way out the door, but she knew if she had, she'd be too late. For what, she doesn't know. Wasn't it the way of nightmares to sow fear beneath the skin? To whisper chaos in the wind? She doesn't know where the fear driving her comes from, but she recognizes the sour taste of it. Knows its hum in her bones.

A vibration that can shatter glass.

Adele pauses to catch her breath; disgusted at her own weakness. Looking back over her shoulder, she can still see her gran's curtains dancing in the breeze. When she closes her eyes, it sounds like the wings of some great beast. A nightmare's child set loose. The sound is what woke her up in the first place. As soon as she wandered into the living room, she knew what must have happened. Her sister liked to sleep-walk, and at first, Adele was sure she would find her curled up on the couch, the same as always. Instead, the door to the backyard was open; emptying the house of warmth and the smell of palo santo and Florida

Water—scents of her childhood for as long as she can remember. She knew then the weekly cleansing her gran performed hadn't worked. If it had, Désirée would still be safe in bed where she belonged.

Adele should stay and get help. She knows this. But something calls to her, a harried cry that tugs her from safety and warmth. Instinct takes over, and she's pulled from the house by a distant shriek so familiar she knows it in her blood and in her bones. No time for shoes or even a coat. No time to dash back through the house and wake Gran. No time to call the police or her father.

It's the screaming that drives her. Denying rest or hesitation, spurring her on for an entire mile, despite her aching, shaking legs, and labored breaths. It is still ringing in her head when she realizes it is now accompanied by something else.

Up ahead, the raucous sounds of laughter and rock music spill out onto the wet pavement. Once upon a time, people danced and prayed for rain during seasons of drought. Ever since they rolled into town several days ago, all the Lost Legion has done is drink. Hell, maybe an endless stream of Corona and tequila shots is a biker's idea of a rain dance because the storm that strolled through the French Quarter last night was as fierce as any Adele has ever seen.

Bottles clinking and the sharp crack of pool sticks finding their target has long since replaced the call of crickets and cicadas. She finds an odd sort of comfort in their beat. Her gran-père never thought the hole in the wall he saved up for would one day turn into a dive bar, but, unlike the women in the family, he'd never been blessed with the sight. The trailer she calls home was only a mile or so from the backdoor of the bar, so her father never has to travel far during the rare occasions he comes into town. In fact, Adele spots him as she darts past the line of motorcycles out front. Disheveled and groggy, he is slumped outside of the building. His chin rests on his chest, and his head lolls from side to side.

Frantic, Adele crouches in front of him. "Rat?" she hisses, slapping his stubbled cheek and trying to tamp down the frustration rising in her breast. "*Dad*, wake up. Désirée's missing." She keeps her voice low, reluctant to draw attention to herself. She's still in her pajamas, and the last thing she wants is for one of the members of the Legion to stumble across her in the middle of the night.

She shakes his shoulder once more, growling in frustration when she realizes how deeply the vodka holds him. He is more drink than man now. She tips him over, and he spills across the ground like a mistake given flesh. He groans, and Adele works his motorcycle jacket off. It stinks of beer and cigarette smoke, stale sweat, and his cheap cologne. Which is to say, it smells both familiar and beloved. Inside the inner pocket are the keys to his bike, and she slips her arms through the sleeves before straddling the mighty beast her father dubbed Pegasus so long ago.

She was five the first time he took her for a ride. She burned her ankle because she wasn't sure where to put her legs. The scar faded somewhat, but you can still see it if you know where to look. Some kids grow up knowing how to swim or ride a horse. Adele was conceived on the back of a Harley. Scar or no scar, the angry growl of the motor coming to eager life left its mark in her blood as well on her flesh.

She peels out of the parking lot, grateful for her father's jacket as the wind whips past. Even encased in leather, icy tendrils of air burrow beneath her clothes and claw at her skin. Adele grits her teeth. Désirée couldn't have gotten far. She'll do a lap, or two, around the block and be back well before her Rat wakes from his stupor.

Adele races through town, eyes scanning one familiar street after another. She tries to ignore the screaming in her mind but finds herself chasing after it. She can't shake the suspicion that if she doesn't follow the ephemeral call, she'll never see Désirée again.

When Adele was seven, her gran-père called for her. She followed his voice only to find him dead in his favorite recliner. Gran says Adele saw the truth of this world and the next. That, for her, it whispered in a way most were deaf to. According to Gran, Adele was blessed by the ancestors and the Lwa alike. But to be beloved of Gods was a rabid thing. A life Adele wanted no part of. Still, she's learned not to ignore her gifts when they have something to tell her. More importantly, she's learned to ignore men like her father, who whisper behind Gran's back. Voodoo, hoodoo, that old Obeah woman living off Main. The crone, the hag, the foul-mouthed priestess with her wrinkled skin dipped in obsidian.

Her gran has a reputation in Louisiana, and Adele wanted nothing more than to escape from beneath the shadow of it. A dream that seems far-fetched some days, especially now when she's chasing down the specter of her sister's voice, on a bike too big for her, in a jacket that will never fit quite right.

*"There."*

A command. Adele jerks the bike to the right. Too fast. Pegasus wobbles, he bucks, and then she falls. The bike skids across the blacktop, trapping her left leg and dragging her a dozen feet before slamming into the trunk of an old oak tree. The world goes dark, and when she comes round again, a light rain trails cold fingers down the planes of her face. The screaming has stopped. She is lying beneath a flickering streetlamp, and the once bustling city is finally still, almost as if it knows what she always has.

That something dark and ravenous is out hunting.

Adele drags herself to her feet, trying not to cry out when pain ricochets down the length of her leg. She glances around, realizing she's driven to the edge of town. The middle school sits less than a block away; a hunched, ornery figure in the dark. It's summer break, but the neighborhood kids like to come and play ball, when the weather allows it. Some kids got hurt a few months back, jumping the fence to explore the swamps beyond, but there is little the police can do to stop them.

She stands frozen, battling the little voice inside urging her to put one foot in front of the other. The voice who *knows* with absolute certainty that she will find Désirée here, in the dark and the damp just beyond the tree line. She won't go any further, she promises herself. She will shy away from where horizon meets blacktop with no waypoint in between, and find her sister back where familiar roads lead the way home.

But Adele doesn't leave. She can't. Because Désirée is waiting for her and she didn't come this far on her own.

"Adele!"

Adele gasps, partially in shock but mostly in relief. Then, icy terror floods her bloodstream. Muscles and tendons fight against instinct and desire. Crying out with the urge to move and stay still. To hide. She needs to save her sister—she's the only one who can now—but fear keeps her small and still. This is the part of the story where shame comes, so fast and hard that tears fill her eyes. The hesitation might have lasted only a breath. But even one breath, as it turns out, is too long.

This time when Désirée screams, there is nothing supernatural about it. Nothing of spirit in the shrill, animal sound she makes. Her terror is real and cuts like a knife. Sobbing, Adele stumbles off the street and into the woods, heart bleeding. Her leg is a bright spot of pain as she crashes through the underbrush, but she bites her lip against the hurt. Here, and now, she is not Adele. Instead, she is Frankenstein's monster, unraveling with every agonizing step. Drenched in sweat and panting, she glances around for any sign of where the cries are coming from.

"*Please,*" she begs her gift, as if it is a God she's long ignored, "*if there's any magic in me at all, please.*"

The ground sways beneath her feet, and Adele grips the trunk of a nearby sapling for balance. This is the reason kids aren't allowed in these woods, and this is the reason they keep coming back anyway. Here, away from prying eyes, the earth liked to dance. It's the water that waits beneath. They are too far inland for the bayou to claim the land, but still she creeps. The result is an expanse of trees writhing like something dark and wild; something howling and hungry.

Just like Adele.

As the trees sway, she catches a glimpse of something through the foliage.

*A hole?*

*No.*

"A grave." Her voice is tight with horror. Adele races forward as Désirée's cries grow louder with every second that passes. Her sister is pleading, begging for her life. Adele can't see who it is she speaks to and is half convinced Désirée is beseeching the woods themselves- begging for mercy from the dirt and worms. She is tempted to do the same.

*The world – this place – is starving. Ravenous. Aching for something to wrap its teeth around.*

That night, it finds what it's looking for in Désirée. When the police ask her later, Adele will tell them the Devil fed Desi to it. That even as she pulled her sister from the grave he dug, he wrapped strong hands around her throat and squeezed so hard she forgot what screaming was. She'll tell them how he shoved her under with Désirée, beneath the rotting leaves and among the maze of roots clinging to the shallow soil. And how, in death and dying, she and her twin were back in the womb together. Deep, deep, deeper to the water lying in wait. The water that made the world dance. She thinks about staying there with her sister, about making their grave their home.

Désirée had been her whole world since Adele took her first breath. She does not know what it was to live without her, to fill her lungs with air not first tasted by her other half. But she will learn. And in a few months, she'll tell a jury about how it feels to claw her way back up from her mother, brown and waiting. About that first breath in a New World. About the motorcycle revving to life in the distance and the insignia of her father's gang emblazoned on the back of an all too familiar leather jacket and shining, in stark relief, beneath the moonlight.

They will not listen. Instead, they will see the blood on her father's jacket and the tread of his bike in the dirt. They will hear how he left the bar and how no one noticed him afterward but Adele. Poor, traumatized Adele. A girl who swore that there was a monster in the woods, dripping fangs and covered in thick fur, red as blood and bearing death in a weighted, feral, grin. The jury will know her father has a history of violence. An anger management problem. A penchant for chaos. And they will take his name, rechristen him Murderer. Child-killer.

But before all of that—before the trial that will soon rock the nation, before the police drag Rat away, there are more visceral things she must concern herself with. Things she will *not* tell the jury. They don't need to know how death grips you hard and lingers close once he's tasted you. How having the breath snatched from your lungs will make you more rage than girl.

*The world doesn't care about things like that.*

Hours later, when the paramedic wraps a blanket around her shoulders and shines a light in her eyes, the woman doesn't ask her about the state of her soul. Oh no. Instead, she asks for her name. Adele's eyes will remain locked on her sister's corpse as they drag her from the marsh.

The paramedic does not make her turn away.

In that bated breath, Death will hug her close and promise that he will come for her next—that he will come for her, always. And it is the girl of rage who answers: "Adele Danielle Burdot." Her voice is hoarse and broken around the edges. It hurts to speak, so she will choose her words with care. "Dusty, for short."

# Chapter One

*The Joy and the Laughter*

This city never slept.

Never slept.

Never slept.

This city never slept, and so dreams came to die there.

It's why Edward loved the place.

He was too full of nightmares to hold much stock in dreams. His mind was a graveyard that discriminated between neither. Briarcliff was a pallbearer of a city. A gentrified version of Gotham, except there were no heroes here. As a kid, Edward learned salvation wasn't found but bought, and he was always low on funds.

On the Upper East Side, in a place of honor right across from city hall, on a plot of grass too green to be real, rested Briarcliff United. The bank had been in operation for over 100 years and was an architectural marvel. Sweeping stone steps lead to a triple set of glass doors with the bank's name embossed in white on each. The domed ceiling boasted not one, but three chandeliers on the inside, while outside, scowling stone gargoyles surveyed all who passed by. Skyscrapers destroyed the monotony of the skyline; scouring for signs of threat and finding none. The windows of the buildings across the street shone like diamonds in the sun. Blinding, but he could just make out...yes. There. A sniper's rifle; scope trained and steady. Or was it three stories up and two over? He couldn't place it, couldn't decide where the shot would be coming from because any one of those rectangular pieces of glass could mean a quick death.

The wind whipped up; a churning cyclone, blowing dust and the scent of roasted lamb from a nearby food truck into his face. Tucked in an alcove against the building, was a figure swaddled in a thick, gray blanket. A shock of curly red hair was the only thing visible, and Edward wondered how long she'd been lying there. His jaw tightened as he strode past, hands shoved deep into his brown overcoat. This was the fourth homeless person he'd seen in his mad dash across the city. Patrol officers would be by soon to pick her up. It was parade day, after all, and the mayor didn't like reminders of whom his many policies were failing. Edward fought the urge to stop, to help, but the cold weight of his watch against his wrist urged him through the doors and out of the wind.

No time. No time. No time.

As always, the opulence inside was a shock to the system after the dreary stone and aging red brick the rest of the city was known for: crystal finishes and gold inlay, marble floors, and soaring ceilings. More gargoyles had been stationed near the curved glass skylight, and a glass cleaner, strapped to a metal piece of scaffolding, hung outside, shining the surface of it until it gleamed. Inside, the air-conditioned air smelled of Lysol and whatever it was they used to mop the floors. Though early, the bank was still packed with people eager to get ahead of the morning rush. There was already a line in front of his usual teller, and he bounced on his heels. Should he go to someone new? Edward discarded the idea as soon as it occurred to him.

No.

Absolutely not.

Him? Talk to someone new? Pure lunacy.

*Cut in line,* came an insidious whisper. *It's the only way.* Edward's jaw tightened, it wasn't something he was keen on, but desperate times; desperate measures. Straightening his shoulders, he strode across the room, his gaze locked on the teller – his teller – Samantha. She was counting out some cash for an older gentleman in a purple tracksuit, but must have sensed him because she glanced up and met his eyes.

Samantha grimaced before turning to Purple Tracksuit with a smile.

"Will that be all, Sir?"

Edward bumped Tracksuit out of the way before he could respond, and Samantha glowered.

"Hey!" the guy complained.

"Shut up," Edward said, not even bothering to glance his way. Tracksuit huffed and puffed for a bit but backed down. It was one of the benefits of being larger than your average bear. Most people were smart enough to leave him alone without things ever coming to blows.

"Mr. Hayes," Samantha said; voice tight. "We talked about this over the phone-"

"I know," he soothed. "It's not company policy. You said that already, and I get it. I do.  But, Sammy," Desperation had him reaching for her much smaller hand and cradling it within his own. "This is an emergency. I wouldn't ask otherwise."

Her cheeks flushed red. She was in her mid-twenties and hadn't been working at the bank for very long. She was too young for him, but she was pretty and he knew, based on her physical responses, that she found him at least a bit attractive. Normally, there'd be some guilt about using her attraction against her, but it *was* an emergency. At the sound of her name, Samantha's blush deepened, and she sighed in resignation.

"I can't get you all of it," she said, keeping her voice low.

"That's fine," he assured her; so earnest she giggled. He couldn't tell her it wasn't all right at all. Or how company policy was going to get him killed. But something was better than the nothing he had. He drummed his fingers on the countertop, the rapid drumbeat soothing something indefinable in his brain as Samantha pulled up his account from memory. An eternity passed before she opened her drawer and pulled out a stack of hundreds. Edward counted along with her, the numbers swimming through his senses like a lullaby. They drowned out the irate grumbling from the people behind him in line and dulled the sharp edge of fear that had driven him since he awoke.

The air in the bank shifted as the doors opened once again. For a split second, he was surrounded by the smell of gyros and fries from the street corner outside. Then, an explosion, a burst of sound and heat, and a wave of air slammed him hard against the teller counter. Samantha was blown clear off her feet as a cloud of smoke filled the air. The smoke, combined with the acrid scent of sulfur, left his eyes watering and there was a sharp ringing in his ears he couldn't shake. At some point, he'd sunken to his knees and pressed his hands against his ears, but he couldn't remember moving. His thoughts were sluggish, but he was already making connections even as he forced his hands back to his sides. The bomb hadn't been meant to kill or even destroy. Just to distract. This was the third robbery, just like it, in as many days so Edward had an idea of what would happen next.

They rushed inside the bank one at a time, guns raised and heels click-clacking in a violent staccato. Gunshots. Reverberations that raised the hair on your skin and left the air thick and wounded.

"Everybody shut the fuck up! This is a robbery, not a roller-coaster at Six Flags, goddamnit! Show some decorum."

Decorum.

*Decorum?*

Edward's laugh verged on hysterical, but it went unheard. He didn't bother looking over his shoulder at the bank robbers. He'd seen plenty of security footage over the last week or so to know what he'd find. It was funny; getting held at gunpoint by the Powerpuff Girls was not on Edward's bingo card for the day. Then again, neither were extortion and death threats, yet here it was, just nine in the morning, and he was already two for two.

Edward clambered to his knees, gathering as many of the remaining bills as he could. Behind him, chaos reigned. Blossom was to the right of the entrance bitch-slapping a security guard like he owed her money while a short, rotund, little Mayor was shaking down the wealthy bank guests with a handgun. *The security cameras are out,* Edward noted. There were bullet holes scattered across the walls and furniture beneath each CCTV. *Someone* was a bad shot, though he wasn't brave enough to test the waters to figure out who.

"On the ground!" Bubbles shouted, firing a bullet into the plaster above their heads to accent the command. Buttercup, giant foam head canted to one side, tsked in disapproval, and Bubbles sighed.

"What?"

Buttercup shrugged, the AK47 he held forgotten. "We talked about this. It's 'Show me your hands!'"

"But I see their hands just fine," Bubbles reminded him. "You're *supposed* to tell them to get on the ground so they don't look at you. Dumbass."

Buttercup jabbed the other robber in the head with his semi-automatic until his companion slapped the barrel away. "You're the dumbass, Dumbass. We're wearing masks." He continued, unphased. "Who cares if they're looking or not?"

He was right, of course. Usually, the giant character heads each of the robbers wore were reserved for kids' birthday parties or the mean streets of Disneyland. They were great for creating a sense of awe and wonder and, in a pinch, were useful for hiding your identity from a room full of witnesses. All Edward could think about were the logistics of fitting through the bank doors in full costume. Bubbles and her Pigtails alone would have required some special maneuvering and one hell of a pivot. As a cosplayer himself, Edward nevertheless admired the dedication. Though the men – six in total - had lost a lot of the plot by not shaving, despite the almost enthusiastic use of fishnets, g-strings, and push-up bras.

*Pretty sure the P-Puff girls haven't gone through puberty yet, so points off for historical accuracy,* Edward thought.

As much as it rankled, he had bigger problems than whether the group was being true to their character design. The robbery part sucked, but he was much more concerned with the fact that if he didn't leave this bank with a quarter of a million dollars in the next fifteen minutes, some intrepid assassin was going to put a bullet in his head.

Which would, as his niece might say, ruin his vibe.

*I like my vibe,* Edward thought, shoving crisp bills down the front of his pants with all the enthusiasm of an aging stripper. How much time did he have left? Ten minutes? Five? "No bitch is gonna kill my vibe."

"Good to know."

Something slammed into his temple, and his vision wavered. "I said on the ground," Bubbles snarled. Edward groaned, his head ringing. Pain, white hot, speared through his skull, and his right eye was awash in red. Copper coated his tongue. All of a sudden he was a kid again with his father looming over him, face a mask of disapproval and disgust. His chest ached, and he forgot to breathe around the panic lying in wait there. He wasn't sure how much time passed as he lay on the ground, panting, his body wracked with chills. A part of him, a large part, wanted to hide, but safety, like salvation, cost more than he would ever be able to afford.

Which was the other thing about Briarcliff. There were no heroes here, so the monsters ran rampant. Day in, day out, the various factions that struggled for control, tore at the city like hyenas at a carcass. If you had the money to pay, you might live to see old age. Everyone else was fair game unless they aligned themselves with one of the gangs. Edward had no money and no affiliation, which meant he should have kept his ass at home this morning and taken his chances with the hitman.

"Three minutes," someone shouted.

When the memory of his father cleared, Bubbles—
the joy and the laughter—was still there, and Edward
gasped in relief. His situation hadn't improved, but
anything was preferable to the asshole who raised
him.

"Put the money in the bag," Bubbles ordered the
teller.

"We don't *have* bags," Samantha sobbed, eyes red-
rimmed as she peeked over the edge of the counter.
Her hair, pulled back in a tight bun, hadn't shifted an
inch. If he survived, he'd ask her what sort of gel she
used. "I'm not a cashier. This isn't a fucking
Walmart."

Bubbles deflated but rallied almost as fast. "Okay,
so where's the safety deposit boxes with jewels and
shit in 'em? Get me one of those."

The teller's lips parted in surprise. "Do you not
know how banks work?" she queried, tone pitying.
"Like, have you only seen them in movies?"

The robber grumbled, large, tattooed hands
tightening around the gun.

Edward spoke without thinking. "Not to pile on or anything"—his voice squeaked, and he cleared his throat—"but you guys are all over the place. There's no way you'll make it out of here before the cops show up." Bubbles' head whipped around like the exorcist, and Edward stared into a pair of blue eyes the size of pizza platters for a full ten seconds before the Powerpuff cursed beneath his breath.

"Goddamnit!" Bubbles glanced toward his comrades, who were busy tearing the rest of the bank apart. Buttercup was trying to get a terrified bank employee to unlock the vault in the back, but the man was blubbering too hard to cooperate. Meanwhile, Ms. Bellum, bright red wig obscuring most of his features—and his vision if the way he kept slamming into counters was any indication—scrambled onto the bank manager's desk, his weapon at the ready in case any of the terrified patrons tried anything. His size fifteen feet had been shoved into a pair of red platforms, and the heels gouged the wood. Still, despite the overflow, Bellum handled the extra six inches they added to his already imposing height with ease.

Edward was sure he wasn't the only one greeted with a handful of nuts dangling on either side of Ms. Bellum's lace underwear as she clambered up on her perch, tight red skirt straining around hairy thighs the size of tree trunks, but he was perhaps the closest. Bellum was shouting at the other tellers to fill a nearby flowerpot with money while the Mayor collected jewelry and phones in a backpack from the people still laid out on the ground. Blossom went to stand near the front door, bouncing from one foot to the other and checking the time on his cell.

"We got one minute," he warned.

Bubbles cursed, then barked at Edward, "Strip."

He blinked. "What?"

"Take off your clothes," he hissed, putting a round in the chamber to accent his point.

*Shit*. They must have seen him pocketing the money. Edward got to his feet, careful to keep his hands in the air as he stood. Bubbles—5'11 in combat boots—had to tilt his big head to look up at him. Petty satisfaction almost brought a smile to his face, but instead, he ducked his head. Undoing the buttons on his shirt with excruciating care even as his mind raced. He couldn't let them take what little cash he had. It wasn't enough to buy his life, but he could use it to get the fuck out of town. For now, it would have to be enough. What had Bubbles said? One minute? He could stall for a minute.

"Will you hurry the fuck up?"

*Okay, maybe not.* Trying out a smile, he said, "You know, if this is what you're into, I *do* have an OnlyFans—"

"No one is subscribing to your goddamn OnlyFans!" Ms. Bellum barked with enough venom Edward was 99% sure the influx of sexy bots over on the interwebs was to blame.

"I might," the Mayor muttered as he stalked past. "Shit, maybe *he's* the hottest eighteen-year-old on the internet?" He seemed unconcerned by their timeframe. "Where do they come up with that shit anyway?" he mused, dumping an old woman's purse out on the floor and rifling through her wallet. "I mean, they can't *all* be the hottest, right? Is this like a holy grail situation? Or maybe a chosen one? Like, is the chosen one some girl on Twitter with her titties out, commenting under my nana's pumpkin pie recipe?"

Bubbles sighed, pressing his foam head into his big black hand as if patience could be found there. "Lenny. Please shut the fuck up about that, man. No one gives a shit about her recipe now, and they didn't give a shit about it three weeks ago."

"Fifty-two likes, Joey," Lenny lost some of his cool. "You ever have fifty-two likes on anything before? No? That's what I thought."

Edward wasn't sure what Joey would have said because there was a pop, and the large window overlooking Main Street shattered in an explosion of glass. Outside, a woman who had been walking her dog screamed and took off, while inside the bank, patrons and robbers alike froze. Blossom fell, as if in slow motion, and Edward's heart dropped.

*Looks like my fifteen minutes are up.*

Getting to his feet, Edward launched himself over the counter, dragging Samantha to the ground with him as another bullet tore through the gaping hole where the window should have been. Someone cried out, and he flinched as a second body hit the ground with a dull thud. Breathe. He had to remember how to breathe.

*In.*

*Out.*

*In.*

*In.*

*In.*

Someone cursed, their gruff voice a fitting accompaniment to the violence. Wrapping his arms over his head and pressing his back against the wall near Sammy, Edward buried his face against his knees. He needed to keep himself under control, but as the remaining Puffs and their companions returned fire, all he could do was rock back and forth where he sat. Stimming helped a bit, but the roar of gunshots was deafening, and his nails dug into his palms.

"Hello," a chipper, strategically casual voice cut through the din. "Are you in need of assistance?"

Edward gasped in relief. Breathing exercises didn't help his anxiety, but the MARCO security bot waiting just a few feet away worked wonders. He scrambled over toward it, leaving the teller curled up on the floor beneath the counter. "Yes," he hissed, grateful for all the noise. Thank God this bank had opted for the upgrade. The police force was so outnumbered and outgunned they were just decoration for the Mayor at this point. MARCO was designed to even the playing field between law enforcement and the criminal organizations who ran Briarcliff. Once it was fully operational, of course. There were still a few kinks left to work out, namely its assessment capabilities, which slowed it down considerably. A disappointment since the bot had run similar simulations based on footage from previous heists. Heists committed by these same intrepid morons, in fact.

"There's a robbery in progress," he whispered.

"Yes," the bot replied succinctly. Could robots get snippy? "I am aware. Authorities should be arriving in ten minutes." A countdown replaced MARCO's digital eyes and mouth on the screen. Ten minutes might as well have been an eternity. Before Edward could give the bot a command, a shotgun blast knocked it on its back and sent it sailing against the back wall, sparks flying.

Edward glanced up as Ms. Bellum launched himself over the counter like an Olympic gymnast, gun over one shoulder and red wig flying in the wind. He crouched next to the bot in his heels, nuts swinging a happy dance below the edge of his red skirt. Edward stared, mystified, as he pulled out a knife and pried open the door hiding the bot's hard drive from prying eyes. Once open, Bellum reached in and removed the small flash drive that was the source of MARCO's code, then pressed the drive against his lips in a kiss.

A surge of overprotectiveness had Edward's eyes narrowing to slits. "What are you doing?"

Ms. Bellum tensed, dropping his knife and turning on Edward with his gun raised, the motion so smooth and practiced Edward was sure he'd done it before. Military? Law enforcement? A lot of cops ended up working for the factions, so it wasn't impossible. There was a confidence in his violence the others lacked; a calculated focus that raised Edward's hackles. Samantha screamed, and the barrel of the shotgun shifted once again. For the second time that day, Edward moved without thinking, hurling himself across the distance separating him from Bellum. He shoved the gun up, and the shot went wild. The chandelier, already hanging on by a thread, spun wildly. A rustle, a crack, like bones breaking, was all that heralded its fall to the marble floor below, taking some of the glass dome along with it. Edward wondered, for the first time, about the glass cleaner as

shards cascaded through the air. The crash from the
chandelier was so deafening it drowned out the
screams from those caught beneath the onslaught.

There was silence.

Then-

"Who the fuck!?" Bubbles roared.

"Sorry!" Came Bellum's insincere reply .

Edward couldn't see his face beneath the hair, but
he'd annoyed plenty of people in his life to know
when someone was glaring at him. Loose wires near
the ceiling sparked a warning that set off the sprinkler
system, plunging the bank into darkness before
Bellum could act on his rage.

It didn't, however, stop the sniper. Another
gunshot, and the Mayor cried out.

"Let's go!" Bubbles yelled over the noise.

Bellum rose to his feet, and, heart racing, Edward
reached out and grabbed for the drive in his hand.
They struggled over possession until Ms. Bellum's
heels slipped on the wet marble, knocking his feet out
from under him. His head struck the corner of the

MARCO bot with so much force Edward cringed, pressing a hand against his mouth in horror even as heavy footsteps sounded on the other side of the counter.

"New guy!" Buttercup pounded an urgent drumbeat above his head. "Let's fucking go. The cops will be here any second."

The room was spinning, and Edward was shaking. Several things occurred to him at once.

One: Someone had just done their best to steal the tech he'd spent his entire life developing. Tech only available to select investors.

Two: There was still a sniper outside, and all he had to show for his excursion to the bank was a few thousand dollars leaving paper cuts all along the Bering Strait that was his taint.

Three: He and Ms. Bellum wore the same size shoe.

# Chapter Two

## *The Fearless Leader*

Edward had never run in heels before, and his skirt kept riding up. He teetered down the sidewalk, trying not to mind the stares. Tugging self-consciously at the hem of his too-small skirt. The guy he'd left passed out on the bank floor had made it look easy, but with the police swarming the streets, it wasn't like Edward could go back and ask him how to be a Bad Bitch.

The people around him cheered as the music from the marching band reached a crescendo, and Edward stopped running. His hands were shaking again. Or maybe they'd just never stopped? The crowd was packed too close, and he imagined their breath crawling into him, wrapping around his lungs like filthy fingers. Feeling dirty and desperate, he shuddered. He didn't belong here. He should be back home in his office, pouring over the calculations for MARCO's next upgrade. Refining the training simulations and eradicating the remaining bugs in the system. Instead, he was shivering on the sidewalk, in the middle of the annual children's parade, trying not to be offended when yet another mother jerked their kid out of his immediate vicinity.

To her credit, Edward was sure her aversion had nothing to do with Drag in general. Several Drag Queens were participating in this year's parade,

though they were much more put together. No.
People were backing away in growing alarm because
of the copious amounts of sweat staining his costume
and, even more damning, the way he planted his
hands on his hips, threw his head back, and groaned
like a dying wildebeest.

He took a deep breath, groaned again. A beat cop
spoke into the radio at his shoulder just a yard away.
Yup. It was the sounds. But in his defense, sprinting a
full block in stilettos was not for the faint of heart. He
was limping toward the officer, eager to ditch the wig
and skirt, when a thought brought him up short. The
cops should have captured the ones responsible for
these heists by now. They weren't criminal
masterminds, after all. Maybe they were still running
free because someone wanted them to be. Not
everyone in the BPD could be trusted, and there was
no guarantee he'd be kept safe either from the sniper
or the gang from today – especially once they found
out he knew Bellum's secret identity.

Ankles throbbing like a sore tooth, Edward continued along the boulevard. Shoving his lace front back a few inches so he could see where he was going as he strutted. It was important to look as if he did this sort of thing all the time and was not, in fact, running for his life. Thanks to the parade, as long as if kept his cool, he didn't stand out. Were the cops at the bank by now? Many of the main roads had been shut down in preparation for the parade, so there was no telling.

*Don't be suspicious.* The clack of his heels on the concrete set up a staccato beat to accompany the command. *Don't be suspicious. Don't be suspicious.*

"Hey, red!"

He froze at the unfamiliar voice and glanced up.

A taco truck was parked at the corner, and a Latino with a goatee and a topknot glared down at him from the serving window. "What the fuck do you think you're doing?" the young man hissed.

Edward glanced first one way and then another. He pointed to himself, and the young man sighed, muttering something beneath his breath in Spanish.

"Get in here," he said, reaching up to unhook the posts propping up the awning. He disappeared from view, and a minute later the backdoor of the food truck swung open.

Edward hesitated, all his mother's warnings about strangers and vans running through his mind. Something about knowing someone out there wanted him dead and being an accomplice to a bank heist had him scrambling inside, regardless. As soon as he closed the doors behind himself, the truck took off. Nothing was strapped down, and Edward clutched the prep table so hard his knuckles whitened as the young man swerved down a side street, punching the gas as soon as they drove beyond the parade route.

"Um, hey…" Edward began, uncertain. "Would you mind dropping me off h—"

The truck screeched to a halt in front of an abandoned laundromat, and Edward slipped in his heels, landing hard on his ass. Legs windmilling, he tugged his skirt back down over his ass, yelping as the doors slid open again. Two men carrying a third between them hauled themselves inside. One of the men was soaked red with blood, his head rolling as his companions lay him on the floor of the truck. The smell of salsa and baked meat was accompanied by fresh blood like copper and stale sweat. On the radio, someone was rapping in Spanish, and the driver turned the volume down. Turning in his seat, he eyed the damage and sighed. "You dicks are getting blood all over the lettuce, man. That's, like, thirty OSHA violations right there." He scowled. "Where's everyone?"

One of the men, shorter than Edward by at least a foot and sporting a massive potbelly and a shock of blond hair, shook his head grimly. "Drive," he said.

Edward went very still. The guy wasn't in costume, but he recognized the Mayor's voice. Dressed in a simple t-shirt and a pair of loose-fitting gray sweatpants with Cheeto streaks along one leg, he was an angry gremlin with a thinning top. He glanced at Edward in his Ms. Bellum get-up in annoyance, before focusing on the task at hand. *Shit. Out of the frying pan and into the fire. How the hell am I supposed to get away from these people?* Luckily, it didn't look as if any of them suspected him. Yet.

"Hospital-" The cry drew everyone's attention. *His* voice was familiar too. The Professor. His shirt and neck were wet with blood, and he was pale as he did what he could to stem the flow. The bullet had struck so close to his neck that Edward feared the shooter might have nicked an artery. This was his fault. The knowledge swallowed him whole where he huddled in the dank, dark interior of the truck. The rap had been replaced by a woman's soft, crooning ballad, and Edward's eyes stung with the urge to cry.

His breathing grew haggard.

"No hospital," the Mayor ordered. "You'll get stitched up in the back of the bowling alley like the rest of us." He turned on his companion. "What the hell was that, Diesel?" the Mayor hissed.

The third man, Diesel, ignored him. "Newbie, hold this," he said, waving Edward over.

Edward hesitated before scooching closer, ducking his head so his wig hid most of his features. There was no time to let his anxiety get the better of him. Having a task to focus on helped.

Diesel pressed Edward's hands against a folded plaid shirt they were using to stem the bleeding. Then he got to his feet and claimed the passenger seat while the Mayor continued his rant.

"So much for being the fucking lookout," the guy snarled. "Don't you have 20/20 vision or some shit? How'd you miss a fucking sniper?"

Diesel shook his head, too busy cleaning his hands and arms with a towel he'd swiped from the prep counter. "Don't start with me."

The Mayor shook his head in disgust. "Leave it to you to fuck up every chance you get." Scrambling forward, he clutched the back of Diesel's seat for balance as the food truck bounced and swayed. "Dusty should have ditched your ass years ago."

Silence filled the cramped space, and beneath Edward's red wig, sweat gathered.

"That's not how the Legion works, dude," the driver said. "At least not since Bobby took over. Even I know that."

"You say it like it's a bad thing, Nico," Diesel replied with an edge of warning in his voice.

Nico shrugged, his expression pensive in the rearview mirror. "Look, I love Dusty as much as the next guy. But I'd be lying if I said I haven't heard rumors."

"What rumors?" the Mayor asked.

"People think Dusty's weak. Soft. Hell, *we* know better, but from the outside looking in…" Nico shrugged. "Me and my abuela would have gone hungry if not for the Legion. And I'm not even a member. Around here, you guys are like Robin Hood and his merry men or some shit." When no one spoke, he shifted. "Anyway, what I'm trying to say is I think you're good, Diesel. I'm sure Dusty will understand."

Diesel scowled.

"You been watching those Hallmark movies again? What did I tell you about that shit?"

"Jesus Christ, Nico!"

"Nico, you dumb little shit!"

"Shut the *fuck* up, Nico!"

"Fine," Nico roared above the heckling. "Christ, I take it back. You're all pieces of dog shit. My bad. I guess we have nothing to worry about then."

*Worry? About what?*

The answer came quickly enough.

Weakness in Briarcliff meant there was a target on your back, and a weak gang was a dead one. Dusty, being known for his kindness, was a failing he wouldn't live long enough to regret unless he was particularly ruthless behind closed doors. An inkling of an idea took root, but before Edward had the chance to explore it, the truck careened to a stop outside of a run-down bowling alley. The neon sign on top of the building was turned off, and the parking lot was empty. The angry gremlin – formally The

Mayor - threw open the truck doors. Still squabbling, he and Diesel dragged their bleeding friend out of the truck and through the doors without a backward glance. Nico wasted no time, pulling away in a cloud of white smoke before they even cleared the entryway.

Still dazed, Edward grabbed another towel from the prep area and took the seat Diesel had just vacated. It brought him closer to Nico, but he wasn't as nervous around him now. Regardless, it was better than trying not to slide around in his heels and failing. "So, we heading back to the bar?" He said, affecting an air of nonchalance. "Bubbles said we should meet up there before we all split up."

"Bubbles?" Nico laughed. "Don't let Joey catch you calling him that." He scowled. "Speaking of Bubbles, why the fuck you still in disguise for, bruh? You walk into initiation looking like that, and Dusty's gonna be pissed."

Dusty. Who the hell was this person? The other men had spoken of him with reverence, so Edward imagined some hardened gang member who enjoyed murder and mayhem. He shook his head. It didn't matter how bad Dusty was. The enemy of his enemy was his friend, and anyone was better than the hitman on his tail and the monster who'd hired him. If Dusty had an altruistic streak, maybe he'd be willing to aim some goodwill Edward's way.

"I don't have anything else to wear," he answered, when it was clear Nico was waiting for some sort of response. Was he convincing enough? Did he sound like a badass who would rob a bank and beat up a robot? He cleared his throat and tried again. "Besides, I look good in red."

Nico shot him a look from the corner of his eye, then nodded. "They're going to eat you alive," he mused. Jerking the wheel to one side, the young man pulled up to a derelict Dollar General. "Grab a new outfit and be back here in five. The parade's going to end soon, and we need to get off the roads before the cops mobilize."

Edward nodded, tripping over himself in his haste to escape the truck. He teetered into the Dollar General, nodding to the sour-faced teenager manning the register. Hurrying over to the clothing section, he grabbed a pair of jeans and a black T-shirt. On impulse, he snatched a sheet of temporary tattoos from the children's aisle on his way back to the register, only to double back and grab the rest of the display just to be safe. The "new recruit" from the bank had been covered in tattoos beneath his disguise. Edward needed to look the part if he had any hope of getting through this. As the kid at the register rang up his items, he considered running for it.

Two things stopped him.

MARCO was the world's first AI-powered security system. Capable of assessing risks with the same discernment as its human counterparts, it revolutionized the industry. Or it would, as soon as it was cleared for distribution. The main issue was AI had no moral compass. When met with resistance, it often chose to ignore human directives if those directives meant failing its objective.

The most recent case involved a simulation of a carjacking. MARCO was integrated into the power grid of an average city. Through security cameras and traffic cams already in place, it was able to track the carjackers as they eluded police. The problem was, rather than following the suspects and gathering intel, MARCO manipulated red lights and, in the end, caused a massive collision. A calculated decision prioritizing the capture of its target over any potential loss of human life. When Edward adjusted the faulty code, MARCO went into preservation mode. Giving the impression that the issue was fixed, even when it wasn't. Running the exercise again with different commands and safety parameters just resulted in disaster.

Edward shared his concerns with his business partner, Andrew, only to be dismissed.

"Look, Eddy, we've got to give our investors something. You've been holding onto this tech for five years, and the shareholders are starting to get antsy. The phone assistant thing is cute, don't get me wrong, but MARCO is the future."

And so it was. He held out for a while, citing bugs and glitches and distracting the board members with other projects he was developing. But at some point, Andrew began negotiations with the military about MARCO and drones, and the next thing Edward knew, he was being threatened with a conservatorship—a loss of everything, including his free will.

Andrew had no idea how MARCO worked, but someone with enough skill could reverse-engineer his own version of the technology based on Edward's code. It's why he was against the beta testing. But Andrew insisted, and the more trouble Edward caused, the more credibility he would lose and the more likely the conservatorship became. Still, he refused to go down without a fight. Last week, he went before the board and gave them an ultimatum. Either they voted in favor of firing Andrew—at which point they could divvy up his shares in the company amongst themselves — or Edward would disband the corporation.

This was around the same time someone cut the brakes on his car.

It was the first assassination attempt, but not the last. This morning marked the fifth time he'd almost died in the last week. It started off small: peanuts slipped into his food, even though his staff knew he was allergic. A car veering too close during his morning run. At first, he thought he was going insane. Living in seclusion all those years could do that to a man. When he got a call demanding money, he knew the danger was all too real. At first, he was relieved. Sometimes he got a little lost in his own head. His eyes and ears liked to play tricks on him, and it was hard to tell reality from dreams, dreams from memories. Even now, it was difficult to believe any of this was happening. He was moving through a thick fog, one he couldn't quite pull himself free from. Drowning.

He was drowning.

"That'll be $52.78," the cashier said, the impatience in her voice an anchor.

"One sec," Edward squatted a bit, reaching down the front of his skirt where he'd managed to stash some of the cash from the bank. It was damp, either from sweat or the sprinkler system at the bank, he didn't know. His smile was stiff as he slid a 100 dollar bill across the counter. "There you go."

The kid stared down at the soggy paper in disbelief.

"Keep the change," Edward said over his shoulder as he left.

Hurrying back out to the food truck, Edward couldn't help but wonder if whoever was blackmailing him was in it for the money, or if it was just a ruse to get him in the bank as it was about to get robbed. Did the Powerpuff Girls work for Andrew?

No. They hadn't been there for Edward, and they'd lost a few of their own in the crossfire. Still, whoever it was had known what they were planning beforehand and would have used the heist as a cover for Edward's murder if he hadn't gotten the hell out of there. At the very least, there was a mole among their ranks. A piece of information he was sure their boss would find useful.

*Dusty.*

He wasn't looking forward to meeting him, but something told Edward this Dusty person might just be his port in the storm. Assuming the guy didn't kill him first.

# Chapter Three

*Lace-fronts and Stilettos*


"Number 3, step forward, please,"
The voice, disembodied and condescending, echoed from the speakers. Dusty stepped away from the wall, squinting.

"Damn, it's bright in here," she groused. All the money she didn't pay in taxes, and they couldn't afford a fucking dimmer switch? "You can't turn that shit down, or something?"

"Line, Ms. Burdot." The voice ordered, and Dusty rolled her eyes. Detective Braxton was a hatin' ass ho and had been since she met the man. She wouldn't be surprised if he were trying to blind her on purpose.

Dusty sighed and capitulated, eager to speed things along. Braxton and his partner had brought her in four hours ago, and she was beyond tired of their company. "On the ground?" she said with zero enthusiasm and no small amount of snark. "Move, and I'll shoot?"

"Ms. Burdot-"

Detective Braxton sounded irritated, and a grin tugged at Dusty's lips.

"Sorry," she called, using her reflection in the one-way mirror to fix her braids. Once they fell just the way she liked, she reached into her cleavage and pulled out a tube of lipstick the cop who'd patted her down had missed for whatever reason. Dusty reapplied a swatch of crimson along her bottom lip, mouth a little O as she cleaned up the excess with the side of one finger. Perfect. Popping the top on and sliding the lipstick back between her breasts, she folded her arms beneath their heavy weight and scowled. "What's my character's motivation again?"

"Their motivation is they're a piece of SHIT-" Detective Kensington's irate interjection – cut short as someone on the other side of the mirror pulled her away from the mic - was a welcome change from Braxton's sanctimonious calm. Nodding as if her response had told her all she needed to know, Dusty cleared her throat and tried again.

"Unless you're ready to die today, Cher," She tried again, gaze unblinking on the glass and voice a low, throaty threat. "You make sure to keep my name out of your muthafuckin mouth, you hear?" The air grew close, heated, until Dusty broke the growing tension with a smile. "How was that?" she asked. "Better?"

There was no response for a full minute. When Braxton spoke again, she could almost taste the defeat. "Number 3, back against the wall. Number 4, step forward and say your line, please."

Dusty did as she was asked, leaning against the wall to take some of the pressure off her bad leg. She had no idea how long she'd been on her feet, but her muscles were cramping. Even worse, she was hungry and needed to pee. Dusty prayed for patience as she waited for the rest of the women in line to take their turn, knowing damn well Braxton and his little lackey weren't going to find their suspect hiding amongst them. A waste of time, but she indulged the whims of the BPD on occasion for the sake of morale. If the police department gave up, things in Briarcliff would get real boring, real fast.

A few minutes later, a beat cop came and led the line of women out of the room. Many of them were returned to a cell, but Dusty was dragged back into the same interrogation room as before. She sat and kicked her feet up. A nap would have been nice, but she didn't think Braxton would keep her waiting for very long. And she was right. Detective Braxton and Detective Kensington joined her a few minutes later, looking grim.

"How's your civilian?" Dusty asked. She was going for 'compassionate,' but the way she bared her teeth as she spoke made it predatory. "Not too shaken up, I hope?"

Braxton sat before her, stormy gaze locked on her face. "You should be proud of yourself," he said. "It's the fastest we've ever lost a key witness. Congratulations." Despite herself, Dusty basked in the praise, and Braxton's hands clenched where they rested in his lap. Tall and lanky, Braxton was all ropy muscle and dark brown skin. He always kept his hair freshly tapered; the waves up top shimmering like obsidian in the light. Dusty tried imagining Braxton at home at night, brushing his hair down and putting on a do-rag, and couldn't. The man was so strait-laced and dedicated to the job he probably fucked with his badge on. Which, in all fairness, wasn't the worst image in the world.

"This is all just one big joke to you, huh?" Kensington asked. Dusty glanced over at her and shrugged.

"Not really," she said. "Jokes are funny."

Kensington's jaw worked. She hadn't bothered with a chair. Instead, she stood with her back against the wall and her hands deep in her pockets. Almost as tall as Braxton, Kensington was an earnest sort with curly brown hair down to her shoulders and sea-green eyes. She was honest like Braxton, but without the confidence to back it. The interrogation room was as hot as Satan's asshole, but the woman refused to ditch the blazer she wore to conceal her flat chest. The city would eat her alive before she learned to accept the faint shadow on her chin or the Adam's apple bobbing in her throat, and that thought made Dusty sad. Still, it wasn't her business, and Kensington wasn't one of her own, so she quelled a surge of compassion to focus on the elephant in the room.

"Can I go now?" Dusty asked, turning back to Braxton. "Last I checked, you can't keep me unless I'm being charged with something."

*And you've got nothing on me,* she thought.

Braxton sat back in his seat, tapping his pen against the tabletop. "I just have one more thing I wanted to run by you," he said. Motioning Kensington closer, he held out a hand. His partner pulled a folded-up piece of paper from her pocket and handed it over. Braxton sent it sliding across the table without glancing down at it. Suspicious, Dusty picked it up and unfolded it. Printed out on cheap printer paper was a faded still shot from a street camera, of a naked man in a G-string sprinting past a Whole Foods. He had a MARCO bot tucked under one arm like a football and a wad of cash stuck beneath the waistband of his underwear.

"You need to buy new ink cartridges," Dusty said, sliding the picture back to Braxton. "I think the office supply place is having a sale-"

"Raphael Holtz," Braxton ignored the photo. "Name ring any bells?"

Dusty shrugged, "No, not really. Should it?"

"Depends," Braxton shrugged. "He's a hired gun—former special ops. He's been off the grid for the last several years, but we've got reason to believe he's working with the Legion these days."

"So?" Dusty snapped. "What's that got to do with me?" When they said nothing, she snorted in derision. "You really think I'm out here running around with mercenaries? I own a fucking bar, for Christ's sake."

"Your father founded the Legion, didn't he?" Braxton asked as if he didn't already know. "It's not farfetched to think you might be running in some of those same circles."

"Rat's been in jail a long time," she reminded them both.

"'Rat,'" Kensington mused. "Not Dad, or Pops, or Papa?" She whistled. "Those daddy issues must run deep."

Dusty's lips tightened, and she cut her gaze towards Kensington's. A look passed between them; there and gone, before she turned away with a shrug. "Well," she said finally. "He did kill my sister, so..." She let the thought trail off. They could fill in the blanks for themselves.

Only Braxton didn't seem inclined to do that. Instead, he sat back in his seat, expression thoughtful. "I've studied your dad's case-" he said, and Dusty's eyes narrowed in suspicion. There was a gleam in his eye - of interest, of knowing. It set her teeth on edge. "-and last I checked, you're the only one who thinks he didn't."

Dusty rested her cheek against the palm of one hand, eyeing them both in silence. "Am I being charged with anything, detectives?" she asked at last.

"It depends," Kensington said. "You see, we picked up a few strays at the bank this morning. Figured we'd bring them in and find out if they have anything interesting to tell us."

There was a knock on the door. Kensington and Braxton both turned, as the knob turned without awaiting a response, and a man entered. Dressed in a gray suit with a red tie, he was taller even than Detective Braxton, and so wide he filled out the doorway. His hair, reddish-brown and peppered with silver, had been slicked back into a thick ponytail at the nape of his neck. Thick, black lines were tattooed across his face like a mask framing his dark, dark eyes, so that when he smiled- like he was doing now - his teeth were a bright flash of white.

"Can we help you?" Braxton asked, getting to his feet. His hand drifted to where his gun rested in the holster at his hip before backing away.

"My name is Iwalani Kiana Natia," the giant intoned, adjusting the glasses on his face before offering a hand to Kensington to shake. "I'm here to collect my client."

Kensington's eyebrows shot up. "You're a lawyer?"

"Graduated at the top of my class," Iwalani said, proud in his brownness and tattoos. At her snort, Iwalani glanced sidelong at Dusty. "Ms. Burdot," he said expectantly.

The room stank like dirty mop water, and Dusty was more than ready to bid the stench goodbye. She stood. "Good luck with those strays, Detectives," she said by way of farewell.

Kensington opened her mouth to protest, but Braxton lifted a hand. "Don't bother Yvette," he said. We'll be in touch with Ms. Burdot again, very soon."

His eyes remained on her as Dusty strode from the room, snatching her leather jacket from the back of her seat as she went. As she slipped past Detective Kensington, their hands brushed. The contact lasted less than a second, but it was long enough for Dusty to palm a slip of paper and tuck it alongside her lipstick.

"What was that about?" Iwalani asked as they made their way down the hall.

Dusty's jaw was tight. She didn't need to look at the missive to know what it said, or who it was from. The invitation came once a year and had done since the day she'd left. "Papa Tate," she said, and Iwalani stiffened.

"Fuck," he breathed, and she nodded.

Dusty would have to burn the paper once she got somewhere safe, but, for now, it was a brand against her skin. Eating away at her flesh. She wanted to tear it to shreds right then and there, but doing so in the middle of a police station would be suicide. If Papa had his claws in Kensington, there was no telling how many more of the fine men and women of the BPD were on his payroll.

*Every time I think I've escaped that old bastard, he finds a way back in my life.*

They left the precinct, trotting down the stone steps to the street below, where two motorcycles sat waiting in the fire lane.

Dusty whistled. "Bold move."

Iwalani grinned, pulling off his red clip-on tie. "What can I say? I'm a helluva good lawyer."

"Whatever you say, Mr. 'Top of my Class.'"

Dusty checked her saddlebags and grabbed her knives, slipping them into their respective holsters. "Where's Diesel?" She asked, tone growing dark.

"Tracking Raphael," Iwalani assured her, taking off his suit jacket and stuffing it into the compartment beneath his seat. Underneath, he wore a white collared T-shirt that strained around his massive arms and across wide chest. In his mid-50s, Iwalani hadn't changed much since he and Dusty first met. He was softer around the middle, but he was still built like punishment on legs. Which was just one of the reasons he went by Ape instead of the good, strong, Samoan name his mother had gifted him with. Dusty nodded toward her second's clothes as he straddled his bike. "Who'd you steal the suit from?"

"Some intern standing in line at the coffee place," He admitted with a shrug.

"You kill him?"

Ape shook his head. "Nah, he's in a broom closet. He'll wake up with a sore head and a public indecency charge, but honestly? Who isn't on a list these days?" He glanced sidelong at her as she straddled her bike and pulled her leather gloves from the pocket of her jacket. "Speaking of killing-"

"Alive," she said, eyes like flint. "I want Raphael alive."

"He gonna stay that way?" Ape asked, more curious than concerned.

"Depends," Dusty said, as she brought her bike to life. "On whether or not he was smart enough to bring me back a consolation prize."

***

The south side of Briarcliff was a restless wanton of a thing. So different from the side of town Edward was used to they may as well have been night and day. This part of Briarcliff wore its sins on its face. A badge of honor for all to see. It was a hidden gem of jukeboxes and midnight dinners. Stray dogs and junkies crouched in doorways like sentries. A place where fluorescent lights were the closest you ever came to rainbows, and smog dragged the street like a woman's skirt. Neon lights painted the shadows, turned them into something beautiful, and Edward wondered if South Briarcliff was just as afraid of what lay beyond the dark as he was.

It would never be dark here, not really, and for some odd reason, knowing as much brought a measure of comfort. Flyers declaring 'Vote Wilks' had been snatched from their perch on lampposts and building sides and now lined the gutters outside where a line of motorcycles were stationed. Next to the bar, was a gated parking lot with a few run-down cars and a couple of dumpsters the bar shared with the wing spot next door.

A bus stop at the corner was decorated with ads for Viagra and an insurance company selling term life insurance. A bum was asleep on the bench inside, and the small space smelled of urine and unwashed skin.

Edward turned around and headed back inside. Now, he sat nursing an iced tea and wondering if he should have asked the guy to scootch over. The company would have been better at least.

"So, a glass eye?" He said. "Nice."

Silence.

Edward cleared his throat and tried again. "Does insurance cover the customization, or did you, like, have to pay extra for…" He gestured at the man's face, realizing he was being rude but unable to stop digging the hole he'd been working on ever since he walked back through the front door.

The old Chinese man blinked in reply, his one Pepto-Bismol pink eye a stark contrast to the subdued brown he'd been born with.

Edward nodded as if his unwilling seatmate had responded. "Right," he said, fingers tracing the lines engraved on the tabletop. "Okay, cool. Cool, cool, cool."

Nico told Edward to "holla" if he needed anything before disappearing behind the bar to work the grill.

Edward's first instinct was to follow him, but he refrained. It was a bit like showing up at a party he wasn't invited to. A party where there was just one familiar face. Edward resisted the urge to holla, but barely. The man glaring at him from across the table they shared did not seem to enjoy his company. Still, since he was the least intimidating of the bar's patrons, he was just going to have to suck it up. Respectfully, of course.

The bar, dubbed The Hellhole, was run down but clean. At least on the inside. There was a mural painted on the brick exterior of a kid who'd been shot last June. Edward remembered watching the story unfold on the news. Remembered how the white men on his board of directors never lamented the loss of life, only the drop in property value. On the inside, past tabletops riddled with old beers, in the far corner, sat an aging jukebox with a cracked face, its lights growing with unsteady, uncertain strength. The speakers on it were uncertain of nothing, however, and the rock music playing at full blast drowned out the television hanging beside a massive wall of liquor. As much as he may have wished otherwise, the lack of sound didn't stop Edward from reading the subtitles as a somber news anchor appeared on the screen. The man was standing outside of an all too familiar building, and Edward's heart skipped a beat.

The closed captions jumped around, but he got the gist. Robbery on the corner of Manchester. Several suspects are in custody. Three members still at large and wanted for questioning in the shooting deaths of at least two people. Considered armed and dangerous. Police urging the public to call in with any information…

Edward's knee bounced - slowly at first and then faster and faster. Soon, his second knee joined the first until he was almost vibrating in his seat. He stilled the motion, but it only made things worse. Lunging to his feet, Edward's mind raced over what his next move should be.

Even if the police caught the hitman, nothing was stopping Andrew from hiring another. If Andrew was

in negotiations with the military about MARCO, and
the only thing stalling the deal from going through
was Edward, going to the police for help might not be
the smartest idea, regardless. Edward needed allies,
and thanks to Ms. Bellum, he had a bargaining chip
and the perfect opportunity to plead his case. He
could use people who weren't afraid to get their
hands dirty, people motivated by something more
than money. He'd play the part of a recruit eager to
join their ranks and get a feel for Dusty and how
much power and influence he held here in Briarcliff.
Even if the guy was only qualified to gather dirt on
Andrew and walk Edward to and from his mailbox so
he wouldn't get assassinated in his driveway, it was
better than nothing.

Edward would need to make a strong first
impression if he were going to convince Dusty of a
partnership, which meant he had some work to do.
From his vantage point, he could see an OUT OF
ORDER sign taped to the bathroom, so he headed
toward the back door instead, sending a shy smile

toward the burly bartender as he hurried past. There was a woman dancing on the pool tables in the next room, and as Edward passed, her boyfriend grabbed her off. Their argument followed him as he slipped through the door and out into the alleyway unnoticed.

Sunlight hit his skin, a stark contrast after being in the dimly bar for so long. He breathed a sigh of relief only to gag on the sharp scent of rotting food and diesel. It might not smell the best, but at least he wasn't surrounded by people. A win as far as he was concerned. The alleyway was crowded with old furniture and a huge metal dumpster. Tossing his Dollar General bag on an overturned crate, he dug past the red wig to pull out the bottle of water and the first sheet of tattoos. He peeled off the plastic covering, ripping the individual images from the larger sheet. Once he was done with the first one, he started on the second. It was tedious, but it soothed him, and soon, all his attention was focused on the task at hand.

Edward got a few of the tattoo sheets on, lining them up and down the length of both arms and up his neck. While he waited for them to dry, he picked at a piece of graffiti on the brick wall at random and tried getting his head in the game. When it came to talking to people, he had done extensive research, and the best way to get on Dusty's good side was to open with an icebreaker of some kind.

"Oh," — he turned as if he'd just noticed someone standing next to him — "you must be Dusty." Holding out a hand to his imaginary companion, he scoffed "What? These old things? Got them in the pen a few years back when I was doing time for…um…for some crime. Ya feel me?" His voice went high and unsure. "You know what I'm saying?"

No, no, no. No African-American Vernacular. He was too white. It would only end up getting him punched in the dick. He tried again, this time throwing in some swag that hopefully said, 'Look at my tattoos and muscles,' but in a non-douchy way. "Hey, Dusty, from one badass motherfucker to another, you're looking pretty swole today." What was Andrew always adding after compliments? Ah. Right. "No homo."

Better.

A husky laugh reached his ears, and he yelped.

"Your *Dragon Tales* sticker is peeling."

Edward turned to find a woman standing at the mouth of the alleyway, a trail of smoke writhing around her like something alive. Dressed in black leather pants and a loose-fitting Tee, her waist-length braids had been pulled back into a ponytail at the crown of her head. He had never seen anything like it before. Brown bled into gold, and gold into silver ash that shone in the sun—just like her skin. Around five-foot-seven, she was built like an hourglass with wide hips and thighs thick enough to save a life or two. As she stalked toward him, Edward found himself transfixed. The way she moved was hypnotic, every step a dance. Like Edward, both of her arms were covered in brightly colored tattoos, though he couldn't make sense of the mosaic when he was so caught up in the canvas. A stranger carved from shades of brown, like something born of the earth instead of man. A goddess born grown from the roots of some old oak tree. She had a heart-shaped face and a rounded, plump little mouth. Her brows, thick wings over eyes like the dark places between the stars. Someplace dark, forbidden, where prayers went to die.

What had they been talking about? He couldn't remember. Those eyes, wide, dark pools with thick lashes, made it hard to keep track of his thoughts.

"Oh, it's not a sticker," he said, feeling stupid. "It's a tattoo."

"No," she assured him, "it's not." Lifting her hand, she took a long drag from a blunt she held - careless and cocky - between her thumb and middle finger. "What you got there?" She gestured with her chin toward the bag at his feet.

Edward shrugged, his hand twitching a sporadic rhythm. "You ever interview for a job and not have anything to wear?" He asked, nodding too fast.

Christ, she made him nervous. "This is the gang version of business casual."

One brow rose, and she gave him a slow once-over that had his body flushing hot. "Lace fronts and stilettos, huh?" she teased, so gentle he didn't even notice. "Well, shit, darling. Looks like I'm under dressed."

Her voice was throatier than anything he'd ever heard before. A little rough around the edges and smooth in the middle. Like aged whisky. He wanted to taste it. Edward stared at her, unsure what to do or say beyond such a startling thought.

He was used to more petite women, slim, blond, and perfect. With the amount of money backing them, they could afford their versions of perfection, so he had come to expect it. There was no room for tattoos or piercings and scars. No room for anything below a size 12 if he were being honest, and even that was pushing it. Nothing like her had existed in his world before this, and something inside him shifted in some fundamental way he couldn't quite understand.

Then her words registered, and with a grimace, he shifted in the heels he'd stolen from Ms. Bellum. To be honest, he'd forgotten he was even wearing them. Of course, Dollar General didn't have his size anyway. No wonder everyone had been glaring at him, despite the fact that his calves had never looked better. His shoulders fell in defeat. At this rate, he might as well just go home and wait to die. There was no way in hell Dusty would ever accept someone like him. Maybe he was just a lost cause, just like his dad always said.

"I'm a dumbass," Edward sneered, voice cracking around the edges and in the middle and all over. Something fragile he wished he'd kept to himself. A soft brush, warm flesh against his own for the first time in a long time, and Edward flinched back like a struck dog.

"Calm down, Pretty Boy," she said, eyes going hard.

He stood still as she tucked the blunt between her lips and reached for his neck. Squinting through the smoke dancing between them, she pulled the ruined tattoo away from his throat piece by jagged piece.

Edward stared down at her, unable to look away as she wiped away any signs of the two-headed dragon. He used to watch the show on television when he was a kid. Back when a metal hanger from the closet shoved into the cable outlet was the best it ever got. He didn't remember much about the show now, just that two little kids chanted a rhyme and were transported to a land of dragons and magic. Even back then, he'd wanted nothing more than to escape from the world he knew, and something about the soft, wondering expression she wore as she touched him said maybe she could relate.

"Want some help with the rest of those?" she asked.

Speechless, he nodded.

One by one, they peeled the paper backing away from each to inspect what had been left behind. She traced a bright yellow happy face with a rose in its mouth and nodded.

"Badass," she said, voice bland, and Edward preened. "What job are you interviewing for anyway? You supposed to be the new cook? Want me to put in a good word for you?"

"Thanks, but I don't think you can do much." He'd been studying the sweep of her lashes, but his eyes danced away when she looked up at him. "This Dusty guy doesn't sound like the type to put much stock in references."

She froze, eyes going cold. "You're trying to join the Legion?"

Edward frowned. "The Legion?"

The woman hesitated, then shook her head. "It's a biker gang." She glared. "You're Initiating and you don't even know what for?"

"It's been a long day," he said, defensive. His fingers twitched, the motion traveling to encompass his entire hand until his fingers were folding on empty air. Was he making a mistake? If he were smart, he'd take whatever cash was left in his underwear and lay low for a while. Hole up on his estate in Michigan for a few months. Andrew didn't know anything about the property. He'd keep a low profile, work on perfecting MARCO's code, and…and…

And what? Wait for life to go back to normal? What was normal anyway?

Edward had been laying low for the last fifteen years. Day in, day out, year after year after year. Sometimes, he lay in bed at night wondering if he were alive or dead. It was hard to find proof his heart was still beating. That he wasn't wandering lost and alone through purgatory. No one spoke to him, no one touched him, and the little interaction he did have with the outside world was riddled with tension. Things had gotten worse ever since he'd developed MARCO. For the last several years, his every move had been subject to scrutiny.

His assistants and doctors, even his fucking cook and the guy who walked his turtle, were all looking at him. Waiting for him to slip up again. Waiting to carry back proof to Andrew that Edward was a walking basket case just as the rumors claimed. It forced him to be very aware of every move he made and every word he spoke. Every piece of him, down to the way he sat and ate his food, was contrived. Forced. Calculated. A desperate man's desperate attempt to appear sane.

Normal.

His heart was racing, but he wasn't sure why. Was he really afraid of going back home? Wasn't home supposed to be the place you ran to, not from? And even if he did run, what would become of Briarcliff? It needed a Hero. It needed somebody who gave a shit. MARCO wasn't much, but it was all the city had to help combat the encroaching darkness. A darkness threatening to swallow this city, and the innocent people in it, whole. He had to-

Fingers gripped his chin, forcing him back into himself, back to the here and now. He glanced down at the woman, and for some reason, it didn't occur to him to resist as she pulled him close.

"Open your mouth, Cher," she drawled, voice all honey and spiced cloves. She smelled of leather and vanilla, of amber and dark smoke.

He should have hesitated, but he didn't. His lips parted, and eyes still on his, she took a drag of her joint. Held it. Then she pressed her lips against his and breathed into him, filling him with a heat that brought something violent and ravenous to roaring life from deep within his soul. Pulling back, she pressed a kiss against the side of his throat, right over the spot where his tattoo used to be. He could feel the imprint of her lipstick on his skin, and his face flushed red.

"There," she whispered. "Much better than a dragon sticker, don't you think?"

The smoke wrapped around his lungs, and he went lightheaded.

She grinned, stepping back as he began choking.

Smoke exploded from his nostrils and mouth. Edward crouched in the alley and dry heaved as the woman snubbed her blunt out against the brick wall.

"Good luck in there, Pretty Boy. You're going to need it."

Tears streamed from his eyes as he caught his breath. He wanted to call out to her, to ask for her name at least, but she strolled into the bar without a backward glance.

"Thanks," he managed. But she was already gone, leaving him alone with his thoughts and a sneaking suspicion that she was someone there would be no coming back from.

# Chapter Four

*The Good, The Bad, and The Damned*

"What took you so long?" Ape asked, waiting by a table near the jukebox. Massive arms folded across his chest, he glowered at her. At some point, he'd changed out of his stolen suit and now wore a sleeveless vest, with no shirt beneath, and blue jeans.

"Don't start with me," she shouldered him aside so she could glare down at Raphael. The smoke break had bought her some time, but she was still running low on patience—had been ever since getting Papa's message. If she didn't check in soon, he'd send someone to find her, which was a confrontation she wanted to avoid at all costs.

Her former enforcer was killed a few weeks back, and she'd held out high hopes for the newbie. Former military, he'd fallen on hard times after being denied his VA benefits. Joining the Legion fulfilled his desire for violence and camaraderie and got him the prescriptions he needed. Illegally, of course, but tomayto, tomahto. Each of the Legion got the chance to bring in a recruit. Raph had been Dusty's pick, so his failure rankled in more ways than one. When she first met him, he seemed like the type who could get shit done, which may have been because the man was a certified sociopath. Whatever, she'd been willing to overlook his condescending attitude if it meant results. The problem was, she'd yet to see any.

Raphael was kneeling on the floor of The Hellhole in a Victoria's Secret G-string and a pair of Ralph Lauren polo sneakers. At the sight of him, anger clawed through the high she'd cultivated back in the alleyway. Ape hated when she smoked, so she bit back a cough as she pulled up a seat.

Diesel stood next to Raphael, a hand on his shoulder and his face a mask of pride. Kiss ass. He was always buttering her up in hopes of taking over Ape's spot as her second. She was sure he thought finding Raphael, before the cops could scoop him up, had earned him some brownie points, which might have been true if Raphael had come with good news.

Dusty sat, resting her forearms on her knees, and grabbed the remote Ape passed over to her. The news was on, and she turned up the volume. Together, the three of them listened to the reporter expound on the clusterfuck that had taken place that morning.

"Three people are dead, and the governor has called for a statewide manhunt. Several suspects have been identified as members of the Lost Legion, a biker gang that has been operating out of Los Angeles for the last several years."

"I can explain," Raph began.

"Shut the fuck up," Dusty said mildly, her gaze glued to the screen. "This is my favorite part."

"Founding member and former head of the Legion, Theodore Morehouse, has been on death row for the last fifteen years. Morehouse was found guilty of the murder of over twelve people — including his own daughter — back in 2008. Police are concerned that today's events may have been orchestrated by none other than Morehouse himself from behind bars. If true, Governor Wilks is considering moving his execution date to early fall."

The reporter disappeared, replaced by a clip of Governor Ronald Wilks at the press conference that had been held less than an hour ago. "We are doing everything in our power to ensure the safety of the residents of Briarcliff. Morehouse terrorized the nation fifteen years ago, and I won't allow him or others like him to treat our justice system like a joke.

I'm personally overseeing a task force to determine the extent of his involvement and whether he has had a hand in other crimes. If he's found guilty, the state of California can no longer tolerate the threat he represents."

Dusty turned off the television. The bartender, David, met her eyes over Raph's shoulder and paled at whatever her expression was. David ushered Nico and the rest of the staff out the door, and soon, the bar was empty but for members of the Legion. Most of the civilians were smart enough to jump ship as soon as her engine sounded out front. She was relieved. It made what came next easier.

"Give me your hand."

Raphael cursed. "Dusty," he said, "listen to me. This wasn't my fault."

Bemused, she turned her head first left and then right. "But, Cher, you're the only one here." Hooking her finger in the strap of his pretty little underwear, she pulled him closer. "And I gotta punish someone, Raph. I can't have you boys going around thinking it's alright to fuck up this bad. What kind of leader would I be?"

They were nearly cheek to cheek. She could smell the fear on him. The sour stink of sweat. Turning her head, she whispered against the shell of his ear, "Of course, all that changes if you brought me what I asked for."

Raphael met her eyes, "I got the bot," he hissed.

"Where is it?"

"I hid it," when she drew back, sucking her teeth in disapproval, Raph hurried to explain himself. "I needed the insurance Dusty, you know that. You would have done the same."

He was right. She would have. But it rankled that he was playing games with her when she'd been after the flash drive for months now.

"He doesn't have it,"

Dusty's head snapped up, and she almost reached for the gun in the holster at the small of her back. She stopped herself just in time. It was the guy from the alleyway and, as she studied him, her second impression mirrored her first. He was too pretty to be there.

*Too…golden?*

He had dirty blond hair, and the curls falling across his forehead shone even in the dim light. Amber brown eyes. Spiked lashes and strong brows. A sharp jaw. Broad shoulders. Her gaze flickered across him, noting each feature as if she were checking off items on a list. Decent amount of muscle for someone so mild-mannered. He was big. Almost as big as Ape and Ox, but he held himself like a man unsure of his place in the world or his welcome even if he found it. His clothes didn't fit quite right, for one thing. For another, he was barefoot now. He must have ditched the heels before coming inside, which meant he wasn't a complete dumbass. She had to admit that despite her doubts, he'd been right about the tattoos. The 'ink' looked good on him, though she found she liked the untouched canvas of his skin just as much. Her gaze caught and lingered on where her lipstick marred the strong column of his throat, and the surge of possessiveness that followed left her shaken. The urge to be the first to mark him, to leave him with a permanent story to tell, a scar that would never fade, made her ache. Made her hungry.

*The fuck is wrong with me?*

Dusty straightened, her hand fisted in Raph's hair to keep him in line. A not-so-gentle reminder she wasn't through with him just yet. "Care to explain?" she asked the stranger. His gaze darted from one of them to the other, as the thoughts raced across his face.

"What you're looking for," he continued, testing the waters. He seemed to sense, somehow, that this wasn't a topic she wanted to discuss with the room at large, and her assessment of him went up a bit. "He doesn't have it." The stranger had the air of a man taking a chance, and she found herself fascinated by the anxious little look on his dumb face. Dusty glanced down at Raph from the corner of her eye, but he refused to look at her.

"Are you going to believe an outside over me?" The mercenary demanded, spittle flying.

Dusty nodded. "Fair point," she said. "What's your name Pretty Boy," she asked, turning to him.

"Edward," he squeaked.

"See, Raph," she teased. "Edward and I are best buds now." Her fingers tightened, and Raphael's breathing hitched. "I bet *he* knows better than to lie to me," she said, her voice darkening. "Do you?"

Raphael finally met her eyes, his own pools of helpless resentment. "You fucking bitch," he hissed, defeated.

Dusty hummed. "That's what I thought." Letting him go, she got to her feet. Ape stepped in, and he and Diesel dragged Raphael over to the next empty table. He struggled with all his strength, but Ape was built like a goddamn silverback gorilla. No one was getting away from him unless he let them go. Diesel, eager to prove he was no lightweight, took it upon himself to shove Raphael's head down on the tabletop, knocking over several glasses in the process.

Dusty pulled her knife and stalked toward the three of them as the other members of the Legion let loose an unearthly howl. She was going to cut off a finger or two, but it was a bitch sawing through bone. Plus, she didn't want to chip her knife. Feeling magnanimous, she picked something a little less conspicuous. Grabbing Raphael's earlobe, she lifted as much of it as she could and pressed the cold steel of her butterfly knife where the soft flesh met his skull.

"Scream," she told him, though he probably couldn't hear her past the curses flying out of his mouth. "It helps."

Lucky for Raphael, Dusty kept her tools sharp. A flash of silver, and then blood was coating her hands. She held Raph's left ear up for the rest of the Legion to see as Ape and Diesel let the man collapse onto the dirty floor. The bikers cheered, beating tables and stomping their feet. She let the visceral sound of their bloodlust wash over her, body flushing hot. She hated making a mess, but damn did she love getting messy.

Dusty turned, excitement dying as she caught sight of Edward again. He was staring, not at Raphael but at Dusty, and he was…sad? It brought her up short. She would have expected many things. Disgust. Disapproval. Even horror. Where the hell had sadness come from?

"Get him out of here," she breathed, shying away from Raph's writhing form.

"You serious?" Ape asked.

Dusty had never seen the big guy look so surprised. It would have been funny if she weren't holding a human ear. She tossed the appendage over to Diesel and snapped her fingers until someone hurried over and handed her a wet rag from the bar.

"Have a bit of decorum, Ape," she said. From across the room, Edward choked as if she'd said something funny, but she ignored him. "There's a virgin in the house and the last thing we want to do is scare him off. After all," she met Raphael's gaze and her lips tightened in annoyance, "we're still a member down."

Ape nodded and, together, he and Diesel drug Raphael to the storage room in the back. "Wait," she called. The two men paused, and she motioned at Raphael's shoes. "They don't match the outfit anyway."

Diesel yanked the shoes off, and Raph was taken away, cursing her name the entire way. Good. He'd need the energy for when she got her hands on him again. Assuming he was still around by then. If he were smart, he'd run while he still could. Taking a seat, she wiped the blood from her hands and motioned Edward closer. "Change your mind about joining?" she asked, half joking.

Ape sent her a look as he came back and took a seat by her side.

"You're Dusty?" He asked, horrified. Dusty couldn't decide whether she was offended or pleased. She settled on tickled.

"Last I checked," she said. Sitting up straight, she extended her arms and posed like she used to see the little beauty queens do back home in Louisianna.

"You like what you see?"

"Great!" he said stiffly, sidestepping her question. "That's…that's great. I've heard—"

God, he was precious. She had to fight the desire to mess with him. His eyes darted down; her hands were still covered in Raphael's blood. *Shit.*

She scrubbed at her hands until the cloth was too filthy to use, and even then, her palms and fingernails were still stained red. She flexed her hand, burying a spark of embarrassment.

*Wait, what the hell do I have to be ashamed of?*

This was her life. He was the one intruding on it. She wouldn't censor herself just to make him comfortable. If anything, knowing what he was getting into was the fastest and easiest way to send him packing. Dusty had a hard enough time ensuring the Legion was taken seriously. Biker gangs were notoriously run by older men. Older white men. Yet here she was, a young black woman. It was three strikes against her and anyone who chose to follow under her command. Despite this, every few weeks, she got random losers trying to join up. Sure, they could get into the Legion even when they wouldn't be accepted anywhere else. But Dusty was picky. Most of the members who made up the Legion had been there since her father's heyday. The rest she had handpicked over the years. This one didn't look like a racist or an incel, confident he deserved to lead more than she did, but nor did he seem useful. Or bright.

Though she was proof looks could be deceiving.

Still, she owed him for his help with Raphael. She'd hear him out, see what he knew about the flash drive, and then kick his ass out of there before he chipped a nail or something. Speaking of…why was he still standing there barefoot?

*Dummy,* she thought.

"Put the shoes on," she ordered.

Edward blinked. "Excuse me?"

"The shoes, Pretty Boy." She waved toward the abandoned Ralph Laurens. "Put them on before you get hepatitis or gangrene or something."

"I don't think—"

Dusty growled in growing annoyance.

"Yes, ma'am," he capitulated.

Ape, Otter, Diesel, and a few others began showing signs of boredom as he took his time, affixing the laces just so. They were not a group known for their patience, after all. Still, she glared them all into silence, and when Edward stood, he seemed braver.

"So," she asked. "What the fuck do you want?"

It wasn't what she was curious about, but there were too many listening in to bring the topic up just yet. She'd get a feel for him first, find out what made him tick, and go from there. It would make torturing the information out of him later much easier. Dusty would see where the night took them. Small talk was Plan A.

Torture was Plan B.

"I wanted to talk to you about your crew." Edward hooked his thumbs in his belt loops and sort of slouched where he stood. The motion made the muscles in his arms bulge, and he winked at the waitress as she sidled past with a tray of beers.

Jeanine should have left with the others, but she was married to Otter and worked for the Legion when they were in town. There was little she hadn't seen before, but even she seemed taken aback by the display.

Dusty cocked her head to one side, wondering what the hell he thought he was doing. She should put a stop to this, but it had been a shit morning so far, and she could use a little entertainment while the cops were busy chasing their own tales. The 'strays' knew better than to talk, so it was just a matter of waiting a day or two until the heat died down.

*If Papa Tate's in town, it might be time to go scorched earth regardless of what the BPD has on us. Speaking of...*

"My crew," she repeated, rolling the words around in her mouth and finding the taste of them strange. Dusty pocketed her butterfly knife, tossed the rag in favor of a beer, and nodded. "Right." Squinting at him over the edge of her glass, she asked, "You a cop?"

The question was a lit match. Instant brushfire. The men at her table surged to their feet. Those who had been shrouded in shadows up until then made themselves known.

Edward's throat worked convulsively as bikers closed in on all sides, hemming him in. Dusty pictured the group as a newcomer might. They were an odd mix of races, ages, and genders, and every one of them presented a threat.

"Of course he's a cop, look at him. Twitchy little shit."

"Fuck him up, Dusty."

"You got a lot of nerve, stepping foot in here."

Edward turned back to Dusty, amber eyes accusing and body tense.

Dusty muffled her laugh with her drink. Not a complete idiot, then. A shame. The pretty ones were only fun so long as they were dumb.

"I'm not a cop."

Dusty was proud of him for managing to sound so calm. He swallowed hard, and his fingers began a nervous promenade. "Then what are you?" she asked, fascinated by the display.

Edward hesitated. Shrugged. "Edward," he said. "Just Edward."

"Alright then, Just Edward," Dusty said, softening despite herself. Maybe there wouldn't be a need for Plan B after all. "Pull up a seat." She waved off the others, and the crowd dispersed as fast as it had formed; satiated. The conversation picked up at a couple of tables, and the rumble of pool balls filled the bar again. Someone Fonzied the jukebox into working, and Stevie Nicks crooned a soft ballad that erased the last vestiges of violence from the air.

Edward did as he was told, pulling a chair from another table so he could perch on the edge of it. When it was just her, Edward, Ape, and Diesel, Dusty dropped the act. "What do you want?"

Edward held up his hands in a show of surrender. "I don't know what you —"

"Cut the crap," she interrupted. Leaning in close so the others wouldn't overhear, she continued, "Where's the bot? What were you doing in the bank? You working for somebody?" Edward's picture was all over the news. He was wanted for questioning, though the media hadn't identified him just yet. The fact that they thought he was one of hers was a complication she didn't need.

Edward flinched, glancing down at his hands in his lap. "I was just in the wrong place at the wrong time."

Dusty glanced at Ape, and he nodded in silent agreement. She had been teasing about the cop thing, but it looking more and more plausible. She asked, "Then why are you here now?"

"Because," —Edward took a deep breath—"I think we can help each other." He reached into his pocket and Dusty tensed, half expecting him to pull a weapon. Instead, he slid a small, rectangular disk across the table to her. Her heart leaped, and Ape cursed beneath his breath.

"Where did you get this?" Ape asked, his expression stormy.

Edward's eyes didn't stray from Dusty. "So, you *were* the one after it." He exhaled, and his shoulders relaxed. That he seemed relieved was odd, since she was two seconds away from breaking his kneecaps.

"Answer the question," she ordered, snatching the drive.

Edward tensed as if he was going to stop her, but he changed his mind at the last second. "I took it from the MARCO bot," he said, chin high. "I figured it was enough to earn me some protection. Was I right?"

Dusty ignored him, too busy staring at the flash drive.

How long had she been trying to get her hands on one of these? The security at the prison where Theodore Morehouse was being held was top of the line. No one had ever seen anything like it before. Which is where Papa Tate came in. Her former guardian had pulled a lot of strings to get her information about the drive, about who had made it, where to find it, and when. She knew it was just a matter of time before he called in a favor, but she wasn't yet ready to play his game. There was still so much left to do if she had any hope at all of freeing her father.

According to Papa, the developer behind the tech- a guy named E.M. Hayes- hadn't been seen in public since his company was founded ten years ago. No one knew anything about him, besides the fact that he was a genius and richer than God. Dusty didn't give a shit about Hayes or his money. All she cared about was the drive. Vance, one of the best hackers in the country, lived right here in Briarcliff. It was the whole reason she'd moved to this godforsaken city. All she had to do was get Vance the drive, and he promised he could use it to customize a virus, one they could use to decimate the prison's security features. Not indefinitely, but long enough for Dusty to get in and out.

*Maybe. Hopefully.*

It was going to cost her, of course, but it was the least she could do after Desi. She owed her spirit this much. A touch, featherlight, across the nape of her neck. It could have been the air conditioning. A stray breeze. But Dusty knew better. She was tired of being haunted. Tired of the ghost shit. Maybe if she made things right, Desi would leave her alone.

"So, you need protection, huh," she mused. It'd been a few years since the Legion had protected anyone. They were always on the move, which meant any alliances were temporary. "What about Drugs?" She offered, hopeful. "You need some Money? If you want girls, you'll need to go to someone else. We don't peddle in that shit."

Edward's eyes got as big as saucers. "No, no, no. I don't...I don't need any of that. I just..." He ran a frustrated hand through his hair.

There was a dimple in his cheek and the sight brought her up short.

*This one's trouble.*

"I just need some help," he was saying. "Someone wants to kill me. I need you to find out who and to help me cancel the hit."

Dusty got to her feet. "Sure thing. You did me a favor. I got you."

"Where do you think you're going?" Diesel asked with a smile. He always said she had the attention span of a rodent, but she'd been still for at least five minutes. A personal best.

Clearing her throat, she zipped up her leather jacket and pulled on her gloves so she wouldn't have to look at Ape. "To see Vance."

Ape shook his head, expression thunderous. "No, the hell you're not."

Edward jumped at the skin-crawling baritone, and Dusty quelled the urge to pet him behind the ears. He reminded her of an anxious kitten, or maybe an excitable golden retriever. Dusty winced, Ape's bellow still ringing in her ears. She often said his nickname should have been Foghorn, but no one listened to her when it mattered. Several members of the Legion glanced at them, and she lowered her voice, careful to keep her expression blank. "And why the hell not?"

"Maybe because of the citywide manhunt?" Ape asked, incredulous.

Grinning, Dusty tightened her ponytail. "Emphasis on 'man,'" she lied, sharing a weighted glance with Ape, and his lips tightened with bitterness as realization dawned. The missive hidden between her breasts was heavier than ever before. Maybe she could take care of two birds with one stone. "Ain't nobody gonna be looking for me," she continued, for the sake of Diesel and Edward. "Joe and Lenny know I'll bail them out once I have the cash. They'll stay quiet 'til then."

"And how are you supposed to find Vance?" Diesel queried.

Dusty breathed a sigh of relief. She had been worried she'd made a mistake trusting Diesel with her plans, but so far, he'd proven he could be an asset. Dusty patted his shoulder. "Manhunt," she said.

"Anyone with a record and a lick of sense will keep their head down. And I happen to know where Vance likes to play."

"Care to share with the class?" Ape asked.

"Nope," she said merrily. "Come on, Pretty Boy." She dragged Edward from his seat as she headed to the front door. "Let's get you initiated."

"Initiated?" His voice squeaked a bit at the end.

Dusty grinned. "It's a rite of passage, Cher," she replied. Throwing her arm over his shoulders, she jerked him closer. "As far as this lot is concerned, you're a new recruit, and new recruits are put through the gauntlet."

He paled. "Oh...fun?"

Dusty kissed his stubbled cheek. He smelled like cedarwood and honey. Something warm and newly blossomed. "Oh," she said, relishing the way his hands shook before he clenched them into fists and tucked them beneath his arms. "It is."

# Chapter Five

*Sweet Poppy*

Dusty led Edward outside to her bike. Neon lights lit up the outside of the bar, and the street beyond bustled with people. The parade had been cut short thanks to the bank robbery, so the main roads were open once again. Her bike, a pristine hog with a red paint job and ROXANNE scrawled across one side, dominated the street in front of the bar. Out of the long line of bikes, Dusty liked to think Roxy gleamed the brightest. Granted, she'd built the damn thing, so she was a bit biased. Roxanne was a collection of parts from several different bikes all crafted together to form something new, slick, and dangerous. The motorcycle was streamlined and built for speed.

Dubious, Edward eyed Roxanne as Dusty straddled the seat and revved her engine. "So do I follow you in an Uber or…?"

Dusty glanced at him over her shoulder, the tail end of her ponytail sliding across her leather jacket like a snake. A serpent just as impatient as its charmer. "Get on."

Scowling, Edward shook his head.

Dusty's lips curled, a hint of mockery waiting and ready. "You're about to join a motorcycle gang," she said slowly. "But you're afraid of riding a motorcycle?"

"I'm not afraid," a fire flickering to life in his amber eyes.

The rev and rumble between her legs was all too familiar, but his frustration made it all the sweeter. "Then prove it, Pretty Boy."

"I'm starting to hate that name," he grumbled, clambering onto the bike behind her. He was so big he had to curl around her, and Dusty rolled her hips as she leaned forward to grip the handlebars.

"Tough shit." As soon as he was settled, she eased off the clutch and let Roxy fly, slipping into the flow of traffic with the ease of long practice. Edward yelped, gripping her hard around the waist.

Pressed against the curve of her back, Dusty could feel the muscled planes of his chest and belly. She took a turn too fast, and his arms tightened further, biceps trapping her in the circle of him. Against her better judgment, she shifted, fitting herself more solidly against him until she wore him like a second skin. His breath teased the back of her neck, the only spot of warmth as cold air whipped past them. The ill-fitting clothes did a lot to hide it, but now there was no missing the sheer strength of him. If he wanted to, he could hurt her.

The thought intrigued.

Dusty was careful never to give a man the physical advantage. She preferred sleeping with women because it was the one time she could be vulnerable enough to enjoy the act. Men Edward's size were to be avoided at all costs. But there was something about him, something insidious and sweet.

Dusty shook the thought away. Pushing her awareness of Edward to the back of her mind, she headed back into the heart of the city. She didn't have time to moon over someone like him. He was running from something, and her job was to keep it from catching him. First things first, pass the flash drive to Vance and see if she could make a little extra cash, since the heist today was a bust. If a certain someone was around, maybe she could charm him into buying her a little more time with Papa. The bastard wasn't known for his altruism, however, and she wondered what it would take to buy his cooperation as they rode. Around them, the world passed by in a blur, a drunken kaleidoscope of color. Something she would always be a part of, but not really. The grief in her heart was an old wound, one she knew better than to pick at anymore. Being around Edward was like digging nails into the edges of scared skin to see if there was still fresh blood underneath, but it was too late now to turn him away.

By the time they pulled up outside Happy Nails, the parking lot was full despite the closed sign and lack of interior lights. There were plenty of other shops in the strip mall to account for the number of cars, but Dusty knew the Party City and Home Depot weren't the reason the parking lot was poppin' at midnight on a Friday.

Edward was quiet as they walked toward the nail salon. Already she'd grown to expect his near-constant stream of nervous chatter. Now, he seemed content to watch, his eyes bright with curiosity as she knocked twice on the salon doors.

A young woman scurried over to the door and inclined her head in a half bow, both apology and greeting rolled into one. "We're closed," she said, pointing to the sign. "You come back tomorrow." Her accent was thick and her English clipped.

Anyone else may have been fooled by the performance, but Dusty knew better. She pressed her forehead against the glass and grinned down at the woman, the flash of teeth hinting at hunger as she took in the lithe body beneath the pink bustier and camo pants. Bone-straight hair framed her rounded face, and her sharp asymmetrical bangs had been dyed dark pink. Slanted brown eyes and a button nose graced a pale face. *There's my girl.* "Come on, Poppy," she purred. "Don't be a fuckin' tease."

Poppy stared at her in silence before rolling her eyes. As soon as she opened the door, Dusty wrapped an arm around her waist and kissed her, lips parted and moist, sweet and soft.

"There's my girl." She buried her face against Poppy's neck as they danced through the doorway. "How long's it been?"

Poppy smacked her upside the head, and Dusty drew back with a grimace.

"Not long enough," Poppy accused, though Dusty liked to think there was still some lingering affection in the outburst. "What the fuck are you doing here?" she hissed.

Dusty always got a kick out of it when she dropped the Korean accent. Poppy was born in Idaho. The closest she'd ever come to Korea was watching romantic dramas with her grandmother, who, coincidentally, just so happened to be the founder of Briarcliff's premier underground fight club.

A worthy gauntlet indeed.

Poppy's eyes darted between Edward and the back of the salon, and Dusty knew she was checking to make sure Mrs. Park wasn't about to appear out of thin air like a pissed-off Dr. Strange. "What part of 'banned for life' isn't sinking in?" she asked through gritted teeth.

"All of it, if I'm being honest," Dusty admitted, slipping past her and hot-footing it toward the back hall. Edward followed, though she could tell he was beginning to second-guess his decision to join the Legion by his expression.

Past the eyebrow station and a wall of nail polish in every color imaginable, was a door. During business hours, they set up a table up inside the small back room so women could get their cooters waxed, but on fight nights, the table was shoved aside and the trap door underneath thrown open. Briarcliff had several tunnels located underneath the city from miners back in the day. Many of them had been sealed away, but Mrs. Park knew there was little a person couldn't accomplish with the help of the Ancestors and a working jackhammer. People would have been trickling in since the shop closed Thursday afternoon. If she listened hard enough, Dusty could hear cheering and drunken shouting as she opened the door. She was a kid in a candy store.

"Oh no you don't, you crazy bitch," Poppy plastered herself against the door as Dusty was about to walk in. "If Halmani finds out you were here after what happened last time—"

Dusty's eyes widened with glee. "You mean she's not even here?" *The old battleax must be losing her edge.*

Poppy winced. "No, Eliot took over." Dropping her arms in defeat, her tone turned accusatory. "Which you would know if you ever called."

Planting a hand on the wall above Poppy's head, Dusty leaned in and pressed her smile against her cheek. "You sound like you missed me," she whispered, pleased when she shuddered.

"Um, should I leave? 'Cause I can leave."

The sound of Edward's voice brought Dusty back to the task at hand, and she straightened. "Sorry, Pops," she said. "I know I should do better. And I will, I promise." When Poppy remained unconvinced, Dusty sighed. "Look, I brought a peace offering."

Dusty sent him a look, and though unsure, Edward nevertheless lifted his hand and waved.

Poppy's lips parted in surprise.

"You've seen the news," Dusty said, talking fast before she could get kicked out. "The bank job went south, and now we're short. Talk to Eliot, let my boy fight."

Poppy stared at Edward, unimpressed. "You think he can win?" She asked.

*Hell no.* "Absolutely," Dusty assured her. "If nothing else, he might give Crusher a run for his money. It'd be a hell of a way to wrap up the night."

"I'm sorry, who?"

Dusty waved Edward into silence as Poppy considered the offer. When the other woman nodded, she almost sagged in relief.

"Fine," Poppy opened the door and led them inside.

They made their way to the trap door,and as Edward was descending the dark staircase into the club, Poppy cleared her throat.

"Dusty," she said, voice low. "Just so you know, things have changed since the last time you were here."

Dusty cocked her head to one side. "Changed how?"

For the first time, Poppy grinned. "You'll see."

At the bottom of the staircase was a room the size of a community theater, with a boxing ring in the middle. At least a hundred people were watching the current fight, and voices rose and fell around them as bets were placed. It was muggy in the tunnel-chamber, and the smell of sweat and blood were heavy in the air. The current fight was almost over, but Dusty could see what Poppy meant as soon as she cleared the last step. Both fighters were buck nekkid. She threw her ex a wide-eyed look of glee and Poppy bit her lip on a smile.

The fighters had been going at it (ha!) for a while. Both men had taken heavy damage, though only one of them was weaving where he stood. The spectators were looking a little rough around the edges, too.

There was no real telling how many days some of them had been here, though it was long enough for their deodorant to wear off. Assuming they'd worn any in the first place.

Eliot, the somber overseer of the fights, was stationed at the bar so he could keep an eye on the proceedings and everyone coming and going. Security manned the staircase and stalked the parameter to keep the audience in line. One of the guards tensed when he caught sight of Dusty, but Poppy was there to give the signal that all was well. An alarmed squeak brought her attention to Edward, who remained frozen at the bottom of the steps.

"It's just a cock fight, Edward. Grow up."

"Grow up!?" Edward struggled to keep his voice down, though it wasn't as if anyone could have heard him over all the noise. Poppy tapped her on the shoulder, nodding towards a privacy screen in the back, and Dusty nodded. Since he didn't seem inclined to follow on his own, she gripped his forearm and drug him after her.

*Patience, Adele,* she thought. If it weren't for being a former employee, she might have been just as overwhelmed as Edward. The nudity was new, but a decided improvement as far as Dusty was concerned.

"Care to explain to me what we're doing here?" Edward asked, as soon as they were behind one of the screens.

Seeing dong always left her feeling amicable, so she nodded. "Sure thing, Chere," she said. "You ever see the movie *Fight Club*?"

Edward nodded, while Dusty rolled the lollipop she'd snatched from the Snack Girl on her tongue. "It's like that," she said. "But with your dick out."

"So, not like that at all."

She shrugged. "I don't know. I've never seen the movie."

"So why assume I have?" He was almost shouting, but Dusty found she didn't mind much.

She snorted at his question. "You're a White guy in your mid-thirties. Please be fucking for real. Next, you're going to tell me you don't have strong feelings about Chris Pratt, and you've never argued with someone about *Star Wars*." She leaned in, eager to tease. "Is Baby Yoda your Roman Empire?"

He bit his lip, and his face turned red. One second passed, then two. He never made it to three. "I just don't understand why you would infantilize such a powerful and significant figure in the Star Wars franchise—" He shook his head, cursed. "You know what? Never mind." Edward paused, but it was clear he couldn't help himself. "For the record, Chris Pratt is a goddamn treasure. His work on *Parks and Recreation* alone is iconic and will be remembered for generations."

"Right." Dusty nodded as if she gave a shit. "Of course." She pointed her lollipop at his crotch and waved it like a wizard's wand. "Now take those off. I can't place any bets until I see foreskin."

Edward reached out, grabbing the hand that held the lollipop and squeezing. Even frustrated and embarrassed, he handled her gently. Carefully. As if she were something that might break. As if he couldn't tell she already had.

*Curiouser and curiouser.*

His touch was gone a second later, and Dusty found that, much like last time, she missed it.

"Do I really have to be naked?" He asked, sad puppy eyes weapons at the ready.

"It's Greco-Roman style, darlin,'" she reminded him, almost unmoved. "Eliot is into that cultured shit."

"There's nothing cultured about two grown men fighting naked."

"There is if you're doing it right."

Edward started pacing.

To be honest, Dusty wasn't sure why Eliot now insisted on full nudity. A few people were stabbed over the years, true, but the bystanders were just as likely to carry weapons as the fighters. Not that she cared either way; she enjoyed the view just as much as the next guy. Why the hell would she tell Edward he could technically keep his underwear on and still fight when it would mean depriving herself of the chance to see…so much?

Poppy poked her head around the screen and Edward yelped.

"Good news I hope?" Dusty said, straightening.

Poppy sent Edward a look and lifted one shoulder in a delicate shrug. "Ban's lifted for the night," she said begrudgingly. "He can fight. A lot of folks saw you two come in and they're already placing bets."

Dusty hooked a finger around the edge of the curtain and pulled it back just long enough to see Poppy was right. The blue slips— small strips of paper representing Edward in the upcoming match— were already piling up before Eliot.

"Have I ever told you how much I love you?" she asked Poppy, half-joking.

"Whatever," Poppy groused. "Don't say I never did anything for you."

"I wouldn't dare."

Poppy gave her the finger and disappeared. Dusty stared at the place she'd been and told herself it wasn't a huge mistake coming here tonight.

"Maybe we should go?" Edward was speaking, and she cleared her throat of regret.

"If you're scared, just go out there, swing your dingle-dangle a bit, and then tap out before he can hit you."

"Why would I need to swing it—"

"The point," Dusty interrupted, "is that you can throw the match. So, a few people see your patty cakes? Big deal. Who hasn't flashed a room full of strangers their upside-down? It's not like you'll be the only one."

Instead of being reassured by her words, Edward clutched his chest, fighting for air. Dusty scrambled out of the way and urged him into her vacated seat. "I can't breathe," he gasped, fanning himself with both hands.

*For fuck's sake.* Trying to remember what it was like to soothe someone and coming up blank, Dusty channeled her inner cheerleader. "Come on, Chere. This is only awkward if you keep doing"—Dusty waved helplessly at him—"whatever *this* is." Crouching next to him, she patted his arm. There. That felt normal. That felt good. She was *good* at this, damnit. "No one likes a sad peen," she said, booping his nose. "So just be confident about your shit, and you'll be fine."

Without warning, Edward surged to his feet. Dusty stumbled back, surprised once again at how much taller he was than her.

"Whelp, I guess I'm calling it," he said, reaching for the privacy screen.

Dusty jumped up, catching his wrist before he could shove the screen aside. "Where the hell do you think you're going?" she asked, all traces of good humor gone. "I've been nice so far because you're cute, but you don't seem to understand the situation you're in. Let me spell it out for you." Stepping into his personal space, she let her head fall back so she could keep her eyes locked on his. "Your face is plastered all over the news. You think the asshole gunning for you is going to just give up? Chances are he's hunting for you as we speak, and if he's anything like me, he has connections all over this city. If you even make it to the cops, what's to stop him from killing you in holding?"

"The police—"

"As far as they're concerned, you're an accomplice, Chere. They'll cuff your ass to a table for a day or two while they go around finding clues and eating Scooby Snacks or whatever the fuck it is they do. Plenty of time for trouble to come knocking." She took a deep breath to calm herself, and when she spoke again, her voice had gentled. "You want my help? Well, this is how you get it without the rest of the Legion knowing what you did for me."

Edward searched her face, his amber eyes darkening to a warm brown. "They don't know what you're up to, do they?"

"No," she admitted, voice hoarser than usual. "And I plan on keeping it that way."

She couldn't tell the rest of the Legion because she knew not all of them could be trusted. After all, it was one of their number who killed Desi and all those other girls. Now, Dusty wasn't one to judge. Every one of them had blood on their hands, including her. But there was a difference between killing and slaughtering. Someone among their ranks was a serial killer.

A monster.

Dusty had no way of finding her sister's murderer. She'd spent the last fifteen years trying, but it was damn near impossible to pin down a suspect. The Legion had hundreds of members spread out across the country, some of whom she'd never met. The ones who weren't dead, in jail, or on the road were busy keeping the money flowing for the rest of them. Besides petty—and not-so-petty—larceny, the Legion also trafficked drugs, weapons, and information. As the Charter President, everything filtered back to Dusty. The bank heist hadn't just been a cover for snatching the flash drive. Families were falling on hard times, and the money from the bank job would keep many of them going for the remainder of the year.

The other robberies had gone off without a hitch, but since the Legion didn't collect protection money, they needed to keep the lights on somehow, and living in Briarcliff wasn't cheap. With the bank job a failure, Dusty needed to make up for her losses if she had any hope of keeping folks fed and a roof over their heads. If she failed, the clubhouse would have several irate spouses and a shit load of toddlers running down its halls come the end of the month. It was funny now, but when she took over the Lost Legion, she thought she'd have enough time to play Nancy Drew and right a few wrongs. In reality, she was too busy keeping this circus running to do anything else, let alone catch a killer and save Rat.

"Can I really throw the match?" Edward stared at the ground, his shoulders rounded as if already waiting for a blow.

Dusty blinked. Sometimes, she forgot there were people whose lives didn't revolve around blood and violence. Against her better judgment, she softened by slow degrees. "I'm *begging* you to throw the match," she said. She touched his chin and tugged until his eyes were on her once again. "You're too pretty to get hit in the face."

The fear in his gaze shifted to annoyance. "Thanks."

"No problem, darlin'."

# Chapter Six

*Chicks, Dicks, and Magic Tricks*

"Next time you see Papa, tell him to kiss my ass."

Eliot didn't bother looking up from his ledgers, too engrossed with his numbers to turn away- even for an old friend. Though, if she was being honest, there was nothing friendly about the things she'd seen him do. Like Poppy, he had bone-straight hair, though his was a rich brown. Shaved short on both sides, ravens had been tattooed in place of his hair. They soared down the back of his neck to disappear beneath the collar of his brown suit jacket and white button-down. The rest of his hair was so long he kept it in a tight bun at the top of his head. His shirt was open to his chest, where several necklaces glinted with every move he made. His olive skin and dark brown eyes glowed like warm honey in the poor lighting.

Like Dusty, he wore a pair of leather gloves, though his were decorated with small silver chains. She didn't know what lay beneath the gloves since he never took them off, but she could guess. She could see the burns marring his wrists, and they spoke volumes. Even after twelve years, he didn't talk about what had caused the scars he always went to such great lengths to hide, and Dusty had never asked him about his nightmares, for fear she would have to name her own.

"That's a hell of a way to repay a man who's doing you a favor," he said, without inflection.

"Please," Dusty said with a sneer. "Papa's not doing me any favors. He's just trying to make sure I stay indebted to him until he can snatch me back into the fold."

Eliot sighed. "If you know, then stop making it so easy for him."

Annoyed, Dusty took a seat on the edge of the table where he was working. From their vantage point, they had a perfect view of the rest of the room. She stared down at the top of Eliot's head for a good minute before impatience got the best of her.

"Hey," she poked him in the arm with her boot. "Pay attention to me." Before she could pull away, Eliot lashed out, grabbing her by the ankle, and she yelped. A high, feminine sound she'd never made before. The damage done to her throat when she was young left her voice too husky for such sounds, and no one knew that better than Eliot. Unlike Edward, he was not at all gentle with her, and her pulse hammered in her ears as he met her gaze from beneath his lashes. They stared at one another as his fingers crept upwards – a game of chicken she was destined to lose. His gloves brushed the bare skin of her calf, and she shuddered.

Eliot smirked. "Happy?"

Dusty jerked her leg back. "Asshole," she snapped, even more irritated when he laughed and licked the fingertip of his glove as if he could taste her on it. Irate and flushed, she slid off the table.

"You're the one who wanted my attention," he reminded her, turning back to his ledgers and calculator, just as calm and collected as he'd been when she first arrived. "Vance isn't here, by the way," he continued before she could respond.

Dusty scowled. "Then where the hell is he?"

Eliot shrugged. "He's supposed to be handling the bets tonight, but he flaked on me." He shook his head in disgust. "You catch him before I do, tell him he's grounded."

"You're such a dad," she teased.

He grunted in response.

Well, there was nothing else for it. Once she and Edward were done there, she'd go searching for the little brat. The last fight had been over for several minutes, so staff could mop up the blood and sweat from the ring. They'd drug the body away, and the winner had already collected his winnings. Which meant it was time for the main event. The lights dimmed, and someone set the smoke machine in the corner on high. The bruiser who shimmied under the ropes and army-crawled to the middle of the stage probably thought no one could see him in the dark. To Dusty's surprise, the crowd didn't even snicker. In fact, when the lights came back on at full strength and he rose to his full height like the Undertaker from WWE rising from his grave, Crusher was met with thunderous applause. Eliot glanced up as his reigning champion bounded around the ring, hyping up the spectators and snatching beer cans so he could chug the remains and crush them against his skull

"Well, *someone* likes making an entrance," she said in disgust, sidling closer so she could be heard over Crusher's entry music.

"Says the woman who *begged* me to find Powerpuff Girl costumes 'for morale,'" Eliot raised his brows at her attitude. "How'd that work out for you by the way?" When she didn't respond, he shook his head in disgust. "Anyway, Crusher's a fan favorite," he said. "Even if he weren't, I didn't peg you as a hater, Dusty. It's not a good look."

"I'll keep that in mind," she replied sardonically. Curious in spite of herself, Dusty took up position behind Eliot so she could see the ring better. The post was so familiar her arm snaked over his shoulder to rest on the bare skin of his chest – her body settling into old habits without thought, or rhyme, or reason. He tensed at the contact but didn't pull away, and neither did she step back. The first one to back down or show that this small touch meant anything at all would lose the game. It was all games between the two of them. It was one of the reasons she'd left in the first place.

It was easy to see why Crusher had remained undefeated for so long. The guy was a giant. Six-foot-five and almost 300 pounds of muscle and body hair, he was so ripped he couldn't turn his head. How the hell had they gotten him through the trap door? Maybe he lived beneath the nail salon, and they'd just built the place around him. Like a bridge troll, except it was some college dropout named Brad hopped up on steroids, coke, and monster energy drinks.

"Talk dirty to me."

"Quarter mil to Crusher if he wins." He shrugged. "Minus my fee, of course. Double to anyone who beats him."

She whistled. Some would take the bet just for a chance to win half a million dollars, but most were smart enough not to risk it. Crusher was the favorite for a reason.

"Let me get in on that," she ordered.

Eliot wrote her name in his ledger without hesitation. "Is your new toy going to be a problem?"

She bristled. "Is that a goddamn tone?"

"No idea what you're talking about." His dark eyes were void of emotion.

Dusty leaned across his back, arms wrapping around his shoulders so she could compare her long division on the page to the amount of money nestled in her bra. They were too close, she knew that, but Eliot was one flame she'd never tire of burning herself on. Eliot's fingers brushed her wrist, and she was opening her mouth to speak, to fan the fire, when Edward came from behind the curtain.

This wasn't WrestleMania or anything. There were no announcers to tell the crowd a fighter had arrived. But when Edward stepped from behind his curtain, golden skin on full, uninterrupted display, Dusty wasn't the only one struck dumb. He was all corded muscle bathed in light and eyes like gems. She imagined he was what Adonis or even Thor would look like if they ever walked the earth for real. Well, maybe not Chris Hemsworth's Thor, but someone's.

Her gaze dropped to his mystery machine, and she broke out in a sweat. "It's like watching a guinea pig fight his way out of a tube sock," she whispered in awe.

Eliot cleared his throat, and his hand dropped, but for some reason, Dusty didn't notice. Whatever objection Eliot may have had to her choice of words was cut short as people swarmed his table, eager to change their bets. Dusty would have been one of them, but Eliot turned her away, his expression so scathing she knew there *had* been a tone earlier. And he had the nerve to accuse *her* of being a hater.

*Whatever.*

Edward might have had a sleeper build, but he didn't have the heart to win. Dusty wondered why the knowledge bothered her. A vibration at her hip brought her attention to her cell. "What?" It wasn't much of a greeting, but it was the best she could do.

"Have you seen the news?" Ape's voice was tense with nerves, which wasn't saying much. The guy always had his panties in a twist about something.

"What part of underground fight club screams CNN to you?"

Ape took a deep breath. He was trying not to curse as much ever since he'd found God or whatever, and apparently, she tested him in ways the Almighty would not approve of. Once he found his inner peace, he was much more calm, "It's him, Dusty. He's the guy."

She frowned. "What the hell are you talking about?"

Her phone buzzed as an image came through, and she squinted down at the little screen, waiting for the jpeg to load. It was a screenshot from Ape's smartphone. A news article with a headline reading, "Genius, Millionaire, Madman. The fall of E.M. Hayes." Below the scathing words was a picture of Edward, just not as she knew him. This Edward was dressed in a suit, his hair slicked back and his jaw free of the shadow of a beard. He was clean-cut, confident, and expressionless.

Ape was yelling, and it took Dusty a second to make sense of it past the ringing in her ears. "Calm down," she said through gritted teeth.

Eliot glanced her way, but Dusty turned her back on him. The referee was going over the rules for Edward and Crusher, and her pulse spiked.

"The news is saying he's been missing since yesterday," Ape said. "Apparently, he's in the middle of a psychotic episode. Dusty…"

This was bad. Dusty didn't need Ape to say it. Hanging up, she shoved through the crowd, leaving Eliot behind without so much as a goodbye. Just like old times. She made it to the stage and used the ropes to pull herself up.

Edward was looking around the room in mounting panic, but when his gaze landed on her relief softened his rough edges. No one had ever been glad to see her before and her throat tightened.

Ditching the ref, Edward hurried over to her. "Dusty, this is a bad idea. I know—"

"Yes." Dusty nodded a little too quickly. "Yeah, the plan is shit. We should go."

How many years could she get for kidnapping a psychotic millionaire and forcing him to fight for money? Her guess? Much more than armed robbery. Her gaze dropped to his dick, then back up again as quickly, and she winced as they made eye contact. Was this an assault charge? It felt assaulty. Or at least assault-lite. Fuck, she was going to jail.

The referee cut through the air with his hands, signaling the start of the fight, and Dusty's stomach dropped.

"What?" Edward squeaked.

Security was in position, and Eliot was lounging in his seat with a smirk on his face as if he already knew what was going on. Asshole. There was no way in hell he was going to let them out of there, not with so much money riding on this fight. Fine, Plan C it was.

"Look, you know what macho sacks of shit like Crusher hate the most?" she hissed, reaching up to grip the back of Edward's neck and tug him close. From over his shoulder, she could see Crusher making his way toward them, so she didn't bother waiting for a response. "Feeling emasculated. They hate anything that threatens their masculinity. Use that."

He frowned. "How?"

Dusty shoved him away as Crusher lunged forward, then she jumped back down into the crowd before Crusher could collide with her. She winced as Edward tripped over his own feet and careened onto the mat. She was holding onto a faint hope that if she sent him home without a scratch on him, no one would ever have to know where he'd been. It didn't look like things would work out, but she was nothing if not optimistic.

"Swing your dick!" she shouted in desperation. Edward wasn't the only one who turned to stare at her as she bent her knees slightly and rotated her hips. "Like a helicopter rotor! No one wants to fight the guy with the dick-copter!"

Crusher was coming for Edward but froze when Edward scrambled to his feet and did as he'd been told. The guinea pig went sailing, slapping against Edward's thighs until he got some good momentum going.

It was mesmerizing.

One of the men who had gone up to change his bet glared down at his blue slip and spat, "God damn it."

For a sweet, sweet moment, Crusher had no idea what to do. She met Edward's eyes and grinned at him, and he grinned back. Naively, she thought perhaps everything was going to turn out all right. She'd get him out of here unscathed, and everything would go back to normal. Then Crusher drop-kicked him in the face, and Dusty hung her head and sighed. She could barely watch as Crusher landed blow after blow. The combos came like a monsoon—without warning or mercy.

Edward was fast, and he could take a hit, but Crusher was living up to his moniker, slamming into Edward again and again with fists and elbows alike. What Edward couldn't dodge, he blocked. His muscles weren't all for show. Edward had been professionally trained. In what, she had no idea because he refused to go on the attack. But the hits that snuck through his defenses were few and far between. Still, he was beginning to tire. Crusher was beating him down bit by bit, and Dusty stared in growing outrage as Edward buckled beneath the onslaught. That's when the real punishment began, with bare-knuckled strikes to his ribs and vicious hooks to his face.

Edward's head slammed back against the floor of the ring. "P-p-please!" he shouted, voice breaking.

Crusher laughed. "P-p-please?" he echoed, staring down at Edward's curled form in disgust. "Fucking pussy," he sneered.

A dozen people laughed, and Dusty's vision narrowed.

*He's shaking*, she noted, and something in her splintered. Cracked.

Edward made a sound like an animal broken and lost, and Dusty lunged for the ropes, ready to shed blood. A hand on her arm pulled her up short, and she whipped around to find Eliot standing behind her. She bared her teeth, but all he did was reach for the sheaths hidden beneath her clothes, divesting her of both her switchblade and bowie knife before letting her go.

"Don't kill him," he ordered.

Dusty jumped into the ring. Unfastening the belt at her waist and tugging it loose as she stalked toward the fighters. Crusher reared back his foot to kick Edward in the stomach, and Dusty clambered up his back. Wrapping the belt around his throat, she looped the ends around her fists and pulled tight, planting her knee in Crusher's spine so she could get the most leverage. He choked and spun, clawing at the belt as he bucked beneath her. Dusty gritted her teeth and held on.

"You bitch," he choked out.

"Those your last words?" she gasped as he sank to his knees. "It's giving, 'Toxic Masculinity'."

He made an inarticulate sound, and Dusty yelped as he brought them both to the ground. She landed hard on her back, with Crusher's thick neck trapped between her thighs. Rearing back, he drove his fist into her left leg again and again. Old agony mixed with the new, and she cried out, pulling herself from beneath him as tears threatened to fall. Crusher turned with her. Climbing his way up her body, he pulled his fist back as an eager light filled his eyes. Dusty told herself not to flinch, told herself not to give him the satisfaction, but in reality she was back in those woods again. Her sister was waiting in the grave behind her, and soon, the beast bearing down on her was going to snap her in half, grind her up like an ancient giant with his horde of human bones.

*Fee-fi-fo-fum.*

Only it was her blood he smelled, and she had no catchy rhymes for the way the world hunted down Black girls like her.

Then Edward was there, his amber eyes so dark with anger they were black. "Don't touch her." His voice was barely recognizable. A tone that brooked no argument and promised only punishment.

Dusty didn't know Edward had that kind of anger in him, but she recognized the wild edge of it. He'd come too close to death once too. He wrapped strong arms around Crusher's middle and deadlifted him off her. The two men grappled, rolling around on the ground until Edward got the upper hand. He punched Crusher again and again, teeth bared in a grimace and face twisted with hatred and…and fear. Blood flew, staining his hands, his face, his hair, and still he continued to pound away.

"Edward!"

He didn't stop. Dusty wasn't sure he knew how. Crusher went limp, and Edward crouched over him, his fingers digging into the other man's eye sockets as the crowd howled, eager for warm, bloody things.

*Shit.*

Edward wasn't a killer. He was nothing like her, or Eliot, or even Poppy. But if she didn't stop him, the only thing he'd have left waiting for him once she got him back to his own world would be a jail cell. Limping toward him, she pressed herself flush against his back and covered his eyes with her hands as if they were kids playing a game of Guess Who. "Edward Michael Hayes," she said, his name rolling off her tongue as if she'd been born to it. As if it had always been a part of her. "You come back to me this instant." She didn't think it would work. Who was she to pull him from the brink? But there was power in names. Her gran had taught her that.

Edward fell still, the fight bleeding out of him like an open wound and leaving him spent. She'd been so focused on him she didn't realize something was off at first. Then Dusty glanced down at her arms to find the fine hairs there standing on end. The air was charged as if awaiting a storm, and she knew what was coming before a familiar voice cut through the chaos.

"Raid!"

Poppy stumbled down the steps, hitting the wall opposite the staircase. A silver canister came bouncing down after her, spilling red smoke. Dusty threw herself onto the mat, dragging Edward down with her as the flash bomb went off with a deafening boom, filling the room with noxious smoke. Her ears rang, and her lungs burned, but she pulled herself to her feet, clutching Edward's hand tight with her own. Blinded, they fell off the stage, into a mass of writhing bodies. Everywhere, people were trying to run. To get away. But the red smoke was a miasma, impossible to see through after the explosion of light.

A pop, and someone cried out. Several more fell as rubber bullets were fired indiscriminately into the room. Dusty never understood the name. Most rubber bullets weren't made of rubber at all, but consisted of a metal core sporting a rubber coating. With enough force behind it, one could tear a hole through Dusty's palm, and she'd seen more than one person lose an eye.

Dusty kept low, Edward stumbling along after her. There was an emergency exit somewhere, a fail-safe for times just like this one. She used to know where it was, but it had been a while since her last visit. Disoriented, she pressed a hand against her aching hip as if that would ease the pain. Was she heading away from danger or toward it? Dusty shoved and elbowed her way through the crush of people, unwilling to slow down long enough to find out. Several times, she lost Edward's hand in the confusion, but they somehow managed to find one another again.

By the time they reached the corner of the room, SWAT was balls deep into Eliot's place. Through the thick red smoke and between the flash of one light grenade after another, she caught sight of their black vests and special-issue goggles.

*The better to see you with, my dear,* she thought, giggling.

Someone grabbed her arm, and Dusty's hand went to her gun, nestled safe and warm in the holster at the small of her back, beneath her jacket.

"The fuck is wrong with you?" Eliot snarled, his hands tracking her movements.

Dusty flushed but tightened her fingers defiantly around the butt of her weapon. Whether she had a gun or not wouldn't matter if it came right down to it, and Eliot knew that just as well as she did.

After a beat, he turned away, jaw tight.

"Are they here for you or me?" she asked, and Eliot gave her a look and she winced.

Edward was now the most sought-after man in America. Duh, this was on her. The real question was, how the police knew where to find him and if they were trying to save him or…

Dusty thought back to their conversation earlier. This didn't look like any rescue operation she'd ever seen before. You'd think they'd show a little tact when it came to bringing in the illustrious E.M. Hayes.

So why weren't they?

Either the cops weren't there for him or didn't care what happened to him either way. He'd said he was in trouble, but Dusty had no idea it was 'get shot by the cops' trouble. Edward's hand tightened around hers, and she glanced back. His eyes were glazed, his face pale. He was shell-shocked, and Dusty wanted nothing more than to shake him out of it.

Eliot snapped his fingers in front of her face, and Dusty turned away from Edward in time to see him motion her to follow him. She complied, sticking to his heels until he led them to a false wall behind more privacy screens. The hallway beyond was narrow and pitch-black, and Dusty drew up short, her heart hammering in her chest and her breath catching. The ringing in her ears was back and, gritting her teeth, she shook it away. She didn't have time for this. She jerked Edward close, urging him inside of the cramped space. If she could just get him back to the bar, she could take a second and figure out what to do. When she hesitated to follow, Eliot grabbed her hand and pressed a kiss to the center of her palm.

"Go on, *sha*," he urged, creole roots peeking through.

Dusty shivered at the intimacy of his words, like a kiss in the dark. *We don't have time for* this *either, bitch,* she reminded her vagina. First Edward and now Eliot? At least Poppy was good for her. Dusty was the toxic one in *that* relationship—which was how she preferred it. She needed to get laid. Like, soon. Though, to be fair, her body had always reacted to Eliot. Physical attraction had never been their problem. Trust, on the other hand…

She bottled the urge to ask him if he'd been the one to rat them out to the police, but a quick look around dissuaded her of the possibility. Never mind her, Eliot would never risk himself this way. He never failed to look out for number one. It was one of the many things she loved about him.

"Before I forget," to her relief, he handed her back the knives he'd taken before she'd stepped into the ring, and she slipped each into place with the ease and speed of long practice as she eyed the entrance to the tunnels. It was like staring down the maw of some great beast, and she shuddered. Edward was already gone, and the darkness loomed over her, reaching for her. Her heart danced an anxious beat, and her mouth went dry.

"Dusty," Eliot said.

She met his eyes and flinched at the impatience there.

"Go."

"Take care of Poppy," she ordered, forcing herself to shake off the fear.

Eliot nodded. "Promise," he said, a smile teasing his lips.

Satisfied he would keep his word, or risk the wrath of Poppy's Hamani, Dusty dove down the hall after Edward. Maybe later, she'd ask Eliot why he bothered helping her at all, but just then, she was too busy running as far and as fast as she could to care.

# Chapter Seven

## *Chaos and Broken Souls*

*Fear*

*Fear*

*Fear*

Dusty knew the taste of it better than her own name. Every morning, she woke up, and it was there waiting on the back of her tongue like a promise long forgotten. Her fingers clawed down her arms, desperate to peel it away but afraid there'd be nothing left of her if she did.

"Edward!" Dusty forced herself to walk faster despite the pain in her leg. In the darkness, she could just make out the dim outline of his back. The farther they descended, the faster he moved until he was running. She took off after him, calling his name, but knew deep down he couldn't hear her. Not now. She wanted to tell him everything would be alright, but she knew better than anyone it would be a lie.

"Slow down!" she called, but her voice was too shredded, too broken. He glanced back at her, his eyes glowing strange and animal-like from the depths of the shadows. Dusty froze and Edward disappeared around a bend in the tunnels. Breath escaping her in a hoarse cry, she pressed her head against the damp stone wall. The air tasted of old metal and stale sewage, but anything was better than the fear. Fuck. She needed to get control over herself. She knew that…but she was *alone*, and the walls were closing in. From the corner of her eye, a sliver of light swam around her. Smoke crawling up the length of her body until she tipped her head back and gasped for air untainted by the stink of decay it brought with it.

The air was cold, like ice, like the kiss of a blade. It could draw blood if she let it. Weight coalesced around her, threatening to drag her to her knees, and a breathless scream built deep within her.

"*Coward.*"

The voice, disembodied, came from just behind her.

"Desi?" Her throat burned as if it were bleeding, and her mouth tasted of metal.

"*What happened to that fire of yours, sha.*"

What was an endearment from Eliot was now a mockery. Shuddering, Dusty glanced back the way she'd come. There was a figure there, backlit by the light spilling from the antechamber where gunshots and screaming still abounded. The voice sounded like her sister's, but the figure was too big to be Desi –

alive or dead. A sob escaped her, and Dusty slapped a hand over her mouth. She clawed her way past the dead trapping her in place as the figure took a step toward her. The tunnel opened up a bit more the deeper you went, but the extra room was offset by the darkness and the stench.

Her boots slapped against the ground as she ran, the unforgiving walls scraping her forearms.

*"That's my girl, make me work for it."*

A scent enveloped her. Something not of the sewers but of the other side, and her thoughts clouded as reason fled. Though she knew of the tunnels, Dusty had never ventured here before. Mainly because she recognized them for what they were. An endless maze through purgatory. A miasma of death and decay. She put her head down and tried to remember what it was like to put one foot in front of the other without the overwhelming fear her next step would send her tumbling into an open grave. That greedy, angry hands would wrap around her ankles and pull her under. There was breathing at her back, an insatiable hunger that clawed her hair and she wanted to lay down. Lay down and die, because anything was better than this rank *terror-*

"Dusty?"

How much farther until she found the light? How much farther until she could reach fresh air?

*How much farther do I have to dig…*

Dusty could hear laughter in the darkness, but there were no answering smiles to welcome the merriment home. Everything was cast in an eerie twilight, interspersed with long stretches of darkness that peered beneath the skin. She wanted to scream and scream and never stop, to rake her nails down her skin until it bled. The scent of wet earth was everywhere and there were earthworms burrowing under her flesh.

There was a wild, sharp cry at her back – like a hunter spotting his prey or a warrior hungry for battle – and she was sure, so sure, the man in the dark would find her. Take her, the way he'd promised to do all those years ago…

"Hey!" A hand on her upper arm, strong fingers on small flesh.

Dusty lashed out, gun up and safety off. Her shot went wild as hands shoved her against the wall of the tunnel. An explosion of sound left her ears ringing, and she bared her teeth, legs kicking. The wall was a cold weight at her back, and her arms were trapped above her head.

"Shit," Edward gasped, breath warm and familiar against her throat. "Be still, be still, be still." Flesh, hot and hard, pressed against the length of her body — a desperate bid to get her under control — but the hunger that rose was instantaneous.

Vicious. A rabid dog snapping sharp teeth at the cold and the dark.

Dusty's finger squeezed the trigger, firing off another shot. The grip on her wrist tightened in warning, and she dropped the gun with a sob. Her back arched, searching, and Edward lowered his head and found her lips with his own.

Dusty was no stranger to kisses. She'd stolen her fair share. But she'd never been kissed quite like this. Never had another's tongue spread her lips wide and delve within her as if he were thrusting into other things. Never had someone swallow the throaty gasps they pulled from her throat as if they were something owed. Her hips lifted, and when she found the throbbing length of him, she tugged at her arms, begging him to let her go so she could snatch his sanity the same way he'd snatched hers.

Instead, Edward used his other hand to lift her off the ground, the cold of the dead vanished beneath his heat. His scent overpowered the rot and the dirt, and Darkness fled as if it had never been. Dusty's legs wrapped tight around his waist. Even through her pants, she could feel how perfectly he fit against the mound of her pussy. How right. She imagined him filling her, shoving so deep she could feel the head of his dick kiss her cervix, and a rush of excitement left her dripping, inner walls clenching on nothing but imagination. Dusty worked one hand free of his hold, then she was clawing at him with nails and canines. Urging him on, searching for the beast living behind those anxious eyes and magician's hands always painting sigils in the air. His control weakened, and that raging, monstrous nightmare, leash already frayed and crumbling from the fight, spilled out of Edward and into her. His hips thrust between her legs, driving her hard against the wall.

Through a haze, she knew her hand was wet with something. The metallic scent of blood was thick in the air. He must be hurt. But Edward didn't slow, didn't stop, so neither did she. His lips traveled down the column of her throat, even as her hand slipped between them to grip his cock. She stroked him, bloody hand working him to rigid attention. He was so hard it was like holding a piece of steel, and frantic, her hips danced in silent entreaty.

Edward pulled away with a growled, "Fuck." He fell away from her as if he were a sinner dragging himself free of the flames. Dusty reached out, pining, all too happy to pull him close once again and lose them both to the inferno. Even in the shadows, she could see the way he shook. He clasped his fingers and pressed both hands against his chest. With another curse, he lowered his head, a man in such ardent prayer that when he went to his knees, she followed. Over his shoulder, the figure from the tunnels loomed large. Its outline was faint, barely a shadow amongst shadows now, but still, she could feel it. Feel *him*, feel his rage, feel his…fear? Between one thought and the next, the figure dispersed. Gone so completely, she may as well have made him up.

Dusty's hand went to the back of Edward's neck, her fingers brushing the soft curls at his nape, and she pressed her forehead against his.

"I can't do this," he gasped, voice thick with unshed tears. "I can't fucking do this."

"Shh, darlin'. Breathe," she said, and laughed, the sound just as wild and lost as they were. "It's only chaos. I ride it all the time." She met his eyes, and the tunnels fell away like smoke.

"If you'll let me, I'll teach you how to do it too."

And God help them both, but there beneath the earth, with blood between them and desire a needle against exposed flesh, Dusty could have sworn he nodded, yes.

***

"Uuugh."

It took an hour to realize he'd been shot, and now, he was dying.

*I'm naked and dying*

The girl who'd done the tarot reading for him over Instagram had said it would end like this, but he hadn't believed her. The entire sexy yoga class—including the instructor—stared slack-jawed as Dusty drug him from behind a wall of mirrors and across the length of the yoga studio. His arm was over her shoulder, and she was supporting most of his weight. He would have felt bad, but she was the one who'd shot him in the first place, so it was only fair. Plus, he *really* liked the way she smelled.

"Namaste," she muttered as they passed one bare mid-drift after another. "Grand rising."

As soon as they were clear, Dusty made a beeline for the men's locker room. Grabbing the first gym bag she could find, she shoved Edward unceremoniously into a pair of stolen jeans and a T-shirt reading *Black Don't Crack Unless You Smoke It.*

"Leave me naked," he begged, but she ignored him.

Together, they stumbled out of the studio and down the steps to the street below. Dusty led them through a few back allies, and before Edward knew it, they were once again at the bar.

"Uuuuuugh," he groaned again.

Dusty muttered beneath her breath in rising frustration, happy to drop him.

"How bad is it?" he asked, piteously. "Should I call my mom? A priest? A lawyer?"

"You would sue me?"

"I mean…" He motioned at the blood soaking through the sleeve of his new shirt.

Dusty sized him up, socking him in the bicep before finally stalking away.

Edward went down like a puppet with his strings cut. Alas. Is this where he was destined to take his last breath? On the floor of a run-down bar? Oh, how his mother would weep if she knew.

"Will you shut the fuck up?" Dusty yelled as he began coughing. "I'm trying to make a call."

Oh, right. Edward had forgotten he'd wandered into the middle of a Quentin Tarantino film. Yes, he was *absolutely* going to die here.

"I'm so sorry," he sassed, somehow gathering enough strength to be bitchy. "I've never bled out before, so there's a bit of a learning curve."

He didn't see her roll her eyes because he was glaring at the back of her head, but he could imagine it. Dusty muttered something rude under her breath, but Edward was too far away to catch the details.

*What the hell is the matter with me?*

What happened in the ring was still replaying over and over again in his mind. He'd promised himself he would never lose control again. But seeing Crusher hurt Dusty had flipped a trigger within him. Edward wouldn't have been able to stop himself even if he had wanted to.

Edward drug a hand down his face. He was a moron. That was the only explanation. A glutton for punishment. There was no way in hell he could afford to get involved with Dusty. She was a means to an end, not some hapless damsel in distress. If anything, she was just as fucked up as he was, which shouldn't turn him on as much as it did.

Edward groaned again, this time in self-disgust, as his hands shook. His fists clenched and unclenched, fingers stretching over and over again as if the bones didn't fit quite right beneath the skin. His jaw tightened. For what may have been the hundredth time, panic suffused him, along with the unshakable belief he'd made a terrible mistake.

***

"How bad is it?"

The line buzzed in her ear as Ape weighed his answer. "Bad," he admitted.

Dusty's teeth worried at her thumbnail before she forced herself to drop her hand back to her side. Christ, she needed a joint.

"*Boondock Saints* bad or…"

"Rat will have to wait," he said. "There's too much heat on the Legion to risk breaking him out right now."

"But the governor—" After everything that had gone down today, her throat was in shambles. The words died on a painful croak. Great. Her voice was almost gone. Knowing she'd need to pick her words with more care, Dusty tried again. "There's not much time."

"With all due respect," Ape hedged. "Fuck Rat. I love him like a brother, but we can't save him if we're caught for this. We need to get the hell out of town while we still can."

Dusty frowned, leaning her butt against a nearby pool table and peeking into the pocket next to her hip. "Hayes?"

"I've been doing some digging on Hayes," Ape said, used to following her train of thought by now. "The guy's loaded, but word on the street is he's bat-shit."

Dusty frowned. "Go on."

"A few years ago, he beat the hell out of some old man during a charity event. Sent his stocks crashing. A guy named Andrew took over running the company, but they've been fielding rumors about him ever since. Been working real close with Governor Wilks to try and improve the company image around the community over the last few years."

"So?"

"So, the kind of shit he's in, we can't dig him out of."

"What does that matter?" she said, truly confused. "We don't need to fix him. We just need to keep him alive and figure out who the fuck wants him dead.

Once I have a name, I'll take care of the guy myself, and Pretty Boy can go home."

"Why?"

Dusty went still. "What?"

"Why are you still trying to help this guy when we've got bigger shit to worry about?"

She wasn't the kind of leader who demanded blind loyalty, but at the same time, Ape was all too happy to indulge her and her various whims. It was a testament to how bad things were getting and how fast, that he was balking now.

"He got me the flash drive," she reminded him. "I owe him."

"Who gives a shit?" Ape sighed. "Look, the drive is useless to us now, especially without a decent hacker. Even if we had time to find one, the cops are so far up our asses we won't be able to take a shit without the Feds kicking down the door, and you're still talking about a Prison break?"

"Iwalani," the sound of his name drew an audible gasp from the older man. Dusty rubbed the bridge of her nose. "Drop it."

It was impossible to shake the tunnels from her memory. The ghosts, the voice and presence of that mysterious figure, and Edward's touch were all seared into her brain. But Ape didn't know anything about that side of her, and she wanted to keep it that way. Something about Edward had kept the figure – whoever or whatever it was – at bay, and that alone was worth the headache that was E.M. Hayes. Besides, Edward might still prove himself a useful ally to have in more corporeal ways. For one, Papa Tate respected men with money and power, and Hayes had both in spades. Maybe he'd get off her ass if he knew they were working together. Besides, if Edward fixed his little problem, maybe he'd help her out with the code. He was the one who created the damn thing, after all, and with him in her pocket, they wouldn't need a hacker.

When Ape spoke again, his voice was neutral. "So, what's the move, Boss?"

Dusty winced. Shit. She'd have to make up for snapping later. Though after learning what she had in mind, he'd have other things to be pissy about.

"Well," she drawled. "Wilks wants to use Rat as a scapegoat, and it's only a matter of time before SWAT raids the bar, looking for something they can pin on him."

"Dusty," Ape groaned. "Come on. Not again."

Dusty grinned. "You got property insurance?"

# Chapter Eight

## *Pretty Boy*

Edward hurt more than he could remember hurting in a long while. His gaze darted to the pool tables where he'd seen Dusty last. She was still on the phone, pacing back and forth and speaking in hushed tones. As far as he could tell, she wasn't paying him an ounce of attention and hadn't been since she'd ditched him beneath a wall of cheap whiskey.

He was sticky in places he didn't care to be and, for some unfathomable reason, now smelled like pee, but, you know…it was still a win. He didn't mind being ignored. For reasons he didn't want to investigate, he didn't like the idea of Dusty seeing him lose his control. Weakness wasn't something he indulged in around other people. It wasn't a luxury he could afford.

Thank God the bar was empty, save for the two of them. The volume at which he'd been complaining about his injuries would have been embarrassing otherwise. Edward had no idea where the others had gone and was too busy to ask, trying to staunch the flow of blood with a pair of underwear Dusty pulled from the corner pocket of one of the billiard tables.

"Don't worry, Pretty Boy. They aren't mine," she assured him before going back to her call.

If anything, knowing made it worse? Edward glanced down at his arm. He was pretty sure he had the clap now. Still, the bar wasn't equipped with a standard-issue first aid kit, so he'd have to take what he could get.

The scent of blood, the sight of it, was painfully familiar. Like bright, copper pennies on the tongue.

*"Come on, Eddy, be a good boy and help Daddy."*

If he didn't know any better, he'd think the whisper had come from right behind him, an insidious snake dripping poison in his ears.

*"This is just what Dad's do, kiddo. It's normal, I promise."*

A sudden wave of nausea had him scrambling back against the counter, his breathing labored. Why was that bastard on his mind so much today? Each time Edward thought he was free of him, he always came crawling back stronger than ever.

Right, what was it he'd learned from Reddit the other day?

Breathe deeply from the belly.

His stomach expanded, and he squeezed his eyes shut—a kid making a wish. He tried again, then again when the trapped lightning in his chest evolved from panic to terror.

Check in with all five senses.

*Right. Make note of five things I can see. Four things I can hear. Three things I can…*

Wait. Was it five things he could see or five things he could feel? Why five? The number seemed excessive. A sickening crunch echoed in his mind as fear slipped expertly through him, chilling him to the bone. The constant replay of Crusher looming over him, fists like anvils, shifted. Now he was going after Dusty, hurting her, and then it was no longer the fighter he saw but someone else.

*Momma cried out and stumbled back, the force of the final blow knocking her off her feet. The edge of the counter rose to meet her, and Edward screamed and covered his eyes. Too little to stop what came next, but old enough to hate himself for it.*

"Oh, for fuck's sake."

Something cold and wet landed on his face. His ensuing gasp was muffled and full of gratitude as the memory was driven back like a demon in the night.

"Shit, Pretty Boy, if I'd known you were going to bitch this much, I would have left you with Eliot."

Edward flushed and ducked his head as he worked to find his breath. It was difficult with the rag over his face. It stank like sour laundry, but he found he was unable to part with it just yet. Maybe because it cleared his head, wiped those dirty memories clean if only for a while. Or maybe it was because he wasn't ready to face Dusty. He couldn't see her face, but he could guess her expression. She'd mock him, just like his father, just like members of the board, just like Andrew. A man like him wasn't a real man at all. Edward had known as much his entire life. Even now, it was easy to imagine the scorn in her eyes, the disgust, and his shoulders rounded as if he'd been hit.

"*Pussy.*"

Edward yelped when, with a low growl, Dusty jerked the rag away.

"What the hell is wrong with you?"

Edward had expected a lot of things—fury was not one of them. "W-what do you mean?" he asked, looking up at her.

A few things worth noting. She'd put her hair up in a bun at the top of her head, exposing sharp cheekbones and placing the scar bisecting her left eyebrow on a pedestal. While he'd been moping, she'd stripped down to a green spaghetti strap top and now held the shirt she'd had on earlier in one hand. In addition to a simple black backpack, she also carried an oblong duffle bag over one shoulder. She was scowling, brown eyes bright with annoyance but no hint of derision.

*One…two…three…four…five.*

"You've been sitting here sniveling for five minutes." She motioned to his arm. "The least you could do is treat yourself so we can get going already."

Edward shook his head. "A pair of used underwear and some tweezers aren't exactly marvels of modern medicine."

Dusty grinned, and like the first time he'd seen it, it was a bright spot of mischief. "Oh, you a bougie bitch, huh? My bad, Pretty Boy. I didn't know."

"Goddammit, Dusty!"

Chuckling, Dusty knelt beside him and ditched her duffle bag. "Adele," she said, then froze. Edward got the impression that she hadn't meant to tell him her real name, but Dusty shrugged and cleared her throat. "You can call me Adele." Her eyes darted to his, then away. The first thing she'd ever been shy about. "Adele Burdot."

*Adele.*

The way she said her name, rolling each syllable along her tongue as if they were made of magic and dipped in moonlight, made him think of Paris. Of Monet painting ballerinas with bated breath and gentle strokes of his brush. Whatever he might have said in response died in his throat, though he found his voice again just as she lifted the sleeve of his shirt away from his wound. Bright spots of pain danced before his eyes, but he gritted his teeth and remained quiet as Dusty reached up to grab a half-empty bottle of vodka. Breath quickening, he turned away.

Common sense told him it would be smarter to cut his losses and go to the fucking hospital. But common sense was easy to ignore. He'd been doing it most of his life, after all.

"This mean I'm in the crew?" he managed, through the nerves. No way in hell he was going through with this without at least a complementary Legion jacket or something.

In the ensuing silence, the only thing shared between them was the sound of their breathing.

*One*, he thought. He met her eyes.

"You're a weird one, Edward Hayes," she said, in her poured whiskey of a voice.

*Two.*

He winced, more from the sound of his name than the sting that accompanied Dusty's ministrations. "So, you know?"

"They got your face plastered all over the news, darlin'," she said, as she cleaned his wound with the wet rag in her hand.

"Oh really?" His fists clenched as she worked on smaller debris in his wound, her eyes narrowed and her face a mask of concentration. "If I'm weird, who's your standard for normalcy? Ape?"

She chuckled, and like everything else about her, it was earthy and warm.

*Three.*

"Ape is a lot of things." She glanced at him, her eyes sparkling with mirth. "Normal ain't one of them."

Edward wasn't a fan of blood—even now, he was shaking at the sight of the red stream pooling beneath his hand—but he found he couldn't turn away again. Looking away meant no longer seeing Dusty, and he was reluctant to deprive himself of the sight of her.

As she worked, he studied how the light played off her tattoos, how the bright reds and greens danced across her brown skin as she moved. Like musical notes spilling across a page, they painted a picture of a song he wanted very much to sing.

Desire was a dark, whispering thing in the center of his being, something fierce and eager. He wanted to explore her, wanted to grow familiar with every rise and curve, see how well her hips fit against the palms of his hands. See if there was more art hidden beneath her clothes and whether she would allow him to paint another, more sensuous masterpiece with his tongue and fingertips.

"Who'd you vote for in 2016?"

Her question derailed his train of thought, and he blinked. "Wait? What?"

Before he could formulate an answer, Dusty poured the vodka over the hole in his arm.

"Fuck-*er!*" Edward slammed his head back against the bar as his vision went black.

"That's more like it," she crooned, pleased.

Through the haze of pain, he could hear a zipper.

*Four.*

Dusty tore a spare shirt from her bag into long strips. Panting, Edward asked, "Care to share with the class?" Maybe she was a sadist. It would explain a lot. He would have liked to say he found her less attractive now because of it, but it would have been a lie.

"You were too quiet. I was starting to worry about you." She wrapped the bits of cloth, pinning the ends in place with pieces of duct tape from a roll atop a dusty mini fridge. He wondered why it was kept there, but the sheer amount of tape holding the pipes beneath the sink together was answer enough.

Slumping, Edward gripped his forearm as Dusty sat back on her heels, satisfied. "*You* were worried about *me*?" he queried.

"That so hard to believe?" She cocked her head to one side.

Edward shrugged, then thought better of it. "Didn't take you for the type to worry about anyone but your crew."

"Please." She held up a hand, her expression pained. "*Please* stop calling them that. We're a street gang, not a club."

"What's the difference?" he asked, feigning cluelessness. He knew a bit about biker clubs, but was by no means an expert. From what he understood, most motorcycle clubs were about camaraderie and individuality. It was a place where like-minded people could come together. The Legion, however, was more of a street gang than a traditional club. The exceptions to the rule, as it were. Being called a 'club' or a 'crew' would rankle, but as far as he was concerned, it was revenge for calling him Pretty Boy. Edward wasn't sure how he would get back at her for the bullet, but he'd figure out something. Without thinking, his eyes darted to her lips as her face flushed with annoyance.

"You—" She took a deep breath and calmed. "You know what?" she continued. "My therapist says I'm in charge of my own emotions, and I choose not to engage further with your bullshit."

"You see a therapist?" He hadn't meant to sound so shocked by the news. He just couldn't picture Dusty sitting in a therapist's office for an hour, playing twenty questions. Somehow, he didn't think she'd have the patience for it.

"Of course I do," she said archly. "So does everyone else in the Legion. Men are hormonal as hell. I can't have you assholes running around with guns, hyped up on testosterone and trauma."

It wasn't something he'd expected, but Dusty spoke as if her gang of misfits getting seen by a mental health professional because they were hormonal was standard practice. And fuck, maybe it should have been.

"We do violent shit and talk about our feelings. You should try it sometime."

He chuckled awkwardly, and Dusty shook her head. "Up," she ordered gruffly, holding out a hand and helping him to his feet.

He'd been sitting still for so long, his legs and back protested. It was the craziest thing. He could exercise for hours at a time, but sitting on the disgusting floor of this hole in the wall was like getting run over by a truck. Once he was upright, Dusty didn't let his hand go and neither did Edward try to pull away. Instead, he breathed in the scent of her—smoke and something dark and sweet. A spent bullet dripping honey. He'd swallow her if she'd let him.

*One*. The thought, filled with a longing he was unused to, brought him up short. He took a step back, wiping his sweaty palms on the side of his pants and hoping she hadn't noticed, stopping the count before it could go any further. There was nothing but trouble down that road.

Dusty narrowed her eyes. "Come on." She turned away, and Edward hustled after her.

"Where to next?" He was nervous but excited.

"To see a friend." She slid gracefully over the top of the bar instead of walking down the length of it.

"Another one?"

Dusty's head cocked to one side in curiosity. "What? You don't like my friends?"

He nodded too fast. "The ones I've met so far seem" — *bloodthirsty?* — "lovely."

"Thanks," she said sardonically. Was he desperate, or was there real affection there?

*'Probably just desperate.'*

Dusty headed toward the front door, turning off lights as she went.

Suspecting he was about to get left, Edward eyed the bar top. Dusty had made it look easy, and he was feeling confident. He considered the logistics, then flopped onto his back and pushed off with his feet. In his mind, he did a little somersault that didn't jar his wounded arm at all. The problem was, he didn't factor in his exhaustion and blood loss. So, instead of flipping like a ninja, he scooted like the Pillsbury doughboy and fell headfirst off the bar, scattering several left-over cups in his mad bid to right himself.

Edward shot to his feet sooner than his sore noggin would have liked, trying to look nonchalant. Had she seen? No, thank God. She'd opened the front door but hadn't reacted to the commotion.

"Hey, Edward," Dusty called, and his eyes narrowed in suspicion. "I'm going to need you to hurry the fuck up."

"Why?" She opened her mouth, but he shook his head. "The truth, Dusty."

Dusty's lips tightened. "It's called *plausible deniability* for a reason, darlin'."

Searching for meaning, he checked in with his other senses. An acrid stench reached his nose, and the blood drained from his face. "Is that gas?"

Before she could respond, a figure appeared in the doorway.

At first, Edward was sure it was one of the other members of the gang, but the knife in the stranger's hand and the hatred twisting his features convinced him otherwise.

The newcomer looked between Edward and Dusty and scowled. "Which one of you fuckers is Bobby Dustflap?" he barked.

Dusty's hand clenched around the straps of her duffle bag. "For Christ's sake," she muttered beneath her breath.

Edward couldn't have agreed with her more.

# Chapter Nine

*Burn Motherfucker, Burn*

Dusty didn't bother waiting to hear an explanation. The knife spoke volumes all its own. Before the intruder could say anything else, she drove her fist into his Adam's apple. He grabbed for his throat, dropping the knife as he fell to his knees. She was about to drive her boot into his face when the butt of a sawed-off shotgun struck her across the side of the head.

She went down, the world spinning above her. There was a burst of sound, a roar and shout joining hands in shared outrage. Dusty rolled over into her stomach in time to watch Edward launch himself at the second man as he stepped into the bar. The tackle was a solid one, even if Edward was working with one good arm, and the two men disappeared through the doorway and back outside.

The man Dusty had attacked was already dragging himself to his feet. There was murder in his eyes, which was fair, given the circumstances. She pulled herself up to her hands and knees, swaying and fighting back the urge to vomit. There was blood in one eye, but she could see what was happening well enough.

Dusty liked to think of herself as mild-mannered. Granted, this was not a sentiment shared by the rest of the Legion, but who the hell cared what they thought, anyway? When the first intruder lumbered over to her, wrapped an arm around her throat, and dragged her to her feet, she lamented that she hadn't hit the fucker harder.

He pressed his mouth against the shell of her ear. "They told us you were free game as long as we killed the prick with you," he snarled, his arm tightening until she was lifted off the ground. Dusty gripped his wrist as black spots danced in the sky above her. A party she wanted no part of.

"Time for a little payback, don't cha' think?"

"Couldn't agree more," Dusty wheezed, pulling her butterfly knife out of her back pocket and flipping it open one-handed, the motion so smooth and practiced she knew exactly when sweet Bess was out and ready to play. She drove the blade into the man's thigh, twisting for good measure before jerking it free.

He fell back from her with a scream, stumbling over a bar stool, hitting the ground so hard even she flinched. Dusty considered going after him, but an outraged roar from outside hinted at bigger fish to fry.

With exacting care, she posted herself next to the open door and peered outside. Edward was surrounded by a semi-circle of bikers. None of them happened to be Legion. In fact, she wasn't sure who they were, which meant they'd come from out of town. Were they trying to take over her territory? Wouldn't be the first group to do so after Rat had been arrested.

*Assholes.*

"Listen, guys, I know this looks bad, but he did strike my lady friend."

*Lady friend?* Dusty's nose wrinkled in distaste. Then she glanced down; Edward had knocked the second biker unconscious, and her irritation ebbed a bit. *That's one fight I would have paid good money to see. Oh well.*

"Statistically speaking," Edward continued, "White-on-White crime is the leading cause of death for Caucasians."

Dusty hummed in agreement as she cleaned her butterfly knife.

"I, for one, know our people can do better. What was your name? K-Killian?"

"Killer," came the gruff reply.

Edward made a sound that would have been considered a squeak from someone fifty pounds lighter. "Right. Of course it is. That's a fine name. My point, Mr. Killer, is we can do better than perpetuate harmful stereotypes. Aren't we all better than that?"

A beat of silence followed, as if they were considering the question.

Then, "No."

*Moron.* Dusty was sitting with her back against the door frame, her gaze trained on the unconscious asshole tangled up in the bar stools. The parking lot was quiet, but for Edward's rambling. If his goal was to buy himself some time, he was doing a fantastic job. That no one had stormed the bar yet to see what had become of their enforcer was an indication of that. Still, a minute had passed and soon people would begin wondering what the hell was going on in here. The gang was so focused on Edward's bullshit, Dusty had been forgotten. She would have been offended if she hadn't caught a glimpse of them. Their bikes were idling behind them, a gentle purr belying the violence about to take place. More than a dozen headlights were aimed right at the front door, blinding Dusty to how many people there were, but it was at least fifty. None of them were wearing a club jacket, though, so there was no insignia or patch to identify them. Intentional, no doubt.

Each and every one of them was armed to the teeth. Crowbars, knives, and a baseball bat with nails decorating the length of the wood. Guns might have been more efficient, but they weren't far from the police department, and there was only so much the cops in this town would ignore. A gunfight across the street from the studio where local housewives went to do Pilates on Wednesdays and Fridays was not on the list.

For a split-second, she considered leaving Edward to the sweet, tender mercies of the rival gang. She could make a quiet getaway and be done with E.M. Hayes, nothing more than a fond memory she rubbed one out to when times got tough. She could pretend the guy had never darkened her doorstep. She let herself imagine it for a bit and was surprised to realize she would miss his company.

*Strange.*

Dusty unzipped her duffle bag, doing her best to stay quiet. The smell of gas was becoming…concerning, and she had another five minutes to get the fuck out of there before everything went to shit. Pulling her prized possession out of the duffle bag, she hiked it up onto her shoulder. Ape would have a field day when he found out she'd used it without him, but it couldn't be helped. Taking a deep breath, she stepped fully into the doorway and whistled.

Edward stopped mid-panicked explanation and turned to look at her. So did everyone else. Eyes widened as they fixed on her, and a sweet thrill filled her veins.

"Oh, Pretty Boy?" she crooned as if they were standing on the set of *Dirty Dancing*. She wondered which one of them was Baby and which was Johnny. Edward's eyes filled with panic, and a lock of curly blond hair fell across his brow and she shook her head. Never mind. She was pretty sure she knew the answer.

"Come here, Pretty Boy," she ordered with a grin.

Edward, Lord bless him, didn't hesitate. He ran toward her, full tilt, leaping over his downed opponent and sliding into the bar as if it were the home plate at a little league baseball game. The bikers scattered, but it was too little, too late.

Dusty fired, and the rocket launcher bucked in her grip, bruising her palms as the shell spiraled through the air to collide with the line of motorcycles. The resulting explosion was a thing of beauty, shaking the ground beneath her feet. She stared at the plume of fire and smoke arching toward the air as bits of metal—and the occasional biker—fell back down and scattered across the parking lot like dandelion seeds. She wasn't sure how long she would have stood there, cast in the warmth of the destruction, had Edward not grabbed her around the waist and took off with her toward the back door.

Shit, he was fast. Still holding the launcher, she scanned the floor for the duffle bag. There it was, still by the front door. She kicked free of Edward with a curse.

"Are you fucking insane?" he barked.

"I'm sorry," she snapped, skidding back the way they'd come. "You pronounced, 'thank you for saving my ass,' wrong." Tossing the strap of the bag over her head, she slid the launcher back in amongst her other goodies, just as an irate biker ran into the bar after them.

Dusty was still crouched by the door when he came in, so he sailed right past her, his eyes all for Edward. The tech guru dodged the fist headed toward his face, ducked under the second strike, and hit the much wider man once in the stomach and again in the chest before a right hook knocked him clean out.

It had taken less than thirty seconds for the guy on the floor to join his brethren by the bar stools.

"Okay," she purred in appreciation. Then she pulled out her butterfly knife and drove it into the throat of the next biker coming through the door without turning to look at him. Heavy-footed assholes, the lot of them. "I see you, White Jet Li. Crouching Caucasian up in here."

Edward shook his head in adamant denial. "Can we stick to Pretty Boy? Please?"

Laughing, Dusty jogged toward him and grabbed his hand. "Gotcha. Let's go." The wrapping around his arm was bleeding again. He didn't seem to notice, so she didn't bother pointing it out.

The smell of gas was almost overpowering, and Edward's nose twitched, his expression grim. The two of them darted past the rows of pool tables, as more bikers flooded the bar. They made it outside, just as another member of the rival gang was reaching for Dusty's hair. She slammed the heavy metal door shut on his hand, until he plucked it back with a howl.

"Hold that, will you?" She left Edward to barricade the door, as more bikers began trying to strongarm it from the other side. Reaching for some broken rebar next to the dumpster, she slid it through the door handle and stepped back. "That should hold them."

Edward stepped back; his every movement screaming doubt. "For how long?"

"Long enough." Dusty turned and jogged down the alleyway.

They needed a car, fast. Thanks to the raid, she'd left her bike parked outside of Poppy's place. These guys probably knew what Roxanne looked like, so maybe it was for the best. A biker was described by their bike, especially when helmets added an air of anonymity to anyone on two wheels. Unfortunately, Dusty never wore a helmet since she couldn't find one roomy enough on the inside to fit over her braids.

And besides her jacket, which wasn't anything like the patched jackets the rest of the group wore, there was no way for an outsider to know who she was or what group she belonged to just by looking. Which worked out great when she was trying to be incognito. But these guys knew they were dealing with a Black woman now, so whatever safety anonymity had offered was shattered now.

Dusty and Edward abandoned the alley to turn left onto the main road. A Dunkin Donuts a block away was just close enough to be a temptation to the Pilates crew and late-night drunks. Dusty could see the glowing sign through the fog saturating the air. She limped toward it, every inch of her aching after the long night. From what she could see of Edward, he was fairing little better, and her jaw tightened as she fought back a wave of guilt.

Another explosion echoed through the night, and they both watched fire arc toward the sky. Dusty cupped her hands around her mouth and whooped. Damn, she loved insurance fraud. By far the most fun she'd had this week. *When you do what you love, you'll never work a day in your life.* Rat had taught her that.

"Take that, you fuckers," she grinned, ignoring the way Edward stared down at her in open-mouthed disbelief.

He must have known a reprimand would land on deaf ears because he just shook his head as they fled the scene of the crime. The flash of lights and sharp cry of sirens pierced the air from across the street as firetrucks and police cars flooded the road. From where they sat, on the curb outside Dunkin, they could see the flames rising from the bar combating with the flashing blue and red lights of police cruisers. Cops and firemen swarmed the block. A long line of men in uniform. Dusty wasn't a fan of civil servants—for obvious reasons—but this season's crop had a lot going for them.

"God, I would let that one spit in my mouth," she muttered beneath her breath, reaching for the box of doughnuts she'd convinced Edward to buy as soon as the first cop car careened around the corner. It had been a long day, and she hadn't eaten, but they needed to stick around a bit longer to figure out how many had survived the initial blast.

One firefighter in particular stood head and shoulders above the rest. His brown hair was cut low, and his dark skin reflected the flames. He was built more like a linebacker than a firefighter. "Love to slide down that pole," she quipped, for lack of anything better to say.

Instead of outrage or embarrassment, Edward sighed wistfully.

The sound was impossible to miss, and Dusty's head whipped around, doughnut half in her mouth, to stare at him. Flushed a dark red, Edward stared straight ahead as a slow grin spread across her face.

"So that's your type, huh?" She nodded to herself. "Good to know."

"I'm not gay!" There was fear in him, hiding alongside the embarrassment - a parasite nestled close and draining him dry. "I mean...I..."

"Calm down, darlin'." Dusty pulled a piece of her cinnamon twist free and stuffed it in Edward's mouth before he could protest. "Nobody's judging. You like what you like."

Choking down the doughnut in the issuing silence, Edward reached for another. "You're the first person I've ever met who thinks so." He spoke around a full mouth.

"Somebody been giving you a hard time for liking men?" *Shit. Shit. Shit.* She shouldn't care, but she did.

"My dad," he began, his words slow and careful, "has very strong ideas about what it means to be a *real* man. Being bisexual is not something a *real man* would do."

Dusty was confused. "So? Why the fuck should you care what he thinks?"

Edward blinked in surprise. "You don't care what your dad thinks about you?"

"Why would I?" Dusty asked, she laughed in derision. "Prick's in jail. I don't take life advice from people I wouldn't switch places with." Edward pulled out the last doughnut and took a bite, and Dusty wondered if she should bitch slap it out of his mouth or just shoot him again.

Seeing her sudden interest, he shoved as much of it in his mouth as possible, chewing so fast Dusty thought he'd choke on it.

She glared.

"Shawee," he shrugged, mouth still full. He swallowed audibly, throat working and tendons in his neck straining. "I was hungry, so—"

Before he could finish, Dusty reached out and grabbed his hand. Pulling it close, she ran her tongue up the length of his sticky fingers before slipping the frosting-covered tip into her mouth. She sucked him clean, eyes locked with his while desire flared like a supernova in her middle. She told herself it was because she liked to tease. Which was the truth. But more than anything, she did it because it'd been too long since last she touched him, and every contact between them demanded more. And more. And more.

Edward went still. No fidgeting, no darting eyes, no hesitation. Just an answering hunger that tightened the muscles in his body and brought an eager growl rumbling up from somewhere deep within him.

He tasted sweet, of course, but beneath was something indescribable. Something dark and clean, despite the layer of smoke, and dirt, and blood coating him. Dusty wondered if he'd ever been fucked while the sun rose. If he'd ever cum on bare skin while storms raged and lightning struck. She wanted him inside her while the world unraveled around them, and the realization left her on uncertain ground. She needed to take back control. Now.

"Sorry," Dusty teased, grinning. "I was hungry."

Edward's amber eyes darkened, and Dusty's heart leapt. She knew she was teasing a caged animal, tugging at a golden tiger's tail through bars worn with age. She wondered what it would take for him to lose his veneer of control.

*Not much*

Dusty went to pull away, but quick as lightning, Edward gripped her by the wrist; the glaze from the donuts leaving their skin sticky. Her mind went back to the tunnels, and she shivered. They couldn't do this. She was using him, and he didn't even know it. Edward had asked her to keep him safe, but so far, he'd been placed in more danger. If she cared about him at all, she'd send him to Ape or even Diesel. Send him to a safe house for a few months until the heat died down. That, or ditch him in the desert somewhere for his rich friends to find. That would be the easiest thing to do. Afterward, she'd go on her merry way with nothing to show from their time together except a stolen flash drive and the knowledge she'd betrayed a man who didn't deserve it.

Her mind rejected the idea almost as soon as it formed. She couldn't let him go. She wouldn't. Dusty's heart did a weird squeezing thing she didn't at all like. *Let him go?* He wasn't hers to keep. If she wasn't careful, if she wasn't smart, this thing between them could end up costing her everything.

*First chance I get, I'm dumping him at Rudy's and calling Ape.*

"Hayes," she said, a gentle reminder for her own sake.

It brought him out of the moment like a slap to the face. He dropped her hand and shook his head. His gaze darted away, once again unsure, and regret soured the pleasure drugging her senses.

"I-I'm sorry. I...I, um...I'm going to get some napkins. You want anything?"

He didn't see her shake her head because he wouldn't look at her. He disappeared inside the Dunkin Doughnuts again, and Dusty pressed her face into her hands.

*What is this?*

Most emotions were unfamiliar to her, but this one was bizarre. It tasted like burning tires on the back of her tongue. Sat like a weight on her chest. Was this guilt? Shame? Attraction she comprehended, but now there was something else going on. Something more complex. Something dangerous and stinking of Edward Hayes.

# Chapter Ten

*Doughnuts and Anarchy*

Dusty took a long drag from her blunt. Several bodies had been loaded up and carted off, but not enough to account for the number of people outside of the bar. She made a mental note to keep an eye out for stragglers over the next few days, though she planned on leaving town expeditiously. With both the police and another street gang on their asses, staying in Briarcliff for another day or two was out of the question. Already, she had Otter out digging up information about their guests, though she wasn't sure he'd be able to find much. Dressed in all black, they sported neither insignia nor name.

The fire trucks had been at it for hours now and showed no signs of slowing. Leaning against the pole of a long dead streetlight, she turned her attention to Edward. He'd collapsed on a bus bench a few feet away, and she could tell from the little furrow between his brows that he was having a bad dream. A kinder part of her wanted to wake him from it, offer comfort. But that part of her was small and rusty from disuse. So, instead, she studied the strong lines of his jaw and the thickness of his eyelashes fanning out across his tanned skin.

In her mind's eye, she could still picture him as he'd been just a few hours ago, coming out of the bathroom, head down as he hurried back outside to her with his large hands full of sopping wet paper towels. It was the way he'd paused just before stepping off the curb, looking both ways as if his momma was at his shoulder, scolding him about safety, that did her in. Even now, something in her softened against her will, and she scowled. She wasn't a fan of unfamiliar emotions, but ever since she'd met Edward, she'd been bombarded by them.

Poor guy must have been exhausted to sleep through all the noise. She drank in the sight of him with unabashed appreciation, secure in the knowledge he wouldn't wake and catch her creeping on him like a horn dog. Dusty didn't go for White boys for various reasons—so many of them had a habit of fetishizing her, assuming they found her attractive at all. But Edward wasn't like so many others, and besides, she liked the look of him. Liked his hands, liked the shape of his collarbones and the column of his throat. He swallowed so hard when he was anxious, and, boy, was he anxious a lot. Though, in his defense, it *had* been shitty day. She enjoyed the play of tendon beneath his skin whenever his throat worked or his jaw tightened.

It made her think about things. Things that would make him nervous. Things that would make him gasp and those amber eyes grow wide. Or make him glare at her with that odd mixture of disapproval and awe he seemed to reserve only for her. The look that said he wasn't quite sure if she was a menace or a gift. She wondered what she would have to do to tease that pacing tiger out of him again, and the train of thought tightened things between her thighs and left her squirming.

Dusty forced herself to look away, annoyed with her train of thought. She needed to get it together. Firming her resolve, she strode over to the bench and sat next to him, scooting close and laying her head on his shoulder. Even so gentle a touch was enough to jerk him violently awake. Head still on his shoulder, she looked up, studying the way his gaze darted about, almost as if he were searching for an enemy.

When he locked eyes with her, he crumbled in relief.

A former member of the Legion used to beat his wife and kids. When Dusty found out about it, she'd put a bullet through both of his kneecaps and drove his ex to one of those shelters that helped battered women and their little ones. She couldn't remember the woman's name now, but she and the kid both had the same look about them. Like a kicked dog eager to avoid another blow and hungry for every scrap of affection it could find.

It made her blood boil. *If I ever get my hands on the piece of shit who did this to him, I swear to God…*

"Dusty?"

Her fingers uncurled by slow degrees and her palms burned from the deep crescents left by her nails. "What?" She asked, voice too harsh. Harsher than she'd meant.

Edward flinched, his shoulders going high before he responded. "I just…you looked…" He stumbled over the words like a drunk with uneven footing, his face flushing red. "Never mind. Sorry."

Rage swamped her and left her shaking. The muscles in her back convulsed with the need to lash out, but she fought the urge down until it was a feral, snarling thing in the darkness of her mind. She took a deep breath and let it out. It wasn't her business. She would remind herself of it over and over again until the words tasted like truth instead of a cop-out. Edward and whatever he was going through was none of her business and never would be. She couldn't save him.

She didn't *want* to save him. Or rather…she had no right to.

*As if I could.* She'd never saved anyone her entire life. Look at how well things were going for Rat. *Hero* was not a moniker she could ever lay claim to. Not since Desi, anyway. And she was alright with that. Honest. She'd had to learn how to be.

"Come on," her voice was huskier than usual but kind in a way she was growing to hate. "Let's go see a man about a car."

The dark bags under his eyes were a stark contrast against his otherwise flawless face. "Okay," Edward said, heavy with exhaustion. Getting to his feet, he ambled along behind her as they left the flames behind.

***

They cut across a mall parking lot to reach the adjacent street. Businesses and streetlamps grew farther and farther apart and were soon replaced by sparse foliage and cracked concrete. They'd been walking for a mile or two, and it was getting harder to put one foot in front of the other. Edward grimaced as the ground swayed beneath his feet. The anti-anxiety meds he'd taken in the bathroom at Dunkin Doughnuts had kicked in a few hours ago, and his brain was sluggish, his body heavy and aching as if he'd been hit by a bus. He wanted to go back to sleep but knew he and Dusty needed to stay on the move.

Stumbling along behind her, he gripped his injured arm with his free hand and tried not to fall on his face. The hurt throbbed in time with his pulse; a deep, blazing pain he hadn't been the victim of in decades. It brought back memories of his father's hands, of his voice roaring and hateful. To love him was to love razor blades and cigarettes. All aching lungs and cuts too deep to ever heal right.

"There's still time."

Startled, Edward glanced up to find Dusty studying him. Forcing his shoulders back, he dropped his hand. "What do you mean?" his voice cracked on the question, and he winced.

Why the hell was he still trying to impress her? None of his efforts had worked thus far. In fact, he was sure Dusty was one of the only people in his life who saw him for who he was. Which was a terrifying thought, considering they'd known one another for less than a day.

She scoffed and turned away, focusing instead on avoiding the cracks in the sidewalk. The sun was low on the horizon, and in the early morning glow, the dilapidated buildings they passed were almost regal. Ruins of a time long past rather than the rotting boards and crumbling foundation of yet another street the city couldn't be bothered with.

"For you to change your mind," she clarified. "You've got enough money to run away to anywhere in the world. You definitely have enough to hire better protection than me. So why don't you?"

Dusty had a habit of refusing to let him shy away from uncomfortable topics, and he knew she'd just keep picking at the thread until it unraveled.

"Because being here, with you, is better than being *there* with *them*," he admitted.

Dusty paused long enough for his footsteps to bring him even with her. "Them?" she queried.

"The doctors." Edward swallowed hard, trying not to shudder with the memory. "I had a little…incident several years ago, in front of some investors. Our stocks plummeted, and the company took a hit. To save the deals we had on the table, we had to prove to the powers that be that I was on the path to mental stability." He tried not to let the old bitterness rear its head. "Which meant doctors, twenty-four/seven. All handpicked by my board of directors, of course, and eager to report my every move. Not only are there eyes everywhere, but I've also taken every anti-psychotic known to man." His stomach knotted. He wasn't sure if he wanted to talk about the next part, but in for a penny in for a pound. "If that weren't enough, I spend every waking second I'm not working undergoing some form of exposure therapy."

"What the hell for?"

He lifted one shoulder in a shrug. His heart was racing despite the meds. "They say I have PTSD," he cleared his throat, uncomfortable. But she hadn't shunned him yet, and it made him brave. "Sometimes I'm able to manage, but other times I get…lost." He nodded to himself. Yeah. That was the right word.

*Lost*. He cleared his throat. "The doctors think the fastest way to cure me is through exposing me to my triggers over and over again until they're no longer triggers." He imagined the VR headset that had been his reality for the last several months and fought back bile.

Andrew thought integrating MARCO into the system would make the sessions more effective. And they had. The problem was, being dropped unceremoniously into hyper-realistic depictions of the worst times of his life—complete with interactive characters!—was much more traumatizing than anyone had expected it to be. Though, now that he knew what Andrew was capable of and how far he would go, Edward wondered if that hadn't been the point all along.

Dusty's silence was chilling, and Edward refused to look at her for fear of what he would see on her face.

"So, *this* is the safest you've felt in years?" she asked gruffly.

Edward flushed. "Yes," he admitted.

She took a deep breath, held it, and when next she spoke her tone was as neutral as it had ever been. "What about your money," she asked. "What's the point of being rich if you can't hop on a jet and fuck off to some uncharted island somewhere?"

Edward rubbed his jaw. He was feeling antsy, as if there were eyes on him. Glancing over his shoulder, he was met with nothing but shadows, and shivered despite the warmth in the air.

"Edward?"

"Huh?" He whipped back around. "Oh, right. The money. I can't touch any of it."

She frowned. "What do you mean?"

"My partner, Andrew, is threatening me with a conservatorship." He wished he could sink into the ground and disappear. "Thanks to my 'violent tendencies,' there's some doubt about my judgment." He smiled but it didn't reach his eyes. "Most of my assets are frozen until the judge decides whether or not I'm of sound enough mind to continue running my own estate. In the meantime, the only money I have access to is whatever is left in my savings. I have a bit of cash stashed away in a safe deposit box, but it's not enough to hire protection. Or book a jet to an uncharted island." *Or pay off a hitman,* he thought. But she could probably guess as much, considering.

Dusty's hands were clenched at her sides, and her gaze was dark with malice. When was the last time anyone had cared enough to get angry for him? When was the last time anyone had taken his side? Not since his mother, and the realization both cut deep but also warmed him. Was this what it was like to make friends? He'd seen her kill several people, and he was pretty sure murder and mayhem made them besties, but he didn't want to ask in case he was wrong. At the very least, they were accomplices, which was still a very special bond, in its way.

Edward had always wondered how adults went about making friends. Since he was currently maneuvering across a parking lot strewn with used condoms, he now knew it involved a rocket launcher and a general lack of self-preservation. Both of which, apparently, they had in spades.

"Anyway," he said, voice too loud to be mistaken for casual. "Here is better. Even with the guns, and the explosions, and the dick-copters. There's nobody watching me, no one plotting. For the first time in a while, I feel..."

"Free?"

Edward met her eyes and grinned. "Free," he replied.

At first, he thought she was going to match his smile with one of her own, but instead, she cleared her throat and turned her face away. "Doughnuts and anarchy," she said in approval. "Fuck, yes."

Her words surprised a chuckle out of him. For a split second, he could have sworn amusement teased the corners of her delectable mouth, but he had no way to prove it.

***

Dusty complained of a headache and dipped inside the corner Bodega under the pretense of buying some Tylenol. She convinced Edward to wait outside, and as soon as the glass door shut behind her, she pulled out her phone to call Ape.

He picked up on the first ring. "You couldn't wait an hour so I could grab my Bud Lights first?"

"I'll buy you more beer," she rolled her eyes. "Now shut up. I don't have a lot of time."

"Go," he ordered.

"I have a plan," she said. "It's a good one."

"As good as blowing up my bar?" Ape grumbled.

"Our bar," she corrected. "And you gotta let that shit go, Ape. It's in the past. It's time to look toward the future." She picked up a Snickers, checked the expiration date, and put it back with a wince.

"Fine," he said, sighing. "What is it?"

She took a deep breath, and her eyes darted to the window. "We kidnap him."

Silence, then a click as Ape hung up the phone.

Tsking in annoyance, Dusty called him back and grabbed a box of off-brand tampons and the Tylenol. It never hurt to be prepared, after all, and she was running low on supplies back at her place. Through the window, the top of Edward's head bobbed back and forth beneath a row of flyers. Anxious bastard was pacing again, and her heart squeezed at the sight.

*Shit.* This was why other gangs called her soft. Because she was.

"No," Ape said without preamble.

"Listen. The guy, Andrew, doesn't want Edward back. At least, not right now. In fact, I'm starting to doubt he even wants him dead."

"What the fuck are you talking about?" Ape asked.

Knowing she'd tickled his curiosity, Dusty breathed a silent sigh of relief. "We can use Andrew to convince Wilks to drop the investigation into the bank heist." Her thoughts were racing a mile a minute, and it took an effort to keep her voice down as she spoke. "Even better, he can persuade the governor to postpone Rat's execution for a few months. It would buy me enough time to get him out. Most politicians are money-hungry assholes. If Wilks will listen to anyone, it'll be Andrew. Hell, for all I know, the two go golfing on the weekends or some shit."

"Why the fuck would Andrew do any of that shit?"

Leaning against a row of chips, Dusty did her best to quell her shaking. "Because Edward's got a court date," She said, barely above a whisper. "And if Andrew does what he's told, I'll make sure Pretty Boy never steps foot inside a courtroom."

Dusty didn't know much, but she wasn't stupid. If Edward missed his day in court, his holdings and control of his company all had to go somewhere. If Andrew was the one trying to push the conservatorship, chances were all those assets would go straight to him in the event Edward was found incompetent.

"You think a missed court date is going to be enough to solve all our problems?"

"If Andrew's as greedy as I believe he is, it'll be more than enough."

She didn't want to get into the details. Not here in the Bodega across from a broken refrigerator full of souring energy drinks. Betrayal left a sour taste on her tongue, but she ignored it. She wasn't just doing this for Rat. She was doing this for the Legion, for the men and women who counted on her the most. Because if the governor went after them, if he truly dug deep, then there was nothing Dusty could do to keep her men from seeing the inside of a prison cell.

Her jaw tightened. "Contact Andrew. Make the offer. In fact, throw in twenty million dollars while you're at it. That should be enough to pay for the bar, right? Your insurance isn't shit, so I doubt it'll cover much."

"Are you insane?"

"Yes."

"There's no way in hell he's giving us twenty million dollars to *babysit* his business partner."

Dusty shrugged. "They're multi-millionaires. This is chump change. Less than they pay in taxes. You know…*if* they pay taxes."

"Dusty…"

"Doesn't matter if we get the money or not, Ape. That shit is just a bonus."

It was risky, but it *could* work. The governor might be willing to show leniency in regard to the heist since no money was stolen and the majority of the casualties were hers. As long as no one found out she was the one running the Legion, they couldn't tie Rat to anything. If nothing else, Wilks could content himself with the members of the Legion already in custody, rather than drag her father into the mix. As for Andrew, Dusty wondered how fast investors would pull out if they thought the CEO of the company—and the brains behind every high-tech security gadget on the market—was being held for ransom. It wouldn't do their precious stocks any favors. No, Andrew would do as he was told, and he'd stay far away from both the press and the police while he did so. Which left the nameless, faceless assassin to worry about.

"Anything on the shooter?" she asked, as she wandered over to the checkout counter. Five minutes had passed. If she stayed any longer, she was afraid Edward would come looking for her. Already, his pacing was bringing him closer and closer to the door.

"Nothing. Trail's about dead on that front, unless some of Otter's contacts come through." He hesitated. "Dusty, I've never kidnapped anyone before."

"Don't worry, Ape, it's way easier than you think." She swiped a bag of chips on her way to the register. "Andrew will want a paper trail or something to cover his ass. Anything to hide his involvement in all of this. Once he agrees and wires you the money as a show of good faith, give him one."

"How the hell am I supposed to do that?"

"How the fuck should I know?" she demanded.
"Get creative. Make Diesel cut some letters out of a magazine or some shit. Send the fucker a ransom note demanding a taxidermy bear stuffed to the brim with heroin and gummy worms. We'll call him Heroine Bear and put him in a place of honor in our brand-new bar in a few months as a reminder of what a goddamn genius I am."

The cashier, a Hispanic kid no older than twelve, rang her up. She took the Tylenol and tossed him the chips and an extra $50.00. He grinned, a high-pitched sound of excitement escaping before she pressed a finger to her lips and winked. "You didn't hear shit, and I was never here," she told him, and he nodded.

Dusty left the Bodega, glancing up and down the street for Edward. He was sitting on the sidewalk a few yards away, his face against his knees, and his shoulders were high and tight.

Eyes still trained on Edward, she kept her voice low. "If Andrew *did* hire the sniper, this should be enough to make him back down. At least for now."

After all, he didn't *need* Edward dead to take him for everything he'd ever worked for. He just needed him out of sight and out of mind long enough for the judge to make a ruling. She wished she could explain all of this to Ape, but she couldn't risk being overheard.

"This had better work."

Dusty ignored the queasy feeling in her gut and let loose the breath she'd been holding, relieved to have Ape on her side. "It will." *It might.* "Just trust me." *Shit, shit, shit, shit, shit.*

"Always have," he said, and warmth suffused her. "Always will."

# Chapter Eleven

*Mustang Sally*

*Dumb Bitch.* Every step Dusty took seemed to whisper the sentiment. She couldn't outrun it and didn't deserve to. Kidnapping. Who the hell does that anymore? All the money was in blackmail. Even kids knew that. But Otter had yet to bring her anything on the mayor. She'd wanted him in her pocket for years, but as far as anyone could tell, the guy was clean.

Dusty hated clean. It's where the darkest truths liked to hide.

The neighborhood she and Edward passed through was a little rough around the edges. Though, after Eliot's, it was practically the Shire. The occasional car shot past, windows dark, and headlights too bright. The pulsing beat of reggae music echoed down the street, and they turned into a gravel-filled lot decorated with cars of every shape and color. More than one was missing tires, windows, or engines. Several seemed in working condition, but the layer of grime on the windows was a testament to how long it had been since anyone had been behind the wheel.

"Let me do the talking," Dusty said in warning.

"By all means," Edward replied. His expression was strained, and the dark circles beneath his eyes spoke of exhaustion. Blood and dirt stained his clothes, but still, he followed her without question or hesitation. Dusty couldn't pinpoint why the idiot trusted her. She wondered if he still would after he found out what she and Ape were planning, and shoved the thought aside. She couldn't afford to waver. The guilt could come later, when she was sleeping, the way it always did for Desi.

*Will he hate me for this?*

Dusty swallowed hard. It didn't matter. As long as he didn't find out, he —

*Wait.*

What the fuck was wrong with her? Was she nervous about how Edward would *feel* when there was so much else on the line? What did it matter if some rando off the street hated her or not? Just this morning, she'd cut off a man's ear. She wasn't winning any popularity contests. Dusty had never cared what someone thought of her, so why start now? With him?

"I'm getting soft," she muttered beneath her breath.

"What?" Edward asked; so loud he might as well have shouted.

The longer they walked, the tighter the cars were packed. Some had been stacked on top of one another, teetering metal behemoths looming over them in the dark. Edward's voice bounced off the narrow corridor they traversed and ran free into the night. Dusty turned, pressing a finger against his lips and glaring.

Contrite, his eyes widened. "Shit. Are we sneaking?"

Dusty hesitated. Was there a reason for stealth? The reggae music was loud, even here. If they were trying to sneak in, no one would have been able to hear Edward over the metallic ring of steel drums and singing. She forced herself to relax and shook her head. "No," she admitted, sheepish. "I'm just jumpy."

Solemn, he nodded. "Want to talk about it?" he asked.

"You always this nice to murderers and troublemakers?" Dusty asked with a snort.

"Only the ones I like."

She couldn't quite read his face, but his voice sent shivers down her spine. Dusty turned away. "Lucky me."

They walked in silence, making their careful way past discarded tires and the occasional bumper.

"What is this place anyway?"

"Salvage yard?" Dusty shrugged. "I don't know what cover Sal is using these days."

"Cover?"

She grinned to herself. "It's a chop shop, darlin'," she confided. "They steal cars, strip 'em, then sell 'em. Lucrative business if you can get into it."

They stepped beyond the car graveyard and into a clearing, of sorts. A set of garage doors had been lifted, exposing the inner workings of the shop. Men and women were dancing, grinding on one another, while outside, several grills had been set up. Long picnic tables took over the driveway, and heaps of food were laid out for partygoers to grab. Dusty could smell the liquor and curry chicken from a dozen yards away. She wanted to run toward the warmth and familiarity of the scene but held herself back, as laughter filled the sky; only to fall like stars.

"How'd you get involved in all of this, Adele?"

The sound of her name was a fist to the heart, and she almost gasped. Her eyes closed for a second as it punched through her. God, the pain was sweet and terrible. She could live in it forever. She didn't realize she'd stopped walking until Edward brushed the weight of her braids to one side, exposing the nape of her neck to the moonlight.

"Came looking for it." Dusty didn't bother pretending she didn't know what he meant. "Just like you."

"You're nothing like me," he said, but not like it was a bad thing.

Dusty laughed, and it was bitter. "You got someone that'll miss you if you don't come home tonight? Come on, Chere. Say yes."

But he shook his head, and the sadness in him was like a falling star too. A quiet light streaking across the horizon. "There's no one."

"Well, there you go." She resisted the urge to step away. He was close but hadn't touched her. Maybe he knew how close they were to doing something stupid. "Guess we're more alike than you think."

"Bobby Dustflap!?"

Dusty jumped and blinked at the sudden light as floodlamps illuminated the junkyard. She couldn't see the person who'd spoken, but she recognized the lilting cadence of her voice. "What chu doing here, girl? Didn't I tell yo narrow ass not to come back 'round here?"

"My ass is not narrow," Dusty forced herself to take a deep breath. She was coming here for help. The least she could do was hold off on being an asshole. "Sal? That you?"

The music was still playing, but the DJ had turned it down. Sighing, Dusty lifted her hands to show she had come in peace. "I'm good. I don't even have a gun on me this time." Not a legal one, anyway. She lasted a full three seconds before snarling, "Can you turn that shit off?"

The floodlights disappeared, and Dusty blinked the spots from her eyes as Sal chuckled.

"There she is," Sal purred. "Same as ever."

A figure stepped forward, fingers loose around the neck of her whiskey bottle and brown eyes bright with curiosity. Dressed in platform heels, a diamond-crusted leotard, and a pink feathered headpiece, it was clear that Sally was prepping for Carnival. Though, knowing her, she was just as inclined to fix a car in the headdress as dirty wind her way across Briarcliff.

Sally glanced beyond Dusty to Edward and made a small noise of surprise. "You bringing White boys to the cookout now?" she teased, the stick-on jewels around her eyes sparkling in the light from the citronella candles stationed around the parameters of the party.

Dusty groaned. She was going to get a lot of shit for this, but there was no helping it. "Bitch, didn't Taylor drop a hard R during karaoke at my spot last year?"

"It was an accident."

"Eight times?"

Sally smiled, nostalgic all of a sudden. "The man knew his way around a Lil Wayne song, didn't he?" When Dusty said nothing, Sal laughed. "Come on. You look like shit. Want some oxtails?"

Dusty started forward, halting a few steps later when Edward failed to move. "Come on," she echoed Sally. "What are you waiting for this time?"

"I don't think…" He was so uncomfortable, so unsure.

It made her sad. Made her soft when all she wanted to be was broken bones and blood splatter. Under cover of the dark and the music that burrowed its way into your empty spaces, she laced her fingers through his. "I got you," she said, searching his face. "Remember? Better here with me than there with them."

He nodded, straightened his shoulders, and, just like all the times before, followed her unflinching into the lion's den.

The cookout. Of course, Edward knew of it. Who didn't?

To White people, it was a magical event. One few could ever hope to see for themselves, sort of like Narnia or Avalon. This was not a wardrobe he ever expected to wander through, and he damn near gave himself whiplash trying to take it all in as he and Dusty followed Sally inside. If he'd had a pen and paper, he would have taken notes just to show it to his frie—

Oh wait…he didn't have friends.

Kids were running around everywhere. More than once, he tripped over someone's offspring and had to choose his steps with care, as if he were maneuvering through rush hour traffic. Several tables were occupied by old Black men playing cards. At a quick glance, he could have sworn they were arguing over UNO, but the amount of vitriol being spewed didn't line up with any UNO game Edward had ever seen before.

The air was fragrant with food, hot from the flames licking the grills, and the music seemed in competition with the conversation and laughter all around him. Edward loved everything about it. He wished he was a little boy again so he could close his eyes and curl up in the backseat of one of the many cars lining the bay. As out of place as he was, no one else seemed to notice or care. In fact, several people smiled at him, and one of the angry UNO players invited him over for a match before Dusty dragged him indoors.

"You don't need that kind of stress in your life," she assured him.

"It looked like fun," he grumbled, but didn't argue the point. This was, after all, a whole new world.

She glowered but said nothing.

Together, they followed Sal past a line of car lifts. At the end of the row, a red Mustang GT with a modified engine hovered a good six feet off the ground. Below it was a metal grate where the mechanics could work. To one side was a hole where a step ladder emptied into a small storage space. A little square room, no bigger than a grave, lined on all sides with tools and various types of lubricant.

Sal lowered herself down into the space, and he and Dusty waited as her green and gold feathered headpiece shimmied with her every movement. A moment later, she was back topside, used to maneuvering the step ladder in her precarious shoes and none the worse for wear. Edward was tempted to ask for lessons but didn't want to push his luck.

"Here," Sal held out a manila folder.

Covered in grease stains and worn from use, at first, it appeared to be nothing more than an itemized list, a receipt for parts purchased, and work done. Then Dusty dug a little deeper and pulled out two fake IDs, one with her face and the other with Edward's.

"Thackary Binx?" He quirked a brow, glaring between the two women. "The moody pilgrim boy from Hocus Pocus?"

Sal tapped the ID with a manicured talon.

"Actually, it's Zachary Michael Binks," she corrected. "Don't want you getting clocked by a bunch of millennials." She winked at him, and he flushed. "I wasn't sure at first, but after getting a good look at you, I can see why Sara Sanderson might want to hang you from a cage and play."

Edward sputtered, his ears burning. Then Dusty was between them with one finger against Sal's forehead, pushing her away. "That's enough of that," she said.

Sal's eyes danced with amusement.

"Keys?" Dusty rasped, tight-lipped.

"Envelope."

Grumbling, Dusty dipped her hand inside for a second time while Edward took refuge behind her. He didn't want it to look like he was hiding, but he was definitely hiding, and the look Sal sent him said she knew it. He made a big show of looking down at his ID just to wince.

"40?" he hissed at Dusty. "I'm 35."

"Not according to those bags under your eyes," she bit back.

*Okay. Well, someone is feeling touchy.* Edward pocketed his new ID. "When did you have time to set all this up, anyway?"

"You're a deep sleeper." She sent him a glance. "Wasn't hard."

"Any more felonious goodies in there I should know about?" he asked stiffly. He could have an attitude too, goddammit.

"Felonious goodies," she repeated deadpan, then squinted at him. Ire momentarily replaced with pity. "We gotta get you out more, baby."

There was something in the way she drawled baby, accent heavy and hugging every syllable it met, that reminded him of what this all was for. He was leaving Briarcliff California, once and for all. Relief flooded him, not just because they were getting the hell out of the way of the shitstorm they'd managed to stir up in twelve hours, but also because running tasted like freedom. Something about standing still always felt like dying, and he'd been dead and buried a long time ago. He *wanted* to run so fast and so far, it put the breath back in his lungs and taught his heart how to beat again.

The music changed, and Sal strode over to the controls for the lift. She swayed her hips in time with the music, even as she lowered the car and released it from its bracers.

"License and registration are in the glove compartment. Even got you a personalized plate."

"Roxanne…"

"Poppy called," Sal interrupted, voice softening. "She's bringing her over tomorrow."

Dusty nodded, slipping into the driver's seat through the open window.

Edward had already learned his lesson back at the bar and was happy using more conventional methods to get inside. Buckling his seat belt, he stared at the side of Dusty's head until she rolled her eyes and followed suit.

"Do I want to know where you're going?" Sal asked.

"Nope." Dusty turned the key in the ignition, purring when the engine came alive with a soft rumble.

"How long you gone?"

Grinning, Dusty leaned back in her seat and threw her arm out the window. "Why? You gone miss me?"

"I charge for babysitting," Sal bent in her heels to grip the bottom of the garage door in front of them and lift it clear. It was one of the few bays closed, and the partygoers outside scrambled out of the way in surprise as the Mustang's headlights flooded the overhang.

"Don't worry, Ape's good for it." The car eased forward, and Dusty sent Sal a wink as they passed. "Besides, Roxy's a good girl."

Sally shook her head. "Keep an eye on that one," she called, and it wasn't until they'd peeled out of the shop that Edward made the connection that she was talking to him.

They made their way toward the edge of the city, and the fake IDs got them past the exhausted patrol officer manning a hastily erected blockade. No one knew who 'Bobby Dustflap' was, and Edward was so haggard as to be unrecognizable, so that helped. The hundreds of other drivers awaiting their turn didn't hurt either. Once on the highway, it wasn't long before the familiar cityscape was lost in their rearview mirror.

"Where *are* we going?" So much time had passed in silence; the sound of his own voice was strange and unfamiliar. He glanced down at his hands. When the cop was examining their IDs, he'd been sure his anxiety would come back, but his hands were still. No dancing. No twitching.

*Weird.*

"Safe house," she said, reaching up to twist her braids in a bun at the top of her head.

Edward yelped and grabbed the steering wheel from her knees to keep them in their lane. She was done in less than a minute, plenty of time for his heart to set up permanent residence in his asshole.

Chuckling, she patted his arm to urge him back into his seat and took the wheel again.

"Get some sleep, Edward," she said. "It'll be a while before we get where we're going."

Had she done it to shut him up? Why wouldn't Dusty want him to ask questions about the safe house? They were on the same side. Or at least, they were supposed to be. What if Andrew had found out about her already, and she was working for him now? A warning tremor in his wrists had him clenching his hands in his lap. No. If Dusty were going to betray him, she'd had plenty of chances to do so. Edward had to trust her to keep her word. Even if the contrary were true, he was already screwed. Might as well enjoy the ride.

*It is, after all, only chaos.*

# Part Two

# Chapter Twelve

*Little Eddie*

The old porcelain sink in the two-bedroom trailer had seen better days, but 8-year-old Edward Michael Hayes had not. It was funny then that the two often found themselves in the same predicament. Smeared in blood and broken in ways few could see, and none could fix. Edward leaned forward, watching the blood from his nose paint the inside of the sink. One drop fell, then a second, racing one another toward the open maw of a finish line.

It was mesmerizing.

Glancing up, he stared at his reflection in the mirror. Unblinking and unseeing, his thoughts hazy with shadows. There was a roaring, a howling in his ears that muffled the rise and fall of his parents' incensed voices. That dulled the bark of sound echoing down the hall as Daddy slammed his way out the front door. His voice—like thunder—nothing but a dull roar out in the dark. A beast retreating to its lair at the bar down the street, content to rest after breaking skin and bruising fragile bone.

Edward imagined himself as Tarzan, or perhaps Mowgli; a boy raised by wolves. He was used to being smacked around by careless paws, used to being gripped by cruel teeth, used to the sting as fang and talon made short work of little boy flesh. To the howls in little boy ears. He was so used to it, some days, he forgot what it was to speak as a human boy would. When Daddy was home, there wasn't much room for words anyway. There wasn't much room for anything but *him*. He made sure of it.

The howling died by slow degrees, and Edward came back to himself in stages. He blinked, a part of him surprised to find himself in the bathroom when hitting the floor was still so fresh in his memory. The clatter of pots and pans as Momma cooked dinner reached his ears. An odd accompaniment to her sobs, perhaps, but a familiar one. He could tell by the way she slammed through the cabinets that she was still mad, but that didn't worry him any. Momma's anger was soft. It lacked hands and teeth.

Goosebumps played down the length of his arms, and Edward shivered, inspecting the damage to his face before claiming the last of the toilet paper from the roll. Wadding it up, he pressed it against his nose. Great. Now, he'd have to chew his food with his mouth open. If that weren't bad enough, the world was going to smell like dirty pennies for the rest of the night. Edward's stomach twisted into knots. He shouldn't let it get to him. Daddy's anger was like a monster. Something big and heavy, intent on blocking out the sun. But Edward knew what it was to live in its shadow and claim what warmth he could find there.

Staring at himself in the mirror, or rather, what he could see of himself over the edge of the counter, he grimaced. His face was bruised, swollen, and his amber eyes were bright and hard. Empty. They reminded him of marbles.

He hated marbles.

Turning away, Edward braced himself and jumped down from his step stool. Picking it up with one hand and staunching his nose with the other, he left the bathroom, careful to avoid the splintered wood and dangling hinges where the door once stood.

*"Privacy is a privilege. One you ain't earned yet."*

How many times had his mother barricaded them inside the bathroom before his father took the door off its hinges, obliterating one of the few havens they'd had? Afterward, when the bottle pulled Daddy over the edge again, she sent Edward scrambling under the bed with his stuffed bear, Marco, and strict instructions to stay quiet and still.

He was used to that too, staying quiet and still, almost as much as he was used to the blood. Definitely more than he was used to the missing bathroom door.

"Dinner in twenty minutes, Eddie."

Edward winced. He hated being called Eddie. It's what everyone called Daddy. But he was too little to be anything or anyone else, unless he was dressing up for Halloween. Outside of that, he was Eddie. Always had been. Always would be. Little Eddie, to anyone bigger than him - which was everyone besides the stray cat he'd claimed unofficial ownership of. And even Tesla, the tabby in question, was putting on enough weight to pose a threat. Especially to a kid like Edward, who was known to start at the sight of his own shadow on occasion.

Still, he didn't mind as much when Ma called him Eddie. She wasn't like Daddy, or the kids who shoved him around at school. No, Ma said he was a genius and that, someday, he'd be someone important. Someone who didn't have time for people like her. So, she was going to keep calling him "my little Eddie" for as long as she could. Like so many other things, Ma's words were soft. No hands. No teeth. Just a warmth that made him want to believe her, even though he couldn't imagine a world where he didn't want to hang out with his mom. He did, however, like the idea of growing up, of going away. He hoped she was right about some things, at least. He wanted to be in charge, so no one would ever touch him again. One day, he'd be Big Eddie.

No. He'd be Edward.

As he wandered through the kitchen, Ma swapped his ball of toilet paper for a damp rag. The cold soothed his aching face, and his shoulders - tensed up to his ears - relaxed by slow degrees. Daddy was gone for the night. The swipe he'd aimed at Eddie had been more of an afterthought than a targeted attack. It hadn't broken anything, which was good since it was almost 9 p.m. He couldn't watch television with a broken nose. Ma would insist on setting it and cleaning him up, and while he enjoyed her fussing usually, there was no time for it. Not at 9 p.m. on a Saturday.

As if his thoughts had given it permission, strains of a guitar solo traveled through the length of the house. He gasped and met Ma's eyes in a brief, unguarded moment of joy. Then he was gone, running, free hand trailing the peeling wallpaper decorating the walls. He couldn't smell dinner, but he could hear the sizzling of the stove as Ma tossed in various meats, vegetables, and whatever else it was mothers did to turn a jumble of ingredients into something not just edible but delicious. They didn't have much in the fridge, but Ma made do, and Edward was young enough not to wonder if he and his family were coming up short. His belly was full more often than not, and that counted for something.

The opening credits came to an end as he slipped on the area rug, and Edward somehow managed to catch himself. It was a close call, but he was too focused on the screen to care. Last week, the Crusader was wounded but still fighting the forces of evil. Plopping belly first onto the rug before the TV, Eddie stared up at the static-riddled screen with wide eyes. The show picked up right where it had left off, and his stomach clenched with dread when Era Dictator, the Crusader's arch nemesis and his alter ego's fiancé – a plot twist neither character was aware of yet- leveled her gun at his head. The black of it gleamed, just as deadly and cold beneath the streetlights as the leather mask covering the top half of her face.

"I've been waiting a long time for this," she said, chuckling and full of malice.

An understatement, if Eddie ever heard one. This confrontation had been in the works for precisely six seasons. Or, 150 episodes thus far, not counting the unaired pilot. Since each season represented at least one to two years within the show, at least ten years had passed since the Crusader, AKA Bradly Star, had met Era at the governor's ball and fallen in love with her. They found out later the bomb set to go off in the governor's mansion that night had been planted by Era in an attempt to threaten the city's leaders into transferring huge sums of money into her offshore bank account. While Bradly had saved her and the other partygoers from the explosion, the irony was not lost on Edward that Era had been rescued from her own dastardly scheme.

Ha. As if she'd ever been in any real danger to begin with!

Era always had something up her sleeve, something the Crusader learned the hard way. Which was why his jaw tightened beneath his mask at her mocking words.

"You don't have to do this, Eradicator," he said between clenched teeth.

She'd shot him in the arm in the last episode, and the pain of it drained some of the color from his face. But he knew, just like Edward did, that while Era didn't have to kill him, she would. It was just what villains did.

As expected, she threw back her head and laughed at the idea of letting him leave the alley alive, and Edward's fists clenched in helpless outrage. He was torn, his heart and mind in chaos. On the one hand, he wanted to swoop in and save the Crusader. On the other, he wanted to shake Era until she realized it wasn't an enemy she threatened but the love of her life. The man figured out when her evil twin kidnapped her and took her place, for God's sake. They both worked together to destroy an alien asteroid from colliding with the city. Sure, it had been Era who had constructed the laser beam, but the Crusader had struggled with his morals long enough to break into the military base and steal the necessary parts. Without the two of them, the entire world would have been in jeopardy, and now they were about to destroy one another.

The unfairness brought tears to Edward's eyes, and his face screwed up as he fought not to sniffle into his rag. His nose still hurt too much for such emotional turmoil, but there was no helping it.

"Eddie? Sweetie, are you crying?"

"N-No," he wailed. And it was true. He wasn't crying. Not yet.

His mother sighed as she began setting the table. "Are you sure?" she asked. "You know how your father feels about crying. We don't know when he'll be back home, so..."

Mention of his father was enough to break the spell the Crusader had woven, and Edward ducked his head in shame. He swiped his face with the rag, shuddering at how cold it now was. Still, he ignored the chill, intent on wiping away any threat or hint of tears until his cheeks were blotchy and red and his shoulders were once more high and tight. His leg shook, a steady vibration he couldn't stop. It soothed him somehow and made the sudden sense of shame seem not so big.

Daddy didn't like criers. It was bad enough when women did it. They were programmed to be weak and emotional, according to Daddy. But for a man to cry, for any reason, was just unacceptable. His propensity for tears had earned him a beating on several occasions. He knew better than to cry after a punishment, but sometimes, he couldn't help it, which made things so much worse for him. Some days it was endless; a cycle that would never stop spinning.

*"Men aren't supposed to cry."*

*"Men are supposed to be strong."*

*"Cooking is for housewives, not little boys."*

*"Books are for gays."*

*"Pink is for girls."*

*"Plays are for Democrats."*

The rules went on and on. A steady stream of expectations and demands. Edward knew, even now, that he was nothing like Daddy wanted him to be. Nothing like a "real man." But, if he wasn't a man— and Daddy was right that he would never be one— then what was he?

"Hey, Ma?" His voice was small, and his eyes were glued to the screen as if it still held all his attention. In actuality, the drama seemed very distant all of a sudden. Unimportant, when before it had been his whole world.

"What is it?"

"Do…do you think I can be strong one day? Like Daddy?"

The ensuing silence was absolute. Edward could hear his heart thundering in his ears.

After a pregnant pause, his mother drew in a careful breath. "Why would you want to be like your father?"

"So he'll love me."

She made a sound, a little exclamation of hurt so small she might have been an animal wounded and scared. "Edward isn't strong."

It was never a good sign when Ma used his father's Christian name. It meant she was angry about something, but he wasn't sure what he said or did to upset her.

"He's stronger than me," he reminded her, daring to look at her over his shoulder, since a commercial had replaced his show. "Everyone's stronger than me," he continued, more than a little shamefaced. "I just want to be a man so maybe Daddy won't hate me so much."

"There are different kinds of strength, Eddie," her eyes darted away from his. Something in her expression was impossible to translate, but she was red-faced and on the verge of tears. "There's no one way to be a man." She turned her back to stir the food on the stove. "Don't let your father brainwash you into thinking otherwise."

He mulled this over. "I want to be like Bradly Star," he ventured, testing the waters.

Ma turned, wiping her hands on a dishrag, her brows furrowed in confusion. "Who?"

He jumped up, lit from within with the idea. "I want to be Bradly Star!" he exclaimed. "I want to be the Crusader!" He leaped onto the couch, bouncing on the cushions and taking off at a sprint. He fell off the arm of the sofa, righted himself, and dashed through the trailer. Circling Ma, he imagined mowing down an army of evildoers.

Later, he would wonder why all the villains wore his father's face in his imagination, but for now, it didn't matter. What did was the joy filling him. He was left so buoyant with possibility that he didn't even mind how much his nose ached.

Choosing another mold for manhood had never occurred to him. He'd always assumed he'd have to be like his father when he grew up. It had seemed the only path open to him. But he didn't want to beat on Ma, didn't want to hurt girls at all. He didn't want to hurt anyone. Well, maybe those mean boys at school, but not much. Just enough so they'd leave him alone. Mainly, Edward wanted to protect people. He wanted to learn big words and do big things, and he wanted to cry if something made him sad, like if Era Dictator shot Bradly Star in the face like she'd been threatening to do for the last ten minutes or so.

He couldn't do any of those things if he were like Daddy. But if he was like Bradly Star?

Grabbing Ma around the knees, he squeezed her as tight as he could and glanced up, beaming through the soft shield of wheat blond hair that had fallen into his face. A hero, mask in place and bravery a weapon at the ready.

"I could keep you safe," he told her. "And I could have my very own Era."

He gasped at the realization. He couldn't imagine falling in love, but he knew already if he had an Era, he wouldn't make the same mistakes as the Crusader. He'd recognize her in a mask, even when she was being a bad guy. Even though their alter egos fought all the time, at the end of the day, Era and Bradly were friends, and that, more than anything else, made the crazy notion of love something worth clutching close, despite the reality of his father looming in the back of his mind.

Edward cuddled against his mother as she laid a hand on his head.

This was yet another thing his father despised. How willing he was to seek and give affection. Daddy said he was a Momma's Boy, and it was no wonder kids beat the shit out of him when he was still wrapped up in "Sherry's umbilical cord." While Edward didn't understand most of the rant, he knew he was being insulted from the tone and the disdain on his father's face. But today, the thought of his father's disapproval wasn't enough to make him let go. If anything, he hugged her even tighter, and something very much like defiance took root. It was just a fledgling, struggling for space and depth, but it was there.

For the first time, it was there. He would keep it. Nurture it. Watch it grow. Not because his father would want him to, but because Bradly Star would have.

Was this strength?

It felt like it. Or at least, it didn't feel like fear.

"Ma?"

"What is it, Eddie?"

"I'm going to grow up to be a badass motherfucker," he promised, coining words the T-Zone Terrorizer had lobbed at Bradly in season five, episode twelve. He wasn't sure what a badass motherfucker was, but promising he would be one was enough to swell his thin chest with pride.

There it was again—that not-fear-maybe-strength feeling—and he liked it.

The glow lasted until Ma swatted him across the butt with her dishrag.

"Edward Michael Hayes, you watch your mouth," she warned, terrifying in her indignation.

"Yes, ma'am," he muttered, though he resolved to do no such thing. At least not if she weren't around to hear him.

He wasn't going to grow up to be Edward, he swore to himself. He wasn't going to be the boss of anybody. He wouldn't even grow up to be important. He was going to be a Bad Ass Motherfucker like Bradly Star, and no one, not even his father, would stop him now that he'd made up his mind.

"Hey,"

Dusty's voice pulled Edward away from his thoughts, and he blinked. It took a few seconds to remember he wasn't back in the old double wide, and it had been a long time since anyone had called him Eddie. So, if not there and then, where the hell was he?

"Order up!"

Oh, right. A little diner a few miles shy of New Mexico. It took him a bit to recognize Dusty as his companion before the fugue lifted, leaving him drained and shaking. Scrubbing the grit from his eyes, he took in the scent of stale coffee and the cheap perfume trailing behind their waitress. His thoughts were scattered - frayed around the edges. What had they been talking about?

Something about where he was going. A safe house for the Legion, operated by a man named Rudy. He and Dusty would be parting ways soon, until she figured out who wanted him dead and took them out. Back at the bar, Edward hadn't put two and two together - asking for help would mean asking her to kill for him - but he should have. He'd been naïve. Selfish. Just like always.

"You alright?" she asked.

Edward clung to the sound of her voice like an anchor in a storm. It was a struggle not to let her see what was raging just beneath the surface. "Is that concern?" he teased, lips lifting in a smile.

When was the last time he'd smiled? Hell, when was the last time he'd slept? It was hard to believe they'd only been on the road for a day or so. It seemed longer, maybe because he didn't get out much. Or maybe it was because Dusty drove like a flaming bat out of hell, and Edward was convinced each second would be his last.

"Tell me again why I can't drive?"

"Because you don't know where you're going." Dusty was straddling her chair, much to the disapproval of their aging server. Leaning her arms across the back of her chair, she grinned at him. "Besides, you don't look like you know how to handle a stick shift, and that beauty out there is a rental."

Edward leaned across the table to hiss a reminder, "It's stolen."

Dusty shrugged, rolling her lollipop from one corner of her mouth to the other with just her tongue. "Same difference." Her tongue was bright pink and her lips sticky.

Edward battled down the urge to kiss her and, instead, glanced back out the window. The farther they got from Silicon Valley, the more animated Dusty became. He didn't mind. He liked knowing at least one of them was having fun. Still, it would have been nice if she understood his anxiety at least a little. By habit, he slipped a shaking hand into his pocket, searching for his case of anti-anxiety meds just to come up empty. Right. He'd taken the last of them back at Dunkin Doughnuts. He was so used to carrying around a dose or two whenever he left his house, just in case, being without felt unnatural.

"Chere!"

Edward's head jerked up. Dusty's voice was hard, a warning edge cutting through the fog in his mind. When he met her eyes, she relaxed, and the grin he'd managed to quell the first time blossomed unhindered.

"You *are* worried about me," he accused.

With a curse, Dusty got to her feet and threw some bills on the table. "I'm gonna go take a piss." Her scowl cast her scar into sharp relief. "Get me a key lime pie to go."

Edward tried his best to stem his smile but couldn't, so he just ended up grinning and nodding at her as she stomped away, heavy boots jarring against the red and white checkered tiles.

There was a pegboard up on the wall in the hallway, and as she stormed past, a row of papers rustled in the breeze she left behind. He couldn't make out the details, but the word MISSING across most of them stood out even from a distance. The door whispered shut behind Dusty, and Edward turned back to his plate. Missing. How long had they been lost? How long had he?

His food was cold to the touch. The last thing he remembered was placing the order, so he wasn't sure what state it had been in when it arrived. It didn't matter now. The eggs were congealed, and the bacon was somehow both greasy and burnt. He crushed the edges between his fingers and winced. No wonder Dusty had been content with lollipops and coffee. It wasn't part of his strict meal plan, but anything was better than this garbage.

Dusty still wasn't back from the bathroom, so he waved down their waitress and put in her request for pie. The server wandered off, and Edward sighed, his head aching. If it were anything like the rest of their meal, it would be a small eternity before she came back.

"But God forbid I get a straw for my orange juice," he grumbled, then glanced around. What if the server could read minds? Or what if her hearing aid could pick up his shit-talking from across the room?

Edward filled his thoughts with white noise and eyed each of the other patrons. Okay, good, no signs of discomfort or irritation. Feeling a bit more confident, he got to his feet and headed out the front door. He had a headache, and Dusty was taking forever. He'd rather wait for her in the car than sit in the diner, breathing in the competing smells of greasy food and stale sweat for a second longer.

Checking over his shoulder to make sure the coast was clear, Edward strode toward the driver's seat. He knew how to drive, dammit. Granted, it had been several years since he'd bothered, but he remembered being good at it. Feeling like a rebellious teenager, he got into the front seat and slammed the door. He regretted his decision almost as soon as he made it. Dusty was smaller than him, much smaller. It was like being jammed ass first into a can of sardines. Searching along the bottom of the seat, he released himself from the leathery coffin and gasped for air.

*Nice. Everything is under control.*

What the hell was taking her so long anyway? It was early morning, but already he could feel the temperature rising. His stomach roiled, and he eyed the glove compartment. Sal had left them several bags of candy. Edward was surprised when Dusty hadn't been inclined to share any of it, but he'd let it go. You didn't get a six-pack by mowing through a bag of Jolly Ranchers for breakfast. Which is what he told himself anyway. But he hadn't eaten since the box of doughnuts the night before, and the sugar was calling his name.

*What would Dusty do?*

*Fuck it.*

With a final glance at the restaurant to make sure the coast was clear, he rifled through the glove compartment and ate as much of the candy as he could find. He'd buy her some more later. It was weird, though. The more candy he ate, the stranger he felt. Lightheaded, he found a few breath mints in a small tin case and popped them on his tongue. He waited for the minty freshness to settle his stomach, but it never came.

"Must be old," he mused, turning one of the tabs over in his hand.

The passenger door opened, and Edward's fists shot up, ready to fight. Years of training in various forms of martial arts had all come down to this.

Dusty slid into the car, slamming the door shut behind her. "Sorry, I was checking in with Ape." She glanced at him, then went still. "What are you doing?"

Edward, still in Kobra Kai mode, lowered his hands inch by inch. "Nothing," he said, narrowing his eyes. Did he look suspicious? He felt suspicious.

Dusty's head cocked to one side as she took in the discarded wrappers littering the front half of the car. She set her to-go bag on the floor between her legs, her lips pursed. "You, um, you ate the stuff in the glove compartment, huh?" she asked. Why did she sound so casual? God, it was hot in here.

"Yeah," he said. "Why? Was I not supposed to?" He was feeling…weird. Had his voice always been so high?

"Oh, sweetie," Dusty cringed. "You might want to strap in for this one."

"Where are we going?" he asked, panicked. Shit, it was hot. Was this global warming? Probably. How were penguins supposed to survive this?

"On a trip," she said, and a second later, the world just sort of melted

# Chapter Thirteen

*Officer Dipshit and the Chamber of Hairy Buttholes*

"Edward, I swear to God, if you don't sit the fuck down—"

"It's not hot in here to you?"

"Please put your clothes back on."

Edward did so. Holding himself still, he stared straight ahead for maybe ten seconds before fiddling with the collar of his shirt once more. "Am I the only one sweating?" he asked for the tenth time in as many minutes. "Christ, I am. Is this menopause?"

"There are several reasons why I'm sure it's absolutely not."

But Edward wasn't listening, which was pretty much par for the course. Thirty minutes had passed since he'd eaten every edible Sal had been kind enough to leave Dusty, including a small stash of Altoids laced with LSD, and a molly.

*Of course, he's sweating,* she thought hysterically. *He's probably hotter than the asshole of a dying star.*

As far as she could tell, the next thirty-six hours could go one of two ways: Either Edward was gonna shit out a lung, or his heart was going to explode while she was pushing 90 down Route 66. Either way, she was fucking screwed.

"A dead millionaire in a stolen Mustang. A dead millionaire in a stolen Mustang." Maybe if she said it often enough, it would stop sounding like the headline for tomorrow's paper. She needed to get him somewhere. Not a hospital, for obvious reasons, but somewhere quiet and away from prying eyes while she helped him come back down.

The road stretched out before them, endless and empty, nothing but the sun and a sky so bright and blue it hurt to look at. Her palms were sweating, and her CBD Lolli was making her nauseous. Or maybe it was the nerves. Either way, Dusty was beginning to think she'd made a mistake. According to Ape, the police were content chalking the fire at the bar up to faulty wiring. The building was old and bound to go up one day, and they had better things to do than to worry about a tinderbox masquerading as some biker hangout. Her conversation with her second was still clear in her mind.

*"Otter's been MIA, so I sent Diesel out for intel."*

*"And?"*

*"It's not good," he admitted. "Lot of whispers. The bar's gone, and you've skipped town. As far as the other*

leaders are concerned, there's blood in the water. Won't be long before more of them move in for the kill."

"Any idea who I dealt with last night?"

"Best guess? The Brotherhood. Rat had some sort of agreement with them a few years back. His execution would nullify any sort of truce we may have had."

"He's not dead yet," Dusty reminded him.

"Like they'd give a shit." When she remained quiet, Ape continued, "Look, ditch Richey Rich at the safe house and get your ass home. If we're looking at a war, we'll need all hands on deck."

"This won't be good for publicity," she reminded him. "The mayor thinks Rat is still stirring shit up from a jail cell. What the fuck do you think is going to happen if he catches wind of a turf war?"

"Don't worry," Ape said. "We'll just clean up the bodies as we go."

Dusty bit her lip. "What about Andrew? What did he say?"

"They ain't buying it," came his gruff reply. "Want proof we got him."

Dusty replied, "Pictures I took weren't enough?"

*"I mean, if you had bothered to take them from a smartphone, maybe, but nobody's going for that blurry ass flip-phone bullshit anymore. Now the iPhone has not one but three—"*

*"Ape, for the last fucking time, stop trying to sell me on Apple,"* she hissed, flicking her blunt away in disgust. She was trying to quit, but it turned out kidnapping was a major fucking stressor. *"You buy one share—one—and now your Steve Goddamn Jobs."* Dusty wasn't a fan of smartphones. They were too easy to track, and she had a powerful need to fly under the radar.

*On the other end of the line, silence reigned.*

*Dusty sighed, then softened her voice. "Look, I know you're proud of your investment portfolio, but now's not the time to try and convert me."*

*"Fair enough,"* he replied.

*"Proof, huh?"* Dusty ran her hand down her face and groaned. *"Give me a day or two.'*

*"You got it, boss."*

When was the last time they'd called everyone home? Not since Dusty had first taken over as leader. As long as money was coming in and deliveries were being made, she was happy to leave the members of the Legion to their own devices. But Ape had a point. The Brotherhood was testing the waters, trying to gauge her response. How she handled this situation would determine whether other factions were dumb enough to take their shot next. If she had any hope of avoiding another ambush, she would need to remind the Brotherhood — and anyone watching — that the Legion was not to be fucked with.

Edward reached out and turned the air conditioning on full blast. Leaning forward, he pressed his face against the vent and hummed along to the music on the radio. The song playing came to an end, and another took its place. The opening lines trailed through the car and Edward held very still. "This is the story about a girl named Lucky," he said, glancing at her with the utmost solemnity

"Oh," Dusty said, distracted. "Okay."

*How the hell is anyone supposed to take me seriously with this golden retriever of a man around?* she mused. The nearest safe house was still a state over, which meant she needed to get them a motel room as soon as possible. His foray into illegal substances would set them back at least a day.

Edward's saucy alto knocked her out of her reverie. "Early morning," he sang. "She wakes up. With a Knock, knock, knock on the door."

"What's happening?"

To her chagrin, Edward stripped out of his clothes again, this time on beat with the music. Dusty damn near drove into a ditch when his shirt came off, obscuring her vision before she shoved it violently toward the back seat. She considered pulling over, then nixed the idea. The top was down, and if he managed to get out of the car, there'd be no catching him. A naked Edward in the front seat was better than a half-naked one running through the desert. Dusty did her best to keep her eyes on the road, but that got harder to do with every piece of clothing lost to the highway. There was a lot of bare flesh in her peripheral, and before she knew it, Edward was using the top of her head as balance while standing in his seat. One foot was braced on his door while the other lay claim to the center console. Gripping the top of the windshield, he threw his free arm wide and let his head fall back as he sang. Dusty dared a glance up, swerving when his gyrating nearly collided with the side of her head. Besides hairy undernuts and a whole lot of butthole, it was an otherwise flawless rendition of the song's choreography.

*Fantastic.*

Edward stared straight ahead, laser-focused, with tears in his eyes and the sky soaring overhead. Dusty tried not to smile at the sight, but it was a losing battle, so she just turned up the volume.

Metal glinted in the sunlight, catching her eye as the song reached its crescendo. Tucked away behind a stray billboard and some shrubs sat a police car. It was too late to slow down, and she was going too fast to stop, so she did neither. Instead, Dusty punched the gas, pushing 70 mph past the patrol car, ready and willing to turn this into a high-speed chase until she came upon the bend in the road. Instinct told her she couldn't make the turn without flipping the car, and her foot slammed on the brakes.

Edward yelped, and Dusty stared in wide-eyed horror as he sailed out of the car and over the metal road divider. He disappeared from view as the flash of red and blue lights reflected in her rearview mirror closed in.

"I just yeeted Edward Hayes off a cliff," she said, her voice dull.

As far as kidnappings went, this one was not going great. Dusty leaped out of the car, scrambling over the hood before she could stop herself. She slid in the dirt before the divider, gripping the corrugated metal and staring down at the rolling hill lined with bushes of varying sizes, where Edward had been sent flying. At first, she didn't see him, but then a rustling branch brought her gaze to a tangle of limbs in a shrub about halfway down the side of the ravine. He broke free of the branches and got to his feet. As far as she could tell, the wound on his arm was bleeding again, and he was covered in scratches but otherwise unharmed. She sagged in relief, remembering how Ape told her once that drunks were more likely to survive a car accident than someone sober because their bodies went limp during impact. Back then, she didn't know enough about physics to call bullshit, but this incident was enough to make her reconsider her stance on the matter.

"Hand's up!" The order was accompanied by a familiar click as the officer behind her disengaged the safety on his gun.

*Shit.* She'd been so focused on Edward she hadn't even heard him pull up. A dumb, dangerous mistake to make. Dusty raised her hands and waited.

Footsteps on the pavement, then in the dirt, were followed by another command. "Turn around, slowly."

She did as she was told, her jaw hard and her gaze like flint. She wanted to lash out, to punish, but she knew better. Out there, in the middle of nowhere, things could go very wrong for her very fast. None of which was lost on the man who'd just pulled her

over. If anything, she recognized the look in his eye.
He was a bully ready to play.

"That your friend out there?"

Without bothering to turn around, she shrugged.
"More of an acquaintance." Which was true.

"He high on something?"

In the distance, Edward was doing his best
impression of Tarzan, and she sighed. He wasn't
giving her much to work with.

"Yes, sir, on life."

"Hm, hm," The guy was tall and thin with green
eyes and brown hair. His no-nonsense cut and clean-
shaven face whispered recent military. He had the
kind of good looks the girls in his small town
probably pined over. A sort of generic, non-
threatening desirability that hid the mean curve of his
lips and his bruised knuckles. "I'm going to need to
see your license and registration," he said.

"It's in the glove compartment," Dusty replied,
still frozen in place.

The cop nodded and stepped out of the way, lowering his weapon enough to ease some of the tension in the air.

Dusty strode around the front of the car, her heart in her throat as she slipped past him to get back into the driver's seat. Leaning over, she opened the glove compartment and pulled out the fake registration for the second time in twenty-four hours. As she made a show of looking for her license, the cop reached up with his free hand and touched the camera affixed to the front of his uniform.

*Fuck.*

Tense, she reached out to hand him everything he'd asked for, but he jerked his chin, indicating that he wanted her to get out of the car. Dusty complied, but she was shaking as he led her to the front of the Mustang. His cruiser was parked perpendicular behind her, blocking any escape. From this angle, his dashcam wouldn't be able to capture anything going on either, and Dusty's palms itched with the urge to reach for her switchblade.

"Here," she held out the registration and her fake ID.

The officer reached out as if he would grab them from her, just to let them both slip out of his fingers and onto the ground. "Oops," he said, deadpan. "Mind picking that up for me?"

*Here we go.* Contrite, she said, "No can do. Bad hip."

He grinned, but there was anger brewing behind his eyes. "Cute," he said. "Turn around and put your hands on the hood of the car."

She eyed his gun, thought about it, but in the end, turned and placed her palms on the Mustang's hood. The cold metal of his gun pressed into the back of her neck, forcing her face first against the bright red steel of the GT. It was hot against her cheek and the bare skin of her chest. Dusty regretted ditching her jacket earlier, but it was too late to take it back now.

"Nice car."

"It's a rental." She gasped as his hands ran down the length of her body. She knew what he was getting at. The Mustang was brand new, bright red, and fully loaded. He was accusing her of stealing it, and he wasn't too far off the mark. Still, she had enough pride to be offended by the implication, regardless of the accuracy. Was it so hard to believe someone like her could have nice things?

*Yes.*

The officer ground himself against the curve of her ass, shoving her so hard against the side of the car that the metal bit into her skin. "You know what I love about being a cop?" he mused against the shell of her ear, his free hand snaking beneath her body to grab roughly at her breast.

"The long life expectancy?" she asked, disinterested.

His hand squeezed harder, his punishment swift, and she grunted.

"The fact that I can do whatever the fuck I want to uppity Black cunts like you," he hissed. God, he was vicious.

Dusty nodded. "That would have been my second guess."

With a growl, he flipped her onto her back and stepped in between her legs, repositioning the gun at her temple. The weight of him trapped Dusty's arms between their bodies, but not before she pulled Bess free and pressed the blade tight against the erection straining the front of his pants.

Officer Dipshit got real still, real fast. "You trying to die today, girl?" he asked, eyes wide and excited.

"Creed," her voice was cold and calm. Since he was doing this in broad daylight on the side of a main road, this wasn't his first rodeo. She wondered how many women he'd hurt along this strip of highway, and the rage came like an old friend. At her words, a muscle in his jaw jumped, and he drew back.

"What?"

"Aventus by Creed," she said, meeting those cold green eyes with her brown ones. Two monsters taking the measure of one another. "A sixteen-ounce bottle runs you, what, $1200 at Macy's?" She leaned forward and took a deep breath, taking in his scent with almost feral glee. "Smells like you've been bathing in the stuff, so it's damn sure not the sample size."

"I don't know what the fuck you're talking about." He tried to rise, but she arched her back and sat up with him, keeping her gaze locked with his. Her free hand came up and gripped his wrist. He could pull the trigger and shut her up for good, but Dusty *knew* he wouldn't. She trusted the knowing more than she trusted herself, and it made her bold.

"Oh?" She feigned surprise as her fingers played with the band of his watch as the gun pressed heavy and loud just out of sight. "What about this? TAG Heuer? Three grand is a lot of money for a watch. I didn't know traffic cops had it like that." She pushed Bess close, and he hissed as the blade bit skin. "Let me guess, you run product for Rudy? Either that, or you're nice enough to look the other way when his mules pass through. Maybe you even take a little off the top, 'cause why not? He's a fucking drug addict.

He won't notice. Right? But me, I noticed. I knew the numbers in this neck of the woods weren't adding up, and I believe I might have you to thank," her gaze darted to the name on his badge. "Officer Conners."

When he went to pull away, Dusty let him. She slid off the hood of the car, her legs shaking and weak, and gripped the hilt of her knife so hard her knuckles turned white. Still, she kept the blade a promise against his cock just because she enjoyed the growing fear in his eyes.

"Who the fuck are you?"

"Me?" She grinned. "I'm the 'uppity Black cunt' who's here to remind you about the chain of command."

Thoughts flashed across his face, so clear it was as if he were speaking them aloud. When he made the connection, his expression crumbled with dread. "Dusty," he said grimly, and she grinned like a proud momma.

Dusty tapped his body cam. "You should have left this on," she confided.

"Ma'am," Conners was pale now, "I didn't—"

"Rudy know you're out here fucking with his business model?"

Rudy was a stickler for presenting a certain image. Many of his clients were staples in the community. He wouldn't appreciate a shady cop putting it all at risk. Conners was a loose thread, and if he fucked over the wrong person and the powers that be gave him a good tug? Well, then, it would just be a matter of time before the trail led them right to Rudy and, eventually, the Legion.

The safe house might not be so safe anymore.

As much as she may have liked to kill him, her hands were tied with Edward around. No, it was neither the time nor the place to punish Officer Conners. He promised to have the footage of her and Edward wiped from his dashcam once he was back at the precinct.

After sending a copy of the footage to Ape, of course.

*How's that for proof, Andrew, you piece of shit.*

Before he left, Dusty turned his body cam back on and patted his cheek.

"You have a good day, Officer Conners," she told him, nice and sweet. "I'll be following up with you about all this real soon."

Conners walked away as Dusty's stomach tied itself in knots. There was no way in hell she could leave Edward with Rudy if he was condoning this kind of behavior. If it turned out the shady cop was on his payroll, she needed to know *before* she left E.M. Hayes on his doorstep. The patrol car peeled away in a cloud of dust. Once it was out of sight, she crouched on the other side of the Mustang and vomited.

# Chapter Fourteen

*You, and me, and Devil Makes Three*

There was a tremor in her hands that reminded her of Edward. Clenching her fists tight, Dusty luxuriated in the way her nails bit deep into her palms. Fear was an interloper. She preferred the pain.

Lucky for her, limping across the Nevada desert was about as painful as it got.

Edward had been missing for two hours now, and it was just as oppressive as it'd been since she stepped foot out of the car. It was the height of summer, and the temperature was well in the triple digits. A heat made all the worse by the glare bouncing off the sand stretching on into infinity. A jolt of agony in her thigh had Dusty stumbling. She fell to her knees and her vision wavered. She needed to keep going. Edward had been out on his own, naked and with no water for far too long. Coupled with the drugs in his system, it would be a miracle if she didn't stumble across his corpse. Unbidden, an image of him, lifeless and forgotten, filled her mind's eye.

*No*

The viciousness of the thought surprised her.

*It's my fault he's lost, drugged up, and dehydrated,* she reasoned. *The least I can do is bring him back. Nothing more.*

But when she stood, panic made her clumsy and slow. Gritting her teeth, Dusty trudged on, her thoughts in turmoil. She was running out of time. She could feel it in the sweat slicking her back and the valley between her breasts. Looking back, the Mustang was nothing but a glimmering red star in the distance. If she didn't find Edward soon, he wouldn't be the only one in danger.

Far off on the distant horizon, a storm brewed. Dark clouds swirling and promising mischief and violence. Another threat prowling close. Dusty stopped, her jaw tight as she stared at the encroaching clouds. In her right hand, she held a handful of leaves she'd grabbed on her way down the side of the ravine. They still had Edward's blood on them, though it was beginning to dry, tacky, against her skin.

*No helping it,* she thought.

Crouching, Dusty reached for the knife in the hilt at her ankle. It was rare she pulled this one free. It wasn't like Sweet Bess, eager for battle and ready to taste skin. No. This one was made for other things, and the steel gleamed as Dusty palmed the handle. If she listened close enough, it was as if the knife whispered, and Dusty echoed the prayer etched into the metal with reverent breaths as her fist crushed the delicate, blood-soaked leaves in her free hand.

She knew most vèvès by heart. While other kids were learning their multiplication table or memorizing the capital city of every state, Dusty and her sister were learning how to call on the primordial deities, the Lwa, who governed the world and man alike. Over the years, Dusty had shied away from the practice she'd been reared on. She was neither initiated nor trained to be the Manbo her mother and grandmother had been. She'd dabbled here and there in hoodoo, just to keep her spirits fed and strong, but a world where miracles were commonplace was no longer her home.

Still, she still knew how to ask for help. Something told her if she spoke, *Someone* would be listening, waiting—just like back in the tunnels, just like the woods that night with Desi, just like always. Setting her knife aside, she pulled off her necklaces and rings, tossing the trinkets aside. Her clothes went next. They were covered in grime and the wrong color for this sort of work. Their energy further tainted by the touch of Officer Dipshit. Once she was as ready as she could be, she crouched on the desert floor. Using the tip of her knife, she carved His name into the earth, splitting packed sand apart with excruciating care. A vèvè was a portal, an anchor, an invitation, but at its core, each one was a name of beings too ancient to comprehend.

Which meant there was no room for error, least she run the risk of calling forth someone…unexpected. The storm edged closer, as if hunting, and her hair danced around her as the symbol took shape. Dusty had left her jacket behind in the car, and the sun was a scorching weight against her back and bare arms. But still, she worked. She was no longer brimming with power and faith – it had been years since she had any altar to speak of. It was hard to pay homage to one's ancestors and spirits while on the back of a motorcycle.

*Hard, but not impossible,* a thought chided, reminding her so much of her gran she winced.

"Sorry," Dusty muttered to her.

A sense of amusement, not her own, before the invisible presence was overpowered by something else. The fine hairs on her body stood on end, as if she were standing too close to a current, and with every pass of her knife, the next line in the sand grew harder and harder to draw. By the time she finished the last symbol, her arms were shaking with strain.

Dusty fell back, gasping in relief – and no small amount of pride. It was perfect, throbbing in time with her heartbeat. In her left hand were the leaves with Edward's blood on them, and in her right was her knife. Was it right? She didn't know. Even the hand you used could determine the success or failure of a conjure. Dusty pushed on. She had no choice. She needed to do something *now*. Edward's face bright in her mind's eye and the touch of his blood an intimate weight against her palm, she spoke her prayers. She could taste him on her tongue, remember the warmth of his skin, how strong he was even at his weakest. She needed him back.

"Èṣù Ọba Ọ̀dàrà," she whispered, uncertain of her welcome. The first time she'd been dumb enough to call for his aid, Desi's death fed life to the conjure. It had been the Devil, after all, who pulled Dusty from the depths beside her sister. Who gave her life. Only, he wasn't the 'Devil' at all. Not to her or those like her, those who felt his spirit at every crossroads, and walked with him through graveyards. Those who tasted him and knew him as Chaos. To be claimed by spirit was to walk the path they'd set for you your entire life, but Dusty had been running for so long she'd long since lost her way. When she was a child, her gran told her she was the daughter of a trickster - but there was so much more to Eshu than the games he liked to play.

The first time she called his name, there had been Desi. This time, Dusty had nothing to offer. Nothing but dirt and blood and steel. And it was enough. Oh, God. It was more than enough. Warmth, both sharper and softer than the heat of the sun on her flesh, suffused her and Dusty's voice grew strong as the magic took hold.

"Èṣù Ọba Ọ̀dàrà," she said again. "Your daughter has come."

The wind stopped, and Dusty glanced up. The storm had inched closer as she worked, but it, too, was frozen. Not even the roiling black clouds bisecting the, otherwise blue, sky moved. The desert was cut in half, part shadow and the other light, and from within the between place stepped a man. The figure from the tunnels, the whisper from the grave, he stomped towards her in bare feet, his footsteps a thousand beating drums she could taste. Black skin, so dark he rivaled the shadows at his back, and sensuous muscle. He was obsidian and strength, lithe and bouncing on the balls of his feet as if he ached to run but enjoyed the pageantry too much to skimp on it. A wide, regal nose and lush lips transformed a strong-boned face from harsh to mischievous. With every step he took, Eshu changed, as if unsure of what form to take.

*Stomp*

A man in traditional tribal gear, staff in hand, and red sash riding low on his narrow hips.

*Stomp*

An old man with a gray beard and wide-brimmed hat

*Stomp*

A little boy palming a necklace of cowrie shells.

When he reached her, he was dressed like he'd been born in the same hood as her, raised on the block, and proud of that shit. His chest was bare, showing off the hard, unforgiving planes of his body. Tattoos ate up every inch of skin, and his hair was in dreads, half of it pulled up, and the rest left to hang down around his shoulders. It framed his strong-jawed face and made his eyes shine like pools of quicksilver. This time, he was wearing the cowrie shell necklace, and his red linen pants hung haphazardly, showing off the deep V where stomach met hips and hips led a trail to other things.

Dusty was staring so she glanced away, flushing when he chuckled. A sound like the cawing of crows in the distance. It called to something primordial within her and her body swayed toward him.

"A shy, Adele Burdot," he murmured, his voice like sins still unforgiven. Lifting a hand to catch a lock of her hair, he ran the braid through his fingers before pressing a kiss to the end of it. "The Gods, they weep, Chere."

"Your daughter-"

"Daughter?" He threw back his head, laughter a sharp bark of sound. "You're no child of mine, Burdot."

Dusty's breath caught, and she dared meet his gaze, as confusion - and the first stirrings of anger - dawned. "My gran says different."

"And you believe her over your own God?"

Dusty grit her teeth. She didn't say as much, but they both knew the answer. Eshu twirled her hair around his finger as he spoke. Around and around. A finger, then his hand, then his wrist. A leash he used to urge her closer and closer still. Up close, he smelled of gunpowder and rum, warm steel and Florida water.

She wanted to bathe in him, clean her soul in him, come up gasping for air with fire in her mouth and a spent bullet for a tongue.

Dusty licked dry lips. "If I'm no child of yours," she rasped. "Then you're no God of mine."

He grinned, revealing a gold grill in the shape of vampire fangs. Between her legs, desire twisted with a violence that drug a gasp from her lungs. Dusty jerked back but he used her hair to keep them less than a breath from one another. "I said you weren't one of my children," he leaned in, scenting the curve of her neck. "I never said you weren't mine."

She was breathing too hard, breasts rising and falling. She wouldn't be surprised if he could feel the ragged beat of her heart against her ribs, even with space between them still. Though they weren't skin-to-skin, a chill emanated from him. His grip in her hair remained gentle, and as much as she wanted to, Dusty knew better than to try and pull away from the ice inching towards her scalp. What would happen if it touched her? Eshu met her eyes, so close their lips almost brushed. She couldn't help but notice; beyond the grills was a yawning darkness, infinity wrapped in rich brown skin, so much like her own that her throat ached with unknown emotion.

"What do you want from me?" she asked, because he wanted something. Everything, above and below, had a price and Eshu was the one who dictated it.

"Everything." He laughed, and Dusty made the mistake of staring too long into those silvery eyes. His lashes were white, she noted, as she was pulled into his gaze. There was no pupil to be found, no iris. It was like peeking through a window into something forbidden. The desert faded and all was light; so intense she quelled before it. In the light was a web, a maze stretching into forever and arching overhead, tangling around her mind and snaking through her veins until she couldn't pull free of it. Each line hummed, screamed, sang, exploding with sound and power where they interconnected with one another.

Dusty fell, and fell, and fell over, and over again. Scrambling to catch herself on the pathways scouring the tender parts of her brain. The scream built from deep within her, tumbling from between her lips to paint the sky a shimmering gold. One of the lines in the distance lit up, echoing her cries until they were all she heard. All she was. From far away, she knew her physical body was thrashing in place, knew there were restraints pulling her away, but Dusty had always gloried in the pain, and her screams turned to howls, rich and wild. Howls to laughter, sharp and broken. And around her the world of crossroads and endless possibilities pulsated and cracked, as if her voice had the power to bring it all crashing d...

Something grabbed her by the throat, the touch so sudden her consciousness was pulled kicking and shrieking from Eshu's own. She was pulled off her feet and to the ground. Dusty struggled, clawing at her neck until similar bands snaked around her wrists and jerked them away. Her feet kicked, digging into the ground as she bared her teeth. She was shaking so hard her body convulsed, desperate to return to that place, even if it meant cutting off her air to get there.

"Be still," Eshu commanded, and the fight leaked out of her so abruptly it was like a spirit being exorcised. A death of self that drug a mourning howl from heart and womb alike. Dusty sagged, realizing the binds holding her were ropes of sand – given life by Eshu himself. Blearily, she glanced down. She was kneeling in the center of Eshu's vèvè, the sand around her neck keeping her head bowed so that she couldn't look up at him as he circled her.

A mercy that felt like anything but.

"I've missed this, sha." He breathed. She shuddered at the endearment, eyes rolling in her head. He 'Spoke' and all of a sudden she was a violin, the strings of her soul plucked with such ease he may as well have been classically trained. Her skin was burning, the sound of his voice crawling so deep it scraped her bones.

"You talk like you know me," she panted, and Eshu chuckled but said nothing more.

*Focus Dusty,* she ordered. How long had it been since she'd called him forth? The storm was almost upon them, bucking his influence in bursts and spats. Lightning was a warning crackle against her skin, and thunder a supernova dying in her chest. But she had to focus.

"Edward," She breathed, calming. His name was a balm against burns too deep to see. "Bring him back to me."

"No."

Another death, Dusty bared her teeth on the grief. Never before had she felt the world so deeply. Never before had she felt every emotion that would call her body home. It would break her soon, she knew, as so many things had already.

"If it's about payment-" she tried again, mind scrambling.

Standing before her once again, Eshu crouched, arms hanging loosely across his knees as he looked down at her. She beat back the urge to meet his eyes again and took a deep breath. Then another.

"For you, Adele Burdot, there is very little I wouldn't do," he confided, his voice gentle. The part of her brain still in possession of a modicum of common sense marveled how a God of Chaos, of destruction, was more careful of her than any flesh-and-blood man—except Edward. But the creature you seek doesn't need to be found."

Confusion cleared some of the fog from her thoughts. This time, when she tried to straighten, the sandy ropes allowed it. Falling away to return to the careful lines she'd drawn earlier. It was as if the vèvè had never been touched. Even rubbing her hands across it didn't clear it away, and a sense of foreboding gripped Dusty harder than any restraint. Eshu nodded towards the distance, and Dusty turned to follow his gaze.

The storm. The darkened sky splitting the Nevada Desert into two worlds was so close she could taste the ozone on her tongue. The sun no longer burned her. It had been blocked out, and now damp air kissed her skin with the promise of rain. A little foreplay before it decimated everything in its path. She squinted, and there, beneath the churning clouds, bathed in a sphere of light breaking through from the Heavens, stood Edward Hayes. He was frozen in place, staring across the distance at her and Eshu. Even from where she stood, she could see the fire raging within him. He shone like a star fallen to earth, his amber eyes blazing with it until he no longer seemed human. His blond hair whipped around him, a shock of light hungry to reach the sky. He was the sun made man, Adonis given teeth to rend and blood to spill.

A scent hit her – so reminiscent of the tunnels she wasn't even surprised to look up and find rage twisting Eshu's features into something monstrous. In his anger, he was all flesh stretched too tight across the bone, so sharp she thought his skin would tear like paper. He and Edward were staring at one another – caught in a stand-off, she couldn't begin to understand.

Who the fuck was E.M. Hayes that he would give a God pause?

"You hate him," she said in wonder. "Why?" There was so much in that one word. It cupped *'what is he'* and *'why is he'* in the memory of Edward's trembling hands and dimpled smiles. Dusty was both frightened and eager for Eshu to turn his banked rage on her. Anything to bring his attention back to where she wanted it most and away from…well, just *away*. Instead, Eshu closed his eyes, snuffing the quicksilver that made the orbs flicker like something breathing.

"I was carved from the heart of the universe, back when it was still wet and mewling," he said, turning to her. "As such, I have seen many things, Adele Burdot." His attention flickered to Edward and back. Just for a second, there and gone, and still the scent of his rage – ripe as old blood, roadkill left to spoil –

gagged her. "*He* is not a creature you make deals with one such as I for."

"I don't know who or what you think he is," she said, voice thick with animal yowls tamped down. If he would bank his fire for her, she would do the same for him. "But Edward Hayes is human," *Lies*, her thoughts breathed. *Desperate lies from a desperate girl.* "He has a family," she spoke louder, drowning out the doubt threatening to take hold. "- a life," more lies. "-a home."

"A half-blood Changeling calls no place home," Eshu spit, surging so close they shared a breath. His words slipped past her lips and down her throat, and power clawed through her body, untamed and raging. A flash of lightning struck, so close, too close, and in the white-hot light, she glimpsed the bone man hiding just beneath his costume of human skin. There was more than just the stirrings of rage within her now, and the familiar heat warmed the touch of death and destruction Eshu's touch had left behind. She stared back at him, unflinching.

"If you're not going to help me," she said, searching his expression. "why did you come?"

He stared her down, expressionless, until he finally pulled away. Stopping her before she could get lost in his eyes once again. A sigh escaped Dusty, shaky with relief.

"To give you a gift," he said, flashing gold fangs as he grinned.

"I don't-" before she could decline, Eshu touched her. Skin to skin for the first time, and the world was fire and light and *agony*. Dusty screamed, and this time, there was no laughter hidden in its depths. Only a feral jubilation that left her throat raw and bleeding. She threw back her head and sang her name to the sky above and the stars beyond while Eshu traced reverent fingertips down the length of her arm. He stepped back as she collapsed to her knees, staring at her arm in horror as the tattoos there morphed and changed. Writhing like snakes, they glowed red hot from shoulder to wrist, where a bracelet made of smooth ivory now rested. Like her ceremony knife, it whispered, and when she pressed cold fingertips against it, she knew it was not ivory he'd placed on her, but bone.

Dusty paled. She couldn't take her eyes off the bracelet. The etchings on it faded in and out of relief like a message disappearing in the sand over and over again, just to be rewritten. Most of it was in a language she couldn't understand, but one word stood out, repeating itself like a cry.

*Hel*

*Hel*

*Hel*

"What is this," she rasped, the Knowing prompting her to speak when all she wanted to do was curl into a ball and whither. Her voice was so torn she could barely hear herself. Eshu had no such issue, and the trickster's glee made the land buck beneath her.

"Reparations," he purred.

"You stole it," she said, her lips numb with disbelief. "Why?" Panic strained her vocal cords. "From who?" *From what?*

"Doesn't matter," he said, waving a hand in dismissal. Then, as if to himself, "It's not like she can come up here and take it back."

For the first time, Dusty looked at what had been done to her arm. There, replacing her tattoos, was Eshu's vèvè. It was much more stylized, much more flamboyant, than her own attempt, but it was his. "You branded me," she accused.

"I blessed you," he countered, smug. "From now on, that which is lost, will always find it's way to you." Fangs glinted in dying sunlight. "And in exchange, for as long as you wear me on your skin, I may come and go as I please, little Pomba Gira."

Pomba Gira.

The name was familiar, but for the life of her, she couldn't remember why. Still, hearing it raised her hackles, and Dusty closed her eyes, muttering to herself in Creole. She wished her grandmother were here. Though, if she were, she would have swatted Dusty upside the head for even calling the lwa forth in the first place.

*I should have let us both die in the desert,* she thought, half hysterical.

Eshu reached for her and whether he would have touched her again or not, she'd never know. He moved and she cried out, jerking out of his reach just as a bolt of lightning danced across the ground between them. They exploded back as branches of electricity licked the air where they'd been. A fiery tongue of sensation rushed through her, and Dusty hit the ground with a groan, rolling to a stop against the base of a giant bolder.

"Seems you have a guard dog," Eshu's voice echoed in the air. Both nowhere and everywhere. She couldn't escape it or him. Not anymore. "Take care - if you are going to run with Beasts, you must learn to tame them," it was a rumbled warning. "I will not spare the Changeling's life again if harm should befall my consort."

"Your WHAT-"

Howling with laughter, Eshu danced away, footsteps echoing the thunder lumbering across the valley floor. His form shifted between all the others she'd seen before. The old man, the boy, the warrior, and Death come calling – cigar between his teeth and rum bottle in hand. One after the other, so fast now they blended together into a form her brain could make no sense of. A scratching - like nails down a chalkboard. A breaking - like teeth crunching bone. The song started in her brain and wouldn't let her go. Licking dry lips, Dusty averted her gaze until her mind fell quiet and still once more. Silence. Stillness. Then everything, everywhere, all at once. Eshu was gone, and so too was whatever had been holding the storm – and Edward – at bay.

***

It starts like this:

A gale storm swallows you whole and lifts you high.

The bone bracelet around her wrist grows teeth and pierces flesh – biting so deep they rend tendons. Blood joins the rain lashing her skin and soaking her hair. The bone bracelet curls into her palm like a skeleton hand grasping her own. She holds each skeletal finger tight, and with a flick of her wrist a handle forms in the palm of her hand as if it has always been there. The whip lashes forth with tongues made of flame. Dripping liquid brimstone on the desert below.

Something, the world perhaps, screams and the wind drops her so suddenly she plummets. The flames lash out once again, and the earth bends around her. Bows. She hits the ground on one bended knee, arm out and red flames snaking through the air. A miasma stinking of sulfur and decay.

His howl is a thing of terror, but Dusty has been touched by God. There is no fear in the way she cuts through the intervening space between them, whip tearing a chasm across the earth until it cries for her. The storm lays tattered above them, a bubble of magic shredded around the edges and leaking power back into the ether where it belongs. Edward is a mad dog, collarless and feral. Ready to bite. The whip drags him howling by the neck to her side, and she straddles the recalcitrant beast. He bucks beneath her, all hard cock and muscles straining, but doesn't hurt her. Leaning over him, her braids fall in a cascading curtain around them, and the scent of gunpowder and rum that has poisoned everything is replaced by something clean and bright.

Oranges and vanilla.

Vanilla and oranges.

So sweet

Sweet

Sweet

they could be kisses. First of their kind and freely given.

For Dusty, he is the sun on a body long cold.

For Edward, she is Master and home both, and he submits to her will with an eagerness that leaves him empty and human once more. The whip slithers back home, and the whispering within the bones falls quiet as it retracts its grip. As Dusty watches, skin once pierced and bleeding re-knits. Good as new, but for the Name resting where her tattoos once did.

She looks down at Edward, eyes shining with unshed tears and her voice shaking with hysteria. "You gotta stop running from me, Pretty Boy," she says, with a laugh that hurts everything she is. "Because God knows what you'll do next time if I'm not around to catch you."

# Chapter Fifteen

*Twisted Steel and Sex Appeal*

"Is he okay?"

"He's fine." Dusty slapped Edward's hand away from her braids for the hundredth time.

"He's covered in dirt," the man commented, and Dusty rolled her eyes.

"He fell."

"You tried to bury me in the desert," Edward accused, still groggy. She opened her mouth to deny it, but the truth was she wasn't sure what had happened out in the desert. Last she remembered, she was debating whether or not to use rootwork to find him... and then nothing. Best guess? The heat had gotten to her, and she passed out. When she awoke, she was butt-ass naked and lying curled up next to Edward. Had she stripped and tracked him down like a fucking bloodhound? It was a miracle she'd been able to find her clothes and Edward's shoes as they trekked back to the car together. Dusty wished there was a Yelp for plugs because God knew she had some feedback for Sal once she saw the bitch again.

*Maybe it's a good thing Edward did everything I had left.* The lollies had hit hard enough, and she hated to imagine what he was going through right now. The good news was that several hours had passed since her run-in with Conners, and Edward was already coming down. Still, he was swaying on his feet, and

Dusty bit back a curse. If he passed out, she wouldn't be able to lift him. She had no desire to drag his limp body across the parking lot. One time was more than enough. Twice, and someone was bound to call the cops.

Speaking of…from the corner of her eye, she could see the clerk's fingers inching toward the emergency call button below his desk. Dusty sighed before sliding a stack of bills across the counter. "You got a room or not?"

Thank God she'd gone with cheap and roach-infested over the continental breakfast option. She wouldn't have been able to afford a bribe on top of the room prices otherwise. Whoever said crime didn't pay never mentioned it was because of inflation.

"Yeah," the clerk said, still doubtful but less inclined to call the cops since Edward was clearly not buried in a ditch somewhere. Still, he glared at Dusty as he pulled out a keycard.

"Room 207," he told her, holding the card just out of reach when she went to grab it. "No freaky shit," he warned.

Exasperated, Dusty snatched the key card out of his hand. If she weren't about to ditch Edward at a safe house, she'd be worried about how she was supposed to fund his kidnapping for the long haul. The money Sal had left in the envelope would only get them so far.

On her way out of the office, another notice for yet another missing person caught her eye. The woman in the photo had her hair pulled back in a bun and was laughing at something off-frame. Dusty turned away, her arm aching. The pain lingered as she lugged Edward down the hall toward their room. Fading only when she burst through their door, struggling to hold Edward upright. Walking him over to one of the two beds, she let him fall backward onto the pillows. As tired as she was, she had a lot of work to do while they were in town, so she didn't plan on sleeping much. It would be a relief to get to the clubhouse so she could relax for once.

Going back out to the car, she searched the secret compartment in the trunk for a few goodies Sal had been kind enough to pack for her—for a fee, of course. Like the drugs, the weapons in the trunk had come with a hefty price tag, though Sal had thrown in some extra magazines out of the goodness of her heart. Dusty stuffed everything into her duffle bag and went back to the room.

Peeling off her jacket, she thought, *God, what I wouldn't give for a shower.* At some point, she'd lost most of her jewelry. All she had left was an ivory bracelet she didn't even remember buying. It was strange. She didn't remember the bracelet, but at the same time couldn't think of a day she'd gone without wearing it. Dismissing the matter, she eyed the bathroom with longing. *Later,* she promised herself, turning away. *When everything's done and there's no more blood to spill. Until then…*

Stripping down to just a cropped spaghetti strap and her leather pants, Dusty undid the button biting into her midsection and crouched on the floor. Her ass looked great, but she couldn't bend at the waist for shit. Unpacking her duffle, she took inventory as Edward swung between consciousness and sleep just a few feet away. She was so engrossed in what she was doing that she jumped at the sound of his voice several minutes later.

"Why do you need so many grenades?" he asked yawning.

Dusty grinned to herself before glancing up at him. He was peeking at her from beneath the pillow he'd thrown over his head. She shrugged. "Better to have them and not need them," she said. "In fact, I keep at least one on me at all times."

Edward stared, "*Where?*"

"Sorry, Chere." She checked the clip on the M92 Beretta and aimed it at the floor, getting a feel for its weight and bulk. "Trade secret." Stretching, she climbed to her feet. She passed the bed, intending to head back outside, when Edward's hand in hers brought her up short.

"Don't leave." His voice was hoarse, his expression pale and strained.

She hadn't seen him like this since the tunnel, and her fingers tightened around his. "I wouldn't," she said, like a dumbass. Cursing herself for the reassurance even as she found herself leaning over him, the fall of her braids to one side of his body a wordless song. Bones stripped bare and rattling along soft palms.

She sat without thinking, let him pull her close and wrap large arms around her. He engulfed her. Like the sun swallowing down Icarus - she'd flown too close. She'd known as much the minute she pressed her lips against his throat. She wondered if he would let her go if she rose. She wouldn't be able to escape otherwise. Like Conners, Edward was strong enough, powerful enough, that he could do whatever he wanted to her.

But unlike Conners, the knowledge didn't disgust. Instead, it tightened things low in her belly.

"Were you really going to take all that crap?"

The question gave her pause, pulling her from the magic of his amber eyes and back into harsh reality. "I mean, yeah," she admitted. "I guess so?" Granted, it wouldn't have been all at once, but Dusty hoped that was self-explanatory.

To her shock, Edward's eyes darkened. "You're no good to me if you're high all the time."

Dusty pulled back with a snarl, but Edward jerked her back and held her still. She said, "What the fuck did you just say to me?"

The look in his eyes… He was still riding the high she craved, but was coming down fast. Though it made him mean, there was clarity in the way he regarded her -a knowing - she couldn't shake free of. "I spent the day thinking I was Mojo Jojo on a goddamn rampage." When she would have said something he held up a hand for patience. "Granted," he amended, "it was thanks to the power of suggestion, but still. That shit rots your brain. Why do you even put it in your body?"

"For fun," Dusty wriggled in his arms like an angry cat. "Jesus, you've never done something to take the edge off?"

He hesitated, and his resolve wavered. "All that just to take the edge off?"

Dusty shrugged. "Some edges are sharper than others. It's not like I have a fucking problem." She didn't like being judged, didn't like the way he looked at her as if he were trying to peer beneath her skin. What? Did he think she was some druggie with a chip on her shoulder? "Not like you'd get it," she said snidely. "You're just some spineless nerd."

As soon as the words left her mouth, she wanted to snatch them back, but it was too late.

Hurt flashed across Edward's face, and his grip tightened to the point of pain. "You don't know anything about me," he said, his eyes ablaze. A heat she could feel, a burn she craved. In the recesses of her mind a flash of memory, too fuzzy to grasp and pull forward. She let the image of a man made of sunlight fade into obscurity. Sleep. Just a few hours of sleep and her imagination would stop running rampant.

"I know enough." Why couldn't she just let up? The sound of her voice was grating on her own nerves, but she couldn't seem to stop. "I know there's a darkness in you," she continued. "A part of you that likes to beats the shit out of innocent old men."

Edward flinched back, eyes dancing away, but she grabbed his chin and forced him to face her once again. "For fuck's sake, Pretty Boy, you're a sinking goddamn ship." She breathed against his mouth. His hold on her slackened, and sensing weakness, she undulated in his arms like a serpent scenting the air. She rose over him until they were so intertwined it was hard to tell where one restless heartbeat ended and the other began.

"Your edges are as sharp as mine, darlin'." She leaned forward, bit his bottom lip between her teeth. "That's how I know they draw blood." She grinned as his eyes darkened, as a growl danced its way from deep in his chest to travel up to his throat.

They'd spent most of the day on the road, and already night was encroaching, leaving their room in a sea of unfamiliar shadows. Dusty knew the dark. She always felt better there. Sometimes, she knew herself only as a half-starved thing. All teeth and twisting hunger. What would it take to satiate the beast in her soul, the dark, salivating serpent eager to consume the world?

A sacrifice, perhaps. Prey with wide amber eyes and hands painting sigils in the air. She would undo the world for a taste of him. But she knew, knew deep down, if she ever sunk her teeth into Edward Michael Hayes, there would be no letting him go. And she had to let him go. If there was one thing she was sure of, it was that he was not meant for this world any more than she was meant for his. He was the sunlight on burnished skin, and she was a dead woman walking. A ghost waiting to return to the grave that had lost her.

*Fuck.*

She could go for a blunt right about now.

"He wasn't innocent."

His voice brought her attention back to the here and now, and she frowned. "What are you —"

"The old man. My dad." His breathing hitched, and she eased back, gripping his hand to steady him as he rose.

They sat on the bed together, legs entangled, tucked in close so the secrets had nowhere to go but where they put them. There, in the shadows and the quiet, he split himself open for her. Told her of the monster living beneath his bed and stalking his dreams every time he closed his eyes.

Once upon a time, there was a little boy. He was too small to fight back, and so he was swallowed down. *"This is love,"* he was told. But what the beast meant was, *"This is what it is to break the thing you love."*

And broken it was.

His hands shaped worlds around them until she gripped his wrists and brought them back home, leaning her forehead against his so those amber eyes couldn't see the rage birthed bloody and screaming in the bayou scrambling for purchase beneath her skin.

"I'll kill him for you," she growled, as she kneaded the tension from his palms.

Usually, she didn't take hit jobs. They were messy. Too many variables to consider. But for this, for him, she would flay flesh from bones. The strength of her reaction should have scared her, but it didn't. Dusty protected what was hers. It would have been the same for any of the members of the Legion. Her reaction, visceral and rending, was nothing.

"You can't," his lips quirked in wry amusement. "He's too powerful for that now."

Dusty scowled. "What do you mean?"

Edward shrugged, uncomfortable, and cleared his throat. His hands slipped from hers, and she fought the urge to pull him back to her. Swinging around, he set his feet on the floor and rested his head in his hands. "Water?"

Rising, Dusty limped to the mini fridge against one wall. She was surprised to find a few bottles of water stacked on the otherwise empty shelves. The owner knew his clientele at least. She tossed Edward a bottle, unsurprised when he went to catch it and missed. Sighing, she leaned back against the wall and crossed her arms beneath her breasts as he drank his fill. The urge to sharpen Bess was strong, but she refrained. For now.

"Who is this guy?"

Edward hesitated, then realizing he'd come too far to turn back, he shook his head. "When I was still a kid, he got involved in politics. He was the relatable good ol' boy. An 'average Joe.' People flocked to him." Edward's voice was bitter, and she could understand why. "Anyway, getting into a good college was the only way I knew how to get away from him, and I worked my ass off to make sure I never needed him for anything once I graduated high school. Having a genius for a son was good for his numbers, especially once I started Marco Enterprises. I was proof he was a family man and a dedicated father. My successes, no matter what they were, were automatically attributed to my dad and how well he'd raised me."

Edward turned away, his throat working. He gathered himself, then continued. "He showed up during a product launch a few years ago to shmooze potential backers for his Senate campaign." His gaze grew distant, empty, as if he were leaving pieces of himself behind in the memories. "I didn't even know he was in town. It blindsided me, and I...I lost it."

Dusty rolled her shoulders, lips tight, but said nothing.

"Remember when I said I get lost sometimes? Well, it's a little more than that," he admitted, unable to look at her as he spoke. "Sometimes it's like I'm someone else. Who I am now kind of disappears, and what's left...what's left takes over and—"

Frustrated, his words died before they could form, but Dusty understood well enough. She'd seen it, those moments when someone else seemed to be looking out at her. There was no fixing this for him, no protecting him from it. Desperate to distract from the unfamiliar sense of helplessness assailing her, she pushed away from the wall. Between getting assaulted and chasing a drugged-out Edward, she didn't have the emotional bandwidth for anything else. She had a drug dealer to see, and she would need her wits about her.

Crouching, Dusty worked on restocking her duffle bag.

"Where are you going?"

"Get some sleep, Edward," she said, gasping when he spilled from his perch on the bed to grip her by the arm. For such a big guy, he was light on his feet when he wanted to be, she noted.

"Don't do that."

"Do what?"

"Push me away." His expression crumbled, and he shook his head. "Like I'm a burden. I can help you."

"Why?" she asked roughly. "Why would you want to help me?"

"Because…" He hesitated. "Because we're friends." He frowned as her resulting silence turned icy, his brows drawing down in earnest confusion. "A-aren't we?"

"We met yesterday. I've had stomach bugs for longer than the two of us have known one another," she jerked her arm away and tossed the bag over her shoulder. "I went to Olive Garden for my birthday last year and kept the leftovers in my fridge for three days. *Three*. After I got my tubes tied, I was constipated for about a week. I waited *seven* whole days to take *one* shit—"

"Okay!" he barked, flushed. "I get it. I'm nothing to you. Less than shit." His voice broke, but his expression was stony. "My mistake."

Dusty buried the knee-jerk reaction to comfort him. To correct him. Things were better this way. She should have been treating him like crap from the start. Now, the two of them had formed some weird connection to one another and things were messy. Complicated. When it was all said and done, Edward would have to go back home, and she didn't want men like Conners and Rudy gunning for him because of his ties with her. She had a weak spot for the goofball, and she didn't want him to suffer because he was dumb enough to think *she* was better than a bullet to the head.

So, she let irritation darken her tone. "You hired me to help you," she reminded him. "To protect you. At first, this whole kicked puppy thing was cute, but now you're just dragging me down. First the fight club, then the tunnels, the bar, the *fucking* cop." She stopped, cursed herself, and turned away. He didn't need to know about what had almost happened with Conners. What happened far too often to women who looked just like her. Not like he would get it even if she did tell him.

*"He's too powerful for that now."* The despair in his earlier words echoed in her mind, and uncertainty tested the firmness of her resolve.

"Adele?" He reached for her, turning her like a dancer and tangling his fingers in her braids so he could cup her jaw in his palm. "What cop?" There was danger in those eyes. Trapped lightning threatening to carve a burning trail in the earth. Another memory threatened, but self-preservation beat it back again.

*Something's wrong*

Dusty held her breath.

"What happened today?" he asked, the gentleness of his tone belying the eruption she could see brewing.

She gripped his wrist, leaning in so she wouldn't have to strain her throat when she said, "I am none of your goddamn business. You're nothing to me, remember?"

Edward's jaw grew tight. "But you're *not* nothing to me," he bit back. "And you can't protect anyone or anything if something happens to you because you're too stubborn to ask for help. What if you wind up dead?" He ran a hand down his face. "My mistake," He breathed. "Dying would be a dream come true, wouldn't it?"

When her eyes widened, he bared his teeth at her, and for a heartbeat, she knew she was speaking to the Edward she'd seen in the ring.

"I know some things about you too," he said with a growl. "I know no one — *no one* — chases Death like you do, Adele Burdot. Keep running, and you'll catch up with him one day."

Dusty stood frozen, tears blurring her vision despite her best efforts to remain unbothered. "Fuck you," she whispered.

"You're not sharp edges and broken glass, Dusty," Edward said, and now he sounded tired. Sad. It enraged her. "You're a fresh bruise, an open wound."

"So what?" she scoffed, pushing away from him.
Her mocking laughter crooked with rising panic.
"You think you can just kiss it and make it better?"

"I could try," he said, gaze was a glittering jewel, a
promise of salvation or a trick. Dusty wasn't sure
which she preferred. "Let me try."

They stared at one another for the longest time.
Dusty searched his eyes, hoping to find…what?
Weakness? Rot? Proof he was just like her? Even now,
she wanted to go to him, let him kiss her all better. It
took an almost physical effort to turn away. She
couldn't trust him, couldn't believe a word he said.
Not without proof. Not without blood. All the best
pacts were sealed in blood, and he'd shed none for
her and never would. In the end, Dusty strode over to
the side table and bent to write a series of numbers on
the legal pad next to the phone.

"This is Ape's number," she said brusquely. "If
I'm not back by morning, call him. He'll take you the
rest of the way."

"Dusty?"

But she didn't linger or hesitate again. Slamming her way out of the motel room, Dusty practically ran to the Mustang; tossing her duffel bag into the passenger seat, she got in and revved the motor. She should have been relieved to be rid of him, even if for a little while. But the passenger side of the car was a black hole, and there was nothing in her large enough to fill it. The familiar rumble of the engine fed the wildness in her spirit, and in a squeal of tires and a plume of white smoke, she peeled out of the parking lot before the memory of Edward's words, and the look on his face as he spoke them, could make her any weaker than she already was.

***

The Mustang's brake lights disappeared down the street, and the motel phone loomed larger than life just a few feet away. Perching just so, on the edge of the bed, Edward tucked his hands between his knees and stared at the far wall.

Minutes ticked by, while the rush of blood in his veins faded to a dull roar. The room wavered; furniture threatening to disappear. Edward knew the signs, knew if he remained stagnant, his mind would leave him behind just like Dusty had. The old voice was back, whispering that he was worthless. Stupid. A spineless nerd.

He scowled. "I'm not a nerd," he whispered to the peeling wallpaper. "I'm not a sinking ship either."

No. He was a badass motherfucker, and it was time he acted like it.

The aging sunflowers on the wallpaper didn't seem impressed by his affirmations, but Edward surged to his feet. Filled with renewed purpose, he stalked over to the side table and stared down at Ape's cell phone number. Reaching out, he lifted the phone just as the motel door flew in. The door bounced off the wall, and one gloved hand reached out and caught it before it could slam shut again.

Ape stepped inside.

*The power of Manifestation.*

"What the hell, man? You couldn't grab a fucking bag or two?" Irate, Diesel pushed past him. By comparison, the second man was more lanky confidence than rippling testosterone, though there was an undeniable charm to the crooked smile he threw Edward's way.

"'Sup, Pretty Boy," he crowed, as if greeting an old friend. "Got any food in this dump?"

# Chapter Sixteen

*No Country for Old Dusty*

Crackhead Rudy lived in a UFO about thirty minutes outside of Roswell. The UFO wasn't a crashed spaceship, it was just easier to say it was. Rudy had seen a show on Netflix about unique homes and spent a cool million last summer constructing his version of the infamous craft. People knew him by his moniker even before Rudy started using, on account of all the crack he'd sold to the good people of Sanderson over the past several years. The nickname didn't roll off the tongue or anything, but there was no denying it had a ring to it.

When Crackhead Rudy wasn't making and selling crack out of the cockpit/kitchen of his UFO, he took refuge in the single-story adobe his father had bought him for his twenty-third birthday. Dusty couldn't remember the last gift Rat had given her, though she knew it sure as shit wasn't a mini-mansion. He did bring her back a single tampon once — unprompted — shortly after she turned fifteen and was annoyingly smug about it for the remainder of the day. Sometimes, she wondered what life might have been like if her dad had been there for her after Desi died. Even before his arrest, no one would confuse Rat for Father of the Year. Still, he tried his best with what he had, and he loved her and Desi with everything he had. Though loving them wasn't enough to save them.

Love wasn't enough to save anyone.

The UFO's lights had gone dark, which meant Rudy was at his main residence. She left the Mustang behind and made the rest of her trip on foot. She didn't want Rudy to see her coming, though the security cameras planted in various cactuses up the long, winding driveway nullified her attempts at stealth.

Regardless, the Mustang *was* a rental, and Sal would be pissed if Dusty brought it back riddled with bullets. Assuming she made it out of Rudy's at all. After taking over the Legion, one of the first changes Dusty had made was ordering her men to cut any ties they might have to dirty cops. Associating with the same men and women willing to put people like her in the ground didn't sit right with her. Some of the Legion had listened. Others had not. Raph had lost an ear for more than just his failure to bring back her drive. The flash drive was supposed to have been atonement for ignoring her orders and feeding the local police department intel. She couldn't blame the boys in blue who were getting rich off jobs meant for her and her men, but she could damn well blame Raph. And did.

*I hope Ape takes his toe. Just for fun.*

In exchange for her silence about his extracurriculars, Raph agreed to keep his mouth shut about why he was assigned to the bank job in the first place. Though, no one would understand the significance of the flash drive, even if they found out about it. She'd left it back at the motel, tucked away in Edward's jacket pocket. If anything happened to her, Ape knew where to find him and would finish what she'd started.

*And Edward?* The question came unbidden. *What happens to him if you're gone?*

*"No one chases death like you do, Adele Burdot."*

One day, she wouldn't be fast enough to escape paying a tithe of soul, and flesh, and blood, but for now, there was only spent bullets and a trail of broken promises—like breadcrumbs—there to lead her back home again.

Dusty was a few yards from the front door when the floodlights came on. She pulled her gun from the holster, aiming down the length of the barrel as the door swung open. It took her sight a bit to adjust to the sudden brightness, and when it did, there was a woman standing on the porch. Her thin, pale body was adorned with a silk chemise and a pair of matching bottoms. Her short crop of curly brown hair was a halo around her face. She reminded Dusty of Poppy and she hesitated, finger slipping off the trigger.

Someone shifted just out of view, a flower-adorned robe peeking out before disappearing just as fast.

Dusty's jaw tightened in annoyance. *Rudy*.

"She cannon fodder?" Dusty motioned to the girl with her gun and the woman grinned, her gaze blank. There were marks on her inner arm as she lifted her shoulders and let them fall. A half-hearted attempt to shift the straps of her camisole back where they belonged. For a moment—a strange, dark moment— the scene shifted, and reality fell away. A woman lay prone on the floor, the front of her Cami soaked with vomit. She convulsed on the ground, the needle still in her arm, and her gaze already far away. A figure stood over her, every inch of skin covered with tattoos that writhed and danced like smoke. He wore a black hood pulled low over his brow, hiding his features from view. When he turned his head, his eyes glowed white hot and eager.

"Depends," Rudy called from around the corner, pulling her back to the present. "You mad enough to shoot me?"

The woman giggled. Apparently, the thought of getting caught in the crossfire was worth a chuckle or two. Dusty should have been annoyed. Instead, she was just relieved the junkie was still alive. The vision was nothing more than that. A few seconds had passed, but Dusty's hands were shaking and clammy, as if she'd caught a fever. She ran her palms down the side of her jeans, trying to get herself under control. She wasn't some naïve teenager anymore. Wasn't dumb enough to believe she had power at her disposal. When she was young, the idea that she was favored by the ancestors—the spirits of loved ones passed—made her feel special. As a grown ass woman, she knew better. If the ancestors loved her so much, then why the hell had they taken her sister? They'd shared a womb, so why favor one over the other? There was nothing special about her, nothing making her more worthy of life than Desi.

Yet here she was, breathing still.

Arm heavy, she let the gun sink by slow degrees.

Dusty talked to a therapist once a month. She knew all the jargon. This was projecting. The 'why' would have to be discussed during next week's session. For now, she had more important shit to worry about than the state of her psyche. She caught the glint of light on glass as Rudy peeked at her through the reflection of his handheld. Paranoid asshole was still inside the house, and after her vision, or hallucination, it was all Dusty could do to control her temper.

"You dumb enough to shoot *me*?" Her fingers flexed around the handle, the gun dipping as she toyed with the idea of taking the shot.

A dark chuckle, and this time, Rudy peeked his head out as if to gauge her mood. "Not right now," he was as jovial as usual. "Might change after a line or two."

"Fair enough." Dusty let the gun drop the rest of the way, hugging it against the side of her leg before sitting it on the ground. Dusty kicked the gun away. Sneering when Rudy stepped into view, gripping the woman around the waist and planting a kiss on the side of her neck. She was still unmoving, unblinking. Dusty might have confused her for a doll if not for the deadness in her eyes.

"That's better," Rudy purred.

A rustle from one of the bushes stationed near the house sent the hair on the back of her nape up. Scanning the darkness with a jaded eye, she found four men surrounding the main building. Dusty's night vision wasn't great, which meant there were more around. Rudy having guards should have been great news. This was Rudy's base of operations after all, the hub responsible for most of her product. The Legion did occasional runs for the cartels, and the consensus was always the same across the board. Rudy made good shit.

Which explained why he was always high. Dusty tried not to think too hard about which came first. Rudy and Crack would forever remain her chicken or the egg. Either way, a chemist of his caliber was in high demand. Rudy, however, preferred leading a more independent life, which is why he worked with Dusty. As long as he adhered to her rules, he was free to do whatever he liked without fear of being snatched up by some intrepid mob boss. He took over the safe house and no one knew where he was except for Dusty and her inner circle. It kept Rudy safe, and it gave the Legion some much-needed leverage amongst some of the more powerful players. A fact

she might be able to use to her advantage,
considering the assholes trying to take her out.

*Do I really want to get any more tangled up in the
mafia? Eliot is bad enough.*

*Nope.*

"You going to invite me in?" she asked, and Rudy
laughed.

It was a good laugh, she'd give him that much.
Rudy may have been handsome at some point—some
of the pretty still lingered in the shape of his mouth
and in his baby-blue eyes—but years of chasing his
next high had left their mark. He was skinny, too
skinny for his slight build. His mousy brown hair was
thinning, and his teeth were blackened in several
places. He had enough money to deal with his
cosmetic issues, but instead, he wore them like a
badge of honor. She was used to seeing him dressed
in suits and cashmere sweaters, his skin sunken and
the marks on his arms and legs a glaring reminder of
just where all his wealth had come from.

"You going to tell me why you're sniffing around?"

"Conners," she said, her voice iron.

Rudy's eyes widened, and without waiting for a response, Dusty strode up the front steps. She half expected someone to shoot her in the back and was relieved when she made it to the door unscathed.

"Got any booze in this shithole?" she shouldered past Rudy.

The door clicked shut behind her, as Dusty took in the safe house. It never failed to astound. Rudy had been obsessed with aliens for as long as she'd known him, and the UFO theme had been carried over to the main house so he could enjoy it year-round. The living room resembled the inside of a cockpit. Silver paneling for every cabinet and door, along with a single, unobstructed sheet of one-way glass, did a decent job of feeding into the fantasy. Dusty knew, from experience, the sliding doors opposite the entrance led down a long hallway where several bedrooms and a bathroom had been designed much the same way. Everything was custom, everything was brand new, and it was all filthy.

Empty cups, plates of rotting food, lines of coke on a glass table. The white carpet—a design choice Rudy likely regretted now—was stained in several places and nothing more than a backdrop for discarded clothes and trash. She imagined Edward living here for any length of time, imagined him even walking through the door, and recoiled.

*Well, there goes that plan.*

A hand gripped Dusty's ankle from beneath the glass coffee table, and she kicked it away. It would seem she'd interrupted Rudy mid-orgy. Men and women in various stages of undress lounged around the room. Two men were fucking in the recliner in the far corner, unconcerned by her arrival.

"Who the hell are all these people?" she asked through numb lips, turning on her reluctant host. There were no cars outside, so there was no telling how long these people had been there or even how they'd arrived. All that mattered was that they were in the last place they should have been. She eyed Rudy, gauging his high. Today was a tuxedo day, though he'd abandoned the suit jacket somewhere, and his button-down shirt lay open to the waist, revealing an ornate Crucifix stretching from the base of his throat and down to the waistband of his pants. The eyes of white Jesus followed her, and Dusty scowled at him.

Rudy's hair was slicked back, and he was wearing bright red lipstick and totting a hunting rifle over one shoulder. He cocked his head to one side, swaying where he stood. "These are my friends." He gripped the girl cosplaying as his human shield by the waist and pulled her close. "C'mon, Candy, let's show Dusty how friendly you can be." Nuzzling her neck, he nevertheless kept his eyes trained on Dusty as the girl sagged against his chest. If he weren't there to prop her up, she would have fallen.

*Gross.*

Dusty wasn't sure what the two of them were on. It wasn't crack-ish behavior, but they damn sure weren't sober. "I spoke to your little friend, Officer Conners, today," she said without preamble, putting an abrupt stop to the love fest.

Bleary-eyed, the woman frowned even as Rudy's jaw worked in annoyance.

"He's not a friend, D," Rudy said, shoving the girl away.

She slunk off, but Dusty's relief was short-lived. Even if she were free of Rudy, there was no shortage of strangers around, eager to take advantage. Already she was being approached by the man from beneath the coffee table, and Dusty gripped her knife. The pommel against her palm soothed her, but the urge to shed blood left her itching for a fight.

"I give him a little product and a few bucks," Rudy was saying, daring enough to step closer. She side-eyed him, and nervous, he laughed and shuffled back. "He makes sure the boys down at the precinct mind their own business," Rudy said. "He's good. We're good." His eyes turned shrewd. "Unless he's on your shit list or something."

Oh, how well he knew her. "How many," Dusty asked, still calm for now.

Rudy frowned. "How many what?"

"How many women has he assaulted since you brought him on?"

Rudy shook his head, and his fingers flexed one by one around his rifle. "I don't…I don't know what you mean."

"I think you do." Tired of the game, Dusty pulled her second gun from the holster at the small of her back and checked to make sure there was a bullet in the chamber. "You know how many missing-person flyers there were on my way here, Rudy?"

He paled.

Idiot. "A *lot*," she continued. "Too many, in fact. So, here's what I think." Before Rudy could say or do anything, she shoved the barrel into the side of his head and drove him to his knees, incensed. "I think you and that pig have been snatching girls instead of running my fucking product."

Profits had been down for a while now, but it had been hard to pinpoint the exact reason why. Dusty had been working through the different angles, ever since running into Conners. Profits were down because less product was being sold. Either Rudy wasn't making as much, or some of it was going somewhere else, like into the veins of the pretty brunette getting pawed at on the living room couch. Women were easier to train and manipulate when they were coked out of their minds. Dusty knew how it worked. Beat them, drug them, fuck them. Do it enough on repeat, and soon, all the soul and the fight simply disappear.

"You're crazy," Rudy gasped, dropping the rifle in favor of raising his hands into the air on either side of his head. He curled into himself, striving to look as small as possible as all eyes turned on them. Even the couple in the corner paused long enough to pull their clothes on.

Dusty raised a brow, "Am I?" She nodded, still thoughtful. "Maybe. Let's see." It took no time at all to think of the name. It had been with her since the hotel. "Hey, Clara," she called. "Your momma's been looking for you, girl."

The woman on the couch stirred, a bit of awareness returning to her eyes. "Mom?" she whispered, so broken and small Dusty's finger twitched on the trigger. Memories of Desi, of Poppy, swam through her blood, and rage rose like a storm, crackled and bit like lightning. She slammed the butt of her gun into Rudy's nose, and he screamed, falling back. Dusty followed him down, straddling him and trapping his arms against his side as she reached forward and pressed her thumb into his eye. He bucked beneath her, but she was anything but petite, and years of drug use had left him nothing but skin and bone. She pushed, pushed, pushed until resistance fled and Rudy's eye popped clean out of its socket. Dusty gasped, open-mouthed and drunk on pleasure.

All around her, people scrambled out of the way, running out of the room, for fear she'd turn on them next. Their fear was something she could feel, something she could swallow whole, and the world was awash in a red, red haze that tasted like blood and terror. Soon, one of the guards from outside would come to investigate, but for now, she gloried in the pandemonium.

Dusty leaned into Rudy, inhaling the stale stink of him as if it were meat fresh from the bone. "I'm going to cut out your fucking tongue," she breathed, pressing the nozzle of her gun hard enough into his temple to bruise. She couldn't kill him, not yet, but she'd have her pound of flesh come hell or high water.

A memory of Edward standing in the bar as she sliced through Raphael's ear, watching her without expression or judgment, crowded into her thoughts, and she hesitated. What would he think if he could see her now? If he knew what she was doing and how far she still had left to go?

Dusty gained her feet but kept her gun leveled on Rudy lest he try and slither away.

Why should she care? She'd only ever done what needed to be done. What others refused to do. Even now. Either she put Rudy in his place, or she slit his throat. The second option was tempting, but once he was dead, she'd lose any hope of finding the girls he and Conners had trafficked. Even worse, she'd have to find a new cook before the cartels came sniffing around. She didn't have thousands of kilos worth of coke just lying around, nor did she have the money to cover the loss of such a sum. So, Rudy would go on breathing for a time, but Dusty would make damn sure he regretted every second of it. Speaking of, Rudy had stopped screaming and was muttering something under his breath.

Dusty scowled down at him. "You better be praying," she said coldly.

"Oh, I am," he giggled, the sound wild with pain. "But not for me. For you."

A pair of long, brown fingers slid over her shoulder. Skin so thin she imagined she could see the white of bone beneath. Her gaze traveled up the hand to the wrist, from wrist to arm, until she met white, bottomless eyes. She had known him, ever since she'd crawled screaming from the dirt, and mud, and grief. She turned because the Devil told her to, and there, standing behind her, dressed in plain clothes and sporting a shit-eating grin, was Officer Conners. He was holding Rudy's abandoned rifle, and at this distance, it wasn't a question of *if* he'd hit her but how big the hole would be after he did.

Once again, she was presented with a choice. Dusty could either abandon Rudy and turn her gun on Conners, or she could blow him away and damn the consequences. Baring her teeth in an answering grin, she squeezed the trigger just as Conners reared back and punched her full force in the face. She and Rudy hit the ground at the same time, and as consciousness fled, she bathed in the fucker's blood and smiled, really smiled, for the first time since Officer Dipshit. And with nothing to stop the memories, the past came rushing forth with painful clarity.

***

"You sure about this?" Dusty met Eliot's gaze, her own heated. Sure about it? She was so excited she was bouncing in place. At the look on her face, he chuckled. "You're a horror, you know that?" He breathed, his fingers tangling in the curls at her nape and pulling her close.

Strange how the words, coming from him, sounded so much like *I love you*. Dusty warmed, glowing under his praise as Eliot pressed their foreheads together. They were so close they managed, somehow, to drown out everyone and everything else. Eliot pressed a kiss against her lips.

"I spiked his beer," he whispered, breath fanning her skin. "You still have about five, maybe ten minutes before the effects start to kick in." He smelled like mint toothpaste and his father's cologne.

Dusty jerked away, brow furrowing in anger, but Eliot grasped her wrist and pulled her back, trying to make the move look casual instead of what it was. A reprimand. "You can hate me all you want later," he hissed. "But I'll be damned if I watch Axel beat you to death over some stupid bet."

The bet.

Dusty had been hounding Axel for weeks. A few hours ago, in front of the entire bar, he'd accepted her terms. They were simple enough. If she won, she got the Legion. If he won, he got her. Axel liked them young. In fact, Axel liked a lot of things, including beating women. His preferences were earning him a bit of a reputation ever since he'd taken over the Legion. Two years after Rat was charged with several counts of 1st-degree murder, violence was all the Legion was known for. Dusty hated this, hated watching something Rat cared for so much become the subject of true crime podcasts and speculation. Her dad had built this club from the ground up and handpicked every single member himself. It was small at first, just him and Ape. Soon, it grew into a bunch of friends, just hanging out and shooting the shit while they traveled from town to town. But somewhere along the way, things had taken a turn, and now the same men who had attended her eighth birthday party after Rat got too drunk to show were on a government watchlist.

The Legion, and the men and women who made up its number, were her people. The closest thing she still had to a family, besides Eliot, and he didn't count anymore. Things had been…weird between them ever since that first kiss, and she didn't think she could ever go back to just seeing him as her foster brother.

Papa Tate would be livid if he knew, but that's what secrets were for. Though, if anyone knew about secrets, it would be Tate. He and Gran had known one another for a long time, and when the media swarmed their small town looking for a traumatized girl with a story, she sent Dusty to live with him and his son for a while. Papa Tate was approaching retirement and in the middle of training his nephew, Eliot, to take over when Dusty landed on his doorstep. Tate was strict but fair. These two qualities came in handy during his rather illustrious career as an enforcer for the mob.

Eliot had no interest in his uncle's business. Dusty, however, was all too eager to learn everything Papa was willing to teach her. For two years, she'd soaked up every lesson he had to impart, and now?

Now, she was ready for war.

Eliot crouched before her, wrapping the knuckles of her right hand. She glared down at the top of his head, shaking. The world around them was loud, knives against her bare skin. She was wearing a sports bra and a pair of boxers, but already she was slicked with sweat. Maybe it was nerves. She wasn't sure. It was hard to tell what she felt sometimes. Most days, she didn't feel anything at all, and she liked those days the best.

"This place is disgusting," Eliot muttered under his breath as wrapped her other hand. "Smells like blood in here." He glanced up, as if waiting for her agreement. When it didn't come, he sighed, his shoulders slumping. "Don't look at me like that," he said. "I know you're mad, but there's no reality where you win this on your own."

Dusty didn't respond. She didn't have to. Her heart squeezed tight, and she turned away, eyeing the room. The bar hadn't changed since she'd left, and there was an air of neglected nostalgia about the place. No matter how far the Legion went, they always ended up back here. The Clubhouse was home, after all. The one safe place many of them had. No one would respect her if they thought she'd cheated. If she was going to win their bet, her victory had to be quick and decisive.

How long had she been waiting for this? How long had she planned? Rat was sentenced just a few months ago. Even for such a high-profile case, the justice system moved at a snail's pace. There was no telling how long things would have dragged out had he not pled guilty from the very beginning.

A dumbass to the very end.

A part of Dusty wanted to reassure Eliot; she had everything under control. But even if she wanted to speak, she couldn't. Sometimes, her vocal cords didn't open and close properly. The doctors said the trauma would lessen over time, but Dusty didn't care either way. What need did she have of a voice when there were men to cut down? It was a task best done in silence, after all.

Axel sauntered to the center of the bar where chairs and tables had been pushed aside to make room for the fight. Jerking her hands from Eliot, Dusty strode forward to meet him. She should have been terrified. For all his faults and vices, Axel was still a grown man and a full head and shoulders above her, though his muscles had turned to fat years ago. Dusty checked the clock on the far wall. Five minutes until the roofie kicked in.

*Shiny,* she thought. *Let's be bad guys.*

There was an answering giggle, but she tuned the voice out. She was getting better at ignoring Desi these days. Gran told her if she ignored the spirits for too long, they'd no longer speak to her. Boo hoo.

"You don't have to do this, sha," Eliot called after her, speaking around the cigarette in his mouth.

Dusty lifted her hand, giving him the finger as she pushed through the crowd. She wished he believed in her, just a little. Maybe it would make what she had to do easier to stomach.

*"Don't trust anyone out there but yourself, Dusty. No one is going to value your life over their own. Not your gran, not Eliot, and not me."*

It was Papa's first lesson, and Dusty was forced to agree. Hadn't she hesitated to save Desi? She loved her sister more than anything, more than anyone, and yet she still woke screaming at night, trapped on the blacktop next to Rat's overturned bike.

Frozen.

In fear.

In indecision.

Her weakness had cost her sister her life.

Dusty would never be weak again. Not for anyone. Not about anything. She would be a horror in human skin, sharp as a blade. Quick and cruel. If she had any hope of killing the monster who took her Desi, she would have to turn into something even worse than he was. The room was full of bikers, full of Legion, and they swarmed around her, watching. Waiting for her to fail and prove she didn't belong there and never had. Everyone and their mother had come out to see Rat's daughter fight for the rights to a legacy no one gave a shit about but her.

Most of the members were much older than her, but some — like Diesel — were around the same age. He was crouched on the edge of the pool table across the room, his red hair in disarray and his blue eyes bright under the fluorescent. He grinned as she passed, and Dusty glared at him. A runaway, Diesel had sought out the Legion about three years ago. It was Rat who'd taken him in and allowed him to join. He used to be nothing more than an errand boy, but he'd just gone on his first job. *Must be feeling himself,* she thought, dismissing him as unimportant. All her focus was on Axel. It had to be.

"Ooh," he crowed drunkenly. "Someone looks serious!" He shivered as if he were scared and laughed. "Come 'ere girl. Let me teach you a lesson your child-killer of a daddy never did."

Several people snickered, and Dusty made a mental note of each.

"Hey, kid." A hand on her arm brought her up short. A man, a giant, stared down at her with dark brown eyes. He was Samoan—the traditional tattoos on his face and arms hinted at a land far from this one. She scowled, and he studied her in silence before nodding as if he'd reached some decision.

"You need help out there, you let me know, and I'll come running. Got me?" He didn't look like he was going to let her go until she agreed, so she nodded and jerked her arm free. Dusty remembered him well enough. He was a big fan of an online first-person shooter game called Apex Predators. Once Rat's right hand, they used to play during the summer at Gran's while her dad slept off his hangover. Ape had never been much of a drinker, though he'd be the first biker she'd ever met who could say such a thing.

Once Dusty managed to work her way past the others, she didn't stop or slow. Instead, she strode right up to Axel, ducked out of the way of the right hook he threw, and drove her fist into his Adam's apple, rabbit quick. He choked, eyes bulging, and rocked forward. She shoved her foot into his knee, putting all the force she could muster into the motion. There was a snap, and he dropped to his good knee with a scream. As he went, she pulled the knife Papa gave her from her belt and flipped it open. She was a little clumsy with it still, so the slash across Axel's throat wasn't as clean as she might have liked.

Still got the job done, though. Arterial blood coated her in a red mist, and Axel fell like some great tree. He hit the ground face first at her feet, just where he belonged. Dusty blinked the scarlet haze out of her eyes and met the stunned gaze of the men and women around her. Toward the back, she caught sight of Eliot, his face a mask of horror and disgust. Turning away, she lifted her arms into the air like a prized fighter at the end of a match. Her heart leapt as the Legion erupted, their cheers filling the clubhouse until the rafters shook.

They were hers now, first by birthright and now by so much more.

Eliot's right, she marveled. It does smell like bloodshed. Dusty's tongue darted out, and she licked her bottom lip as a crimson curtain consumed her and the Legion, both.

# Chapter Seventeen

*Girls Just Wanna Live*

Edward had few expectations in life. A hermit for the last several years, he'd been getting most of his information from television. Sort of like when he was still a kid, tinkering in the living room and imagining a better life for himself and his mother. He liked

Lifetime movies in particular. Lifetime, unlike Hallmark, showed the gritty reality of life. For instance, three days ago, he'd seen a film about a young gymnast who got caught up in drugs while dating a boy from the wrong side of the tracks. She went missing, so her mother had to go looking for her. The suburban housewife entered the drug den expecting the worst and found it in the form of her dead daughter. Riveting stuff for the first ten minutes. Edward wasn't sure how the mom went about finding justice because he fell asleep halfway through the two-hour premiere. Still, he remembered the scene at the crack house very clearly. A drug den had a certain vibe.

A burning UFO in the middle of the desert with a bunch of half-naked people dancing around it did *not* pass the vibe check.

"You sure this is the right place?" he asked.

Rather than use his words, Ape grunted his displeasure. Edward's jaw went tight. He was beginning to think the guy didn't like him, though he couldn't fathom why. He was a goddamn delight.

The smoke trail disappeared against a backdrop of stars, and the fire was so large it warmed him, Ape, and Diesel, even from several yards away. Funny, this was the second arson he'd seen in as many days. Of *course* Dusty was involved somehow, but he didn't see her anywhere among the spectators. They'd found the Mustang down the road, so at least she'd made it to Rudy's. But if so, where the hell was she?

"You can let go now," Diesel said.

Edward glanced down. Ape was too big to ride with anyone, and Edward was too big to fit into the sidecar attached to his massive bike. In the end, he'd found himself perched on the back of Diesel's dark blue Harley and spent the entire ride trying to think of less Yaoi-coded ways to clutch another man around the waist.

Spoiler alert: He never found any.

He released the biker, shivering a bit. The scent of melting plastic was heavy in the frigid air. Edward was surprised none of the people outside had passed out from the fumes. Though they were probably on something a lot stronger than micro-plastics if their yelps and euphoric howls were anything to go by.

"Take the druggies on the right," Ape barked, his expression hard and cold as he dismounted his motorcycle. In just the span of a few minutes, his entire demeanor had shifted from affable overlord to hardened second in command. "I'll handle the ones on the left. See if any of them have seen her and meet back here in five."

Diesel nodded, slipped out from in front of Edward, and took off at a jog.

"What about me?" Edward asked.

Ape hesitated, then forced a smile. "Stay and watch the bikes, would ya?" He left before Edward could protest.

Ape had been acting weird ever since the hotel, and Edward wondered what was going on but knew the Goliath wouldn't tell him even if he asked him outright. Feeling antsy, he yelped when a tug on his sleeve brought his attention around. Heart beating a mile a minute, Edward's hands came up. He was a badass now, which meant he was ready and willing to fuck up whoever was brave enough to accost him.

A young woman stumbled back in shock, and contrite, Edward surrendered. "Sorry," his hands shot up, hoping to calm the animal panic in her eyes. "Reflex." He cleared his throat, hoping he at least sounded confident. "When you live life on the edge like I do, you have to keep your guard up. Know what I mean?"

The woman shook her head, and Edward lowered his arms. She seemed calmer now that he wasn't on the offensive, but still doubtful. She glanced over at Ape and Diesel stomping toward the fire, and Edward could see the gears turning in her mind as she assessed their threat level. He knew the look all too well. It reminded him of his mother.

Somber, he reached out, bringing her focus back to him. "Are you alright?" he asked, this time, dropping the pretense.

Some of Little Eddie must have bled through because she relaxed enough to speak. "You're looking for her?" she asked instead of replying. "For Dusty?"

Edward's breath caught, and he didn't bother hiding his relief. "You've seen her? You know where she is?"

The woman nodded. "The cop took her," she said. "Put a bunch of us in the back of a truck and loaded her up in the cruiser." She pointed down the road, dark and empty. "You don't have much time," she said, Edward tensed. Without a backward glance, he rushed after Ape and Diesel with a muttered "Thanks," to mark his departure. There was no telling how much of a lead they had, which meant he and the others needed to move now.

What would a cop want with Dusty? He thought back to the hotel, to the things she'd almost said but left buried instead, and went cold. Panic was a wolf, pacing back and forth in his mind, scratching at an old trailer door, sniffing at the cracks, and looking for a way in. Edward shoved it down, ignoring jaws that snapped and threatened to rend and tear, and stumbled toward the UFO with his lungs struggling to draw a full breath.

There were about a dozen people laid out on the ground, celebrating before the blaze. They weren't dirty, just entrenched in their own skin. Most of them were under dressed for the frigid weather. There was a carelessness going beyond the dirt and grime. It was something hot water and soap couldn't wash away. There was a vacancy to the eyes, a listlessness or over excitement to their gestures, or lack thereof, that seemed a silent testament to the hollowness beneath the skin. Whatever hole they wanted to fill was still gaping and hungry. An emptiness so impossible to hide, it was visible even to the naked eye.

Most people hid their cracks and broken pieces beneath the bravado of sheer personality, but the drugs took that away. Those who met his eyes were matchstick men, gazes unsteady, glassy. Broken Golems with eyes like mirrors—as much a reflection of the world outside as the one within. They were contradictory by their very natures. Fragile, breakable things, but somehow untouchable. The world was a predator, hungry for the soft, vulnerable underbelly of the ones who found themselves separated from the herd. While they hadn't prevented the tooth or the claw from doing its damage, they had managed to place a barrier between themselves and the agony of being ripped to shreds.

They knew the wolf just as well as he did, and finding himself in people so far removed from everything he knew was jarring. It fed the beast, and his hold on the door slipped just a bit. With a gasp, he crouched where he stood, unable to take another step for fear he'd shatter. The firelight played on his skin, and shaking hands dove into his hair, nails scraping his scalp in silent punishment for his weakness. He gritted his teeth, a whimper slipping past as he stemmed the flow of terror.

*"I got you,"* Dusty said, *eyes searching his face. "Remember?"*

His head echoed with the throaty sound of her laughter, as endless and dark as those eyes.

*One.*

*"You can call me Adele," she said. "Adele Burdot."*

There was a rising phoenix winding the length of her upper arm, feathers a watercolor of red and yellow. Flames come to life. Edward had always been too distracted to appreciate it properly.

*Two.*

*"You're a weird one, Edward Hayes."*

A memory, then, of rushing through the desert. Of trying to escape the wild specter of his father. A figure so large he blocked out the sun, the sky. Then Dusty was there, gripping him by the sides of the face. Her hands cool and callused against his skin. In this memory, dulled by the haze of too many drugs, she was panting for breath. Even now, the memory anchored him.

*Three.*

*"You gotta stop running from me, Pretty Boy,"* she said with a laugh. *"Because God knows what you'll do next time if I'm not around to catch you."*

"I don't have time for this shit," he gasped, lifting his head. The door slammed shut, and the wolf backed down, dissatisfied but willing to be patient. After all, it'd always gotten its fill before. This time would be no different, but it would have to be later. Dusty was in danger, and he had to get to her, no matter what.

With a start, he glanced up to find Diesel standing just a few feet away, staring at him from beside the blaze. He was unblinking, and so still he seemed carved from the shadows around them. There was a dark, savage thirst twisting his features until he met Edward's eyes. His expression shifted, softened, but it was already too late. Edward had *seen* the monster hiding in plain sight. His hands took to their nervous dance, and he fought not to shrink back into himself. Tight and small. Edward was a little boy again, and emotion, unnamed and unwanted, was crippling him.

He recognized this feeling. It had come so often in childhood that he was able to shrug into it without thought.

A heavy hand on his shoulder had him seizing with terror, but it was only Ape, his expression tight with dread. "Get to the Mustang," he ordered. "Drive back to the motel and lock the door."

"Someone took her," Edward managed. "A cop." The woman from before was nowhere to be found. To his relief, she hadn't taken off with either of the bikes, but he worried for her out on her own.

"Shit." Ape ran an anxious hand through his hair, loose and flowing around his shoulders. The tattoos on his face cast stark, black lines across his visage. "He must have loaded her up with the others."

"Others?" Edward frowned.

Diesel joined them, looking just as amiable as always, his red mane in wild disarray.

Edward ignored him, still unsure what to make of what he'd seen or what it meant, if anything. "What others?"

"Rudy's been running a little business on the side," Diesel answered, falling in line with Ape and Edward as they walked back the way they'd come. "Most of these people have been missing for months. I recognized a few of them from the flyers posted on the way here."

Ape's lips tightened, eyes blazing. "I want his head."

A ferocious grin of approval from Diesel. "Duh," he said. "Let's go get our girl."

*Our girl.*

Without realizing what he was doing, Edward's arm shot out, and he gripped Diesel by the collar of his shirt, jerking him off his feet as he pulled him close. "*My* girl," he snarled in the other man's face, livid in a way he'd never been before. "Mine."

"Whoa," Diesel's eyes went wide. "calm down, big guy." The redhead patted the back of Edward's hand. Even now, something about his expression was off. Was he…laughing? It was almost as if he was enjoying this. Edward's grip tightened, and Diesel's flushed red.

"Hey," Ape's voice, ripe with concern, cut through the tension. "Chill, Pretty Boy. You're hurting him."

Edward flinched, forcing his fingers to uncurl one by one. He took a stumbling step back.

*What the hell was that?*

Both men stared at him, and Edward scratched compulsively at his wrist—anything to keep his hands busy. "I can help." Why didn't anyone believe him when he said that? He'd been screaming it into the void all his life.

"Of course, you can help," Ape said. "By waiting for us back at the hotel." Ape spoke as if he were dealing with a child, and Edward wanted nothing more than to lash out like one. The larger man hesitated, then continued softer than before. "Don't worry. We'll bring her back."

"Yeah," Diesel interjected from a safe distance. "We'll take good care of Dusty. Don't you worry."

Ape was already heading for the bikes, and after a final look, Diesel followed.

Edward found himself wishing he'd squeezed just a little harder. He didn't know what it was about Diesel that was rubbing him the wrong way all of a sudden. Had he seen something earlier? Or was it all part of his imagination?

Regardless, he hadn't come all this way *not* to see Dusty again. With a final glance, he took off for the Mustang at full speed, thrilled when his last-minute decision to slide across the hood didn't send him flying off the other side and into a ditch. He got into the driver's seat, praying Dusty had left the keys beneath the floor mat just like all the other times before.

*Jackpot.*

The Mustang started with a purr, leaping forward as if eager to get back on the road. He punched the gas, shifting the car into gear and gripping the wheel as the world skipped past at breakneck speed. His headlights illuminated the road ahead, and soon he caught sight of the twin motorcycles racing just out of his reach. He pulled up even, met Ape's gaze through the driver's window, and gave him the finger as he sailed past. The Mustang, heavier and much more cumbersome than the bikes, had to work to outpace Diesel and Ape, but the souped-up engine managed it.

The highway rocketed past, darkness and stars streaking overhead, enclosing him, until it was just him, the open road, and the Mustang's engine thrumming in time with his thoughts. The wolf scratched, pacing, and his hands clenched around the wheel.

*Dusty.*

For some reason, she held the monsters at bay, kept his broken edges from leaving his mind in tatters. So, he would think of only her, hear only her, taste only her until everything else faded, and she was all he had left. The wind tore through his hair with long fingers, and Edward threw his head back and howled, letting the sound carry up, up, and away. A warning to the Gods themselves.

*She's mine*

The back of the semi-truck came out of nowhere. Its lights were off as it cruised down the highway, following behind a solitary police car. Edward whipped around the truck and reached across the console to unzip Dusty's duffel bag with one hand. Grabbing the first thing he found. Dusty had been talkative during their long drive. Explaining with a certain amount of relish how a car of this caliber could hit 155 mph with ease, but thanks to the mods Sally had been working on, their "rental" could go twice that. His thoughts ran, numbers flying as he worked out the math. How far ahead would he need to be? How many seconds would he have? How much distance between...

*Fuck it.*

Edward paid no heed to the oncoming traffic swerving out of his way, cars spinning out in the dirt on the side of the road as he sped past the cruiser.

When he was several hundred yards ahead, he pulled the pin of the grenade with his teeth, down-shifted gears, and whipped the Mustang around in a clean 180. The grenade went flying, and Edward upshifted, hit the gas yet again, and sailed back the way he'd come, the smell of burnt rubber fouling the air. He was working with 0 to 60 in 4.2 seconds and had just five seconds to escape the blast radius.

The countdown started in his head, numbers ticking away, both too fast and yet never fast enough. By the time he reached three, he was already pushing 40 mph, and his pulse was a wild thing trapped in his throat. What if his math was wrong? If he hadn't gotten far enough ahead of the cruiser and haul truck…

*Fuck.*

The two cars passed one another, and Edward met the gaze of the man in the front seat.

*"I want his head."*

*So do I,* Edward thought, and there was venom in those words.

He hit 60 mph, and in the next breath, the world exploded around him. The firestorm knocked the wheel out of his hands and lifted the back end of the Mustang into the air. The car crashed down a split second later, and Edward hit the brakes, jerking the wheel to one side. The Mustang came to a halt, and he paused to catch his breath. The cruiser had flipped, while the haul truck was cab first in a ditch, its hood smoking. Up ahead, a line of flames blocked the road, but otherwise nothing moved.

Then the door to the haul truck burst open and a man jumped out. Edward scrambled. He hadn't thought beyond this point. Which was okay. Really. He could improvise. The duffel bag was still open next to him, and he pulled the AK-47 with its scope from the depths of it, practically singing the hallelujah chorus as he gripped the cold metal. It fit in his hands as if it had been made for him. Getting to his feet in the seat of the car, he stepped onto the passenger's side door and jumped down onto the pavement, ready to kick ass and take names.

Bradley Star with a license to carry.

Then he tripped on the uneven pavement and hit the ground face-first. The AK-47 went off, sending a spray of bullets arching through the air. The tires exploded one by one on the haul truck, and the driver screamed as a bullet went right through his upper thigh. He dropped his gun and hit the ground, too intent on army crawling beneath the truck to bother returning fire.

"Sorry," Edward called.

"Fuck off!"

*Okay.*

New plan. Maybe this time, one *without* a high-powered assault rifle he had no idea how to use. Maybe he could just take names? Leave the ass-kicking to someone more qualified? An itemized list was more his speed.

Edward climbed to his feet, pushed the gun over into the grass with his shoe, and then ran toward the overturned cruiser. The windows were all busted out, and the man in the front seat was hanging upside down from his seatbelt, the gash on his forehead dripping blood onto the ceiling of the car.

Bypassing him, Edward opened the back door, sucking in a sharp breath when he found Dusty curled up in a ball where she'd fallen. She was handcuffed to the oh-shit bar, and a strip of bloody cloth had been stuffed in her mouth. She was unconscious and covered in cuts and bruises, but alive.

Edward's knees went weak with relief.

"Hey, Pretty Boy!"

He glanced over, surprised to find Diesel and Ape had arrived. He'd been so focused on stopping the cruiser, he'd forgotten about them. Diesel was busy wrestling the key to the trailer from the driver while Ape stalked over to help Edward.

"We need to get the hell out of here," Ape said.

Edward pointed to the handcuffs, then turned to brush Dusty's braids back so he could examine the blood on the side of her face. Ape cursed, then went to the driver's side and ripped the door open.

Reaching inside, he riffled through the cop's pockets. When no key was forthcoming, he slammed a fist into the side of the unconscious man's head. Edward wasn't a fan of gratuitous violence, but in this case, the violence wasn't gratuitous enough.

The flames were dying down, and on the other side of the inferno was a line of people. In the distance beyond the growing crowd, the flash and dance of fire trucks and ambulance lights could be seen, even past the blinding white of dozens of headlights.

"Ape," Edward warned.

"Move over," the other man shoved him out of the way.

Gripping the oh-shit bar in one massive fist, Ape's muscles bulged as he pulled. Edward was about to lecture him about the sheer force necessary to make what he was attempting possible, but before he could, the bar snapped clean in half. His jaw dropped, but Ape didn't pay him any mind. Instead, he reached into the car to pull Dusty into his arms. Climbing to his feet, Ape hot-footed it to his bike.

"Go help Diesel." When Edward didn't move, Ape met his gaze. "I got her," he assured him.

Edward nodded, still reeling, and lunged to his feet. He found Diesel at the back of the semi, already removing the lock and a set of chains holding the back shut. Together, the two gripped the door handles, glanced at one another, and pulled.

Edward wasn't sure what he hoped to find. Nothing would have been nice. Instead, tucked inside were about thirty women and children. They were crying, many of them clutching one another. While there were some White women amongst them, the majority of them were Black, Hispanic, and Native. Some were as young as three, toddlers confused and terrified. The crash had knocked them around, but most of them seemed unharmed. If you didn't count the bruises and the haunted look in their eyes. Edward didn't have to guess at what they'd been through. He knew.

The wolf rumbled a warning, and he stumbled back from the truck, almost falling a second time.

"Let's go," Diesel grabbed Edward by the arm and pulled him away.

Numb but obedient, Edward followed, jumping back into the Mustang. The people in the back of the truck were pouring out, slowly at first and then faster as safety beckoned. Some of them didn't move at all, already long dead. There was one body on its side in the middle of the truck. Dressed in a white chemise and little else, she had curly brown hair cut short and wide brown eyes. The lower half of her face was covered in dried vomit, and there was a white band tied tight around her upper arm. No one had bothered to loosen it, and Edward wondered if she'd died before or after they'd thrown her onto the truck.

As he, Ape, and Diesel sped away, those sightless eyes watched him through his rearview mirror. He couldn't shake the suspicion that if he'd been just a few minutes slower, Dusty would have shared a

similar fate, and the knowledge left a bitter taste in
his mouth.

# Chapter Eighteen

*Sharp Edges and Open Wounds*

It took Dusty a bit to recognize her surroundings, but when she did, she sighed in relief. She lay on a hospital bed in the back of an abandoned bowling alley. Her memories after Conners were fuzzy, but she was able to piece together enough to paint a picture. Conners had drugged her; the familiar pinch of the needle heralding the fog in her mind.

She remembered a gentle hand against her face. She remembered Ape and Diesel, and the confines of Ape's sidecar hugging her close – the way the night sky sailed overhead, endless and beautiful. Little else had made it through, but she didn't care. They were back in Briarcliff, and all was right with the world. A byproduct of the 90s, the bowling alley was shut down a few years ago after some kid climbed up into the pin lift on a dare, got stuck, and died.

Everything still worked, but his death really brought the mood down, and without the random birthday party to keep the place afloat, it soon went under. Tucked off in a dead-end lot, overlooking the highway, the bowling alley wasn't easy to get to, and when it became obvious no developer worth their salt would buy the place, the seedier residents of LA claimed it as their own.

These days, the Rinky Dink was just as popular as it used to be back in its heyday, just in a very different way. For the most part, it was used as a med bay for all the criminals and degenerates in town who couldn't afford health care, which was pretty much every one of them. In fact, the youngest member of the Legion—a six-year-old named Lane—had been born there.

The bowling alley was neutral territory. For now, at least, she was safe. Dusty sat up, glancing down as a painful tug in her arm alerted her to the presence of an IV. She pulled the needle out with a hiss, wondering where the others were. She was hungry for the sight of Edward and, for once, unwilling to question it.

Dusty had been placed in one of the back offices; the only room with a door big enough to fit the stolen hospital bed. Some real VIP treatment, as far as she was concerned, since the bed was reserved for those on death's door. Either the Rinky Dink wasn't very full, or she'd been hurt worse than she'd thought. The machine next to the bed beeped and a second later, the door flew open.

Poppy glared as she stepped inside, juggling a clean towel, some clothes, and a shit ton of toiletries. Dusty sniffed surreptitiously beneath one arm when Poppy passed the bed to dump her wares on a desk shoved against the back wall.

"Didn't know you were working tonight," Dusty croaked, wincing at the sound of her own voice. Holy shit, how many days had it been since she'd spoken? Too many, if the state of her vocal cords was an indicator. Poppy came around the side of the bed and pulled a lever. The head of the bed jerked backward, and Dusty went flat on her back with a yelp.

"Hey!"

"That's what you get." Despite her tone, Poppy's hands were gentle as she adjusted Dusty's blanket. "You know better than to touch the IV. Do it again, and I'll cuff you to the bed."

"Oooh," Dusty purred, unable to help herself.

Poppy rolled her eyes, but there was a smile on her face. She was wearing dark eyeliner and big faux lashes, the same pink as her bangs. The matching pink tutu went well with the scoop-neck Metallica tee and combat boots. Dusty's eyes traveled down the length of her fishnets, and Poppy squeezed her arm in warning. "Behave."

"You ever hear of a little thing called bedside manner?" Dusty pouted. "Might want to work on it before you finish your doctorate. Criminals have feelings too, Pops."

"Yeah, they do. You, though?" She searched Dusty's face. "When it comes to you, sometimes I'm not so sure."

Dusty cleared her throat. That stung. Just because emotions were hard to access, and even harder to identify, didn't mean she didn't have them. Did it? "Where is everyone?" she asked, more than happy to change the subject. If she couldn't flirt with Poppy, she might as well focus on more pressing matters.

"You mean the peanut gallery?" she asked with a sigh. "I sent them out for supplies. It was the only way I could get the three of them out of my hair."

*Those three?* Striving to sound casual, she asked, "Edward was with them?"

Poppy, like always, saw right through her, nodding as she reinserted the IV.

"He's fine, by the way," she said. "Since you're too stubborn to just come out and ask."

Dusty relaxed, turning away so Poppy couldn't see the look on her face.

Considering the way they'd left things back at the motel, she was afraid she'd seen the last of him. But worse than the thought of never seeing Edward again was knowing he'd gotten caught up in her mess. She had to get him the hell away from her before the cartels found out about Rudy. For all she knew, they were involved as well. In which case, she'd slaughtered *two* cash cows for the mob, not just one.

"Hey," Poppy murmured, frowning. "What happened to your sleeve."

Dusty glanced down, her brain slow to register what Poppy meant. She examined the black lines bisecting her skin where a bejeweled phoenix once flew, and her thoughts ground to a halt.

"Dusty?" Poppy sounded scared and Dusty frowned and turned away.

"What?" She asked. What had they been talking about again? Something about Edward? *Yeah. Sounds about right.*

Poppy searched her eyes, then shook her head with a curse.

"Sorry," she said, brushing her fingers down Dusty's arm. "I thought…never mind."

Dusty let her work in silence for a full minute before her nerves got the best of her. She sat up again. Poppy sighed, crossing her arms beneath her breasts. "What now?"

When Dusty didn't respond right away, Poppy softened. Sitting on the edge of the bed, she reached around for Dusty's hair, gathering the heavy mass of braids up in expert fingers and winding them into a neat bun.

They stared at one another across the small distance separating them. Dusty breathed her in, finding peace in the softness of her skin. The ministrations against her scalp were soothing in more ways than one.

"Better?" Poppy asked.

Dusty nodded. Wrapping her arms around Poppy's waist, she pulled her into her lap, nuzzling the side of her neck like a cat begging for a kind hand. The fact that Poppy allowed it was an indication of just how worried she must have been. She brushed gentle fingers across Dusty's brows. First one and then the other. It brought her eyes up once again to meet Sweet Poppy's.

"I think your boy is in love," Poppy said, soft.

"He's an idiot if he is."

A sadness in the shape of her smile. "I think you love him back."

*Well, that's because I'm an idiot too.* But what Dusty said aloud was, "You sound jealous, Chere."

Poppy thumped her on the forehead, sliding off her lap as Dusty's hands came up to rub the sting away. "Maybe I am," Poppy said.

Before Dusty could dig any further, there was a knock at the door.

Poppy straightened her tutu. "Right on time," she crossed the room to answer the door and, if Dusty didn't know better, she would have said Poppy was running from her. She grinned but her smile died when Eliot stepped inside. Doleful, he pouted when Poppy snatched the lit cigarette from between his lips and stubbed it out on the bottom of her boot.

"No smoking around my patients."

"My bad, Pops," Eliot said, staring after her as she left.

As soon as the door shut behind Poppy, Dusty's fingers drifted over to her IV once again. "You guys set up shifts?" she asked, incredulous.

"Had to make sure you were alright. You're a popular woman, Dusty."

Her eyes narrowed. "What's that supposed to mean?"

Eliot paced the room, picking up random objects and putting them down, one by one, once they lost his interest. "You've been out of it, so you don't know, but that Cop in New Mexico has been giving interviews for the last few days. Says he busted a sex trafficking ring run by none other than the infamous Adele Burdot."

Dusty lunged forward, but Eliot grabbed her and held her still.

"What's the plan?" he asked, face pressed tight against her temple so he spoke into her hair. "March back to Nevada and shoot him in the head?"

Since that had, in fact, been the plan, Dusty sat back, seething. "There were witnesses," she hissed, only to freeze.

What good would the testimony of a bunch of women and children really do? Even if some of them were brave enough to point the finger at a cop - without any idea of just how many on the force were also involved - they'd all been drugged. If their memories of what happened were anything like Dusty's, no judge or jury would consider them credible.

Maybe she *should* have shot him.

Once she was calm, she nodded, and Eliot released her, though he remained wary.

"What are you doing here, anyway." She asked.

Eliot shook his head. "Oh, I don't know. Could have something to do with my place getting *raided* a few days ago."

Dusty groaned. She'd forgotten.

"Speaking of," Eliot continued. "You still owe me."

"I'm not paying you shit," she snapped. After Rudy, she wouldn't even have enough gold in the coffers to keep her men fed, let alone pay off such a massive sum. "That fight was rigged, and you know it." She ignored the fact that *she* was the one who'd tried to rig it.

*Semantics*

"Who said I wanted money?" Eliot asked gruffly, pulling another cigarette from the pack in his front pocket. "Don't worry. As soon as the cops stop riding your dick, I'm coming to collect."

Dusty flushed - and shocked - Eliot laughed. "You've changed," he said with a tsk.

"What do you mean?"

"You're softer than you used to be," he replied. "Makes me wonder what you were like before Desi." Leaning against the wall beside the door, he glanced down at his feet, and his Adam's apple worked. "I wish I could have seen you smile more back then," he admitted. "Before all of this took over and ruined anything good in either of us."

How did she tell him she didn't remember that part of herself? That the Adele before the woods was like some fever dream? Even before Desi, there had been something broken within her. Wrong. Dying had breathed life into it; made it strong. There had never been anything good in her. Not really. Once upon a time, she might have agreed with Poppy about not having any emotions, but it didn't ring true anymore. If anything, ever since meeting Edward, Dusty found herself feeling *too* much.

What did you call it when the people who claimed to know you best proved they'd never known you at all? Dusty muttered something about taking a shower and got to her feet. This conversation was the last thing she needed right now. Poppy would be pissed when she found out that Dusty had removed her IV again, but all she could think about was getting the hell out of the room and away from Eliot. Poppy was confusing enough. Adding Eliot to the mix was unconstitutional.

Dusty slipped out of the room without a word from Eliot. For which she was relieved. So much for being on guard duty.

It wasn't until she was in the hall, her arms laden with supplies, that she was able to breathe again. Over the years, the space where all the shoes were kept had been converted into a functioning bathroom. It wasn't up to code, and Dusty was sure it violated several health and safety regulations, but otherwise, it was a marvel of modern ingenuity. The combined effort of dozens of people with different skills, all with the same goal. Which made it Dusty's favorite room in this dump – though the food court was a very close second.

Inside, Dusty set her clean clothes out of the way and turned on the shower, wincing at the way the pipes groaned and shook before freezing water shot out and caught her arm. She was eager to get out of the shit she'd been wearing for the last several days. As soon as she stripped down, she checked the water temperature, cautious lest the pressure peel off a layer of skin. Once it was hot enough to boil a lobster, she stepped under the spray, moaning as dirt and blood sluiced off her aching body. Once under the water she was able to take full stock of the damage that had been done. The deep, purpling bruises that decorated her torso, as if Conners had kicked her around some before dosing her. There was a myriad of cuts decorating her arms and legs, and as she leaned forward to wash her braids, more blood from the blow to her head bathed her face in red and left the shower awash in pink splatter. Her lashes were spiky with blood, and her tongue ripe with the taste of metal. Her fingers traced a path on her tattooed arm, but she didn't turn to examine it. Something urged her not to, and she was compelled to listen.

What had Eliot called her all those years ago?

A horror.

She was one now more than ever before.

How many times had she done this? How many more times would she have to before she could stop?

*As long as it takes. As many times as it takes.*

Dusty ran her palm across her cheeks, fingers brushing along first her bottom lip and then the top. She traced each feature with bloodstained fingers until the water ran clean. Then she grabbed the soap Poppy had brought and began all over again.

Homesickness reared its head, and she wished she were back with Gran. Her grandmother would fill the porcelain tub in the backyard with water and herbs, and Dusty would sit there amongst the honeysuckle and apple blossoms and let her ancestors and her grandma's magic cleanse her bruised soul. A pipedream, of course, nothing more, but she ached for it just the same.

Dusty didn't know what made her turn. She didn't hear the door open so much as feel the air shift. Didn't hear the aging floor creak, as catch the shift of his breathing. Braids slicked back from her face, Dusty blinked the water out of her eyes to find Edward standing just a few feet away. The air crackled around him and he took in the sight of her like a man starved.

"I'm sorry," he managed with a shake of his head. "Poppy sent me... She didn't say you would be..."

"Close the door," Dusty ordered, and the desire transforming his expression was so sharp it hurt to see.

Edward kicked the door shut, dropping his shower supplies on the ground as he strode to her. There was no talking this time. No push and pull. No hesitation as he drove his fingers into the labyrinth of her hair and lay claim to her mouth. Like the first time, kissing him was like breathing. Better, because there was no wrong way to do it. Edward's teeth nipped her bottom lip, and she lay a gasp on his tongue even as he drove her back against the wall. The spray from the shower soaked them both, but Edward didn't seem to care.

"Two days," he growled, lifting a hand to grip her by the chin and hold her still. He glared down at her, tortured with memory. "I've been without you for *two* fucking days." His voice broke on the last.

Dusty ran her fingers through his blond curls. "You make me sound like a drug."

He met her eyes, his own lost. "Aren't you?" Before she could respond, Edward leaned in, teasing her wet mouth with his own until heat permeated every inch of her. "Shut up," he breathed. "You can tell me how dumb I am after I've had my fix."

Then he was working his way down her body, tongue marking her breasts only briefly, a sweet pain that unraveled her, left her in pieces in his arms. A gentle kiss against her stomach was more of a benediction, a prayer, than a seduction, and Dusty blinked back a sudden rush of tears. The tenderness was unexpected. Unwelcome. Her hand still in Edward's hair, she jerked his head back and stared down at him on his knees. His shirt was plastered to his skin, outlining every ridge along his arms and chest. She said nothing, didn't have to. Still holding her gaze, he gripped her waist and lifted her higher, higher still, until she had no choice but to hook her legs over his shoulders, her back against the shower wall for balance. The sheer size of him held her spread wide, and he wasn't shy about looking his fill.

Dusty wouldn't call herself shy, but no one had ever looked at her like Edward. No one had ever spread the lower lips of her pussy with two gentle fingers and licked - long and slow - across her opening, tongue swirling as if savoring the very taste of her. She cried out, already trembling.

*Come on, Adele,* she thought in disgust. *Stop acting like a lil' bitch. You've had your pussy eaten before. Keep it together.*

But Edward made keeping it together impossible. In fact, he delighted in leaving her an unraveled mess. He delved in and out of her with just tongue alone, until her thighs were slick with excitement. Then she urged him closer, squeezing with her thighs as his teeth nipped her delicate folds. A surge of excitement as she curled over him, her hips rolling in time with his tongue until he held the entirety of her weight in his arms. Dusty rocked back against the wall; body a rolling wave of desire that brought her nipples, tight and swollen, directly beneath the pounding water as she fucked Edward's waiting mouth.

There was something dark and ravenous about the way he devoured her. Something in those amber eyes that was possessive and eternal. She should have bolted. But she couldn't make herself push him away again, not so soon after the last time. Not when being forced to watch him leave for good was a question of when and not if.

Edward came to his feet, rising through the spray from between her legs like some golden-haired God. Hair a messy halo, he hooked her legs over his forearms, bending her almost double so he could position the head of his cock against her throbbing entrance. She had no idea when he'd undone his pants, but there they were, bare flesh against bare flesh. Heat against heat. His hips rocked forward, thrusting his length into her, the motion slamming her back. Dusty reached out, gripping his shirt by the collar and ripping it down the middle until his bronzed chest was on full display as he worked, fucking her so hard and fast she could feel him against that sweet spot deep, deep inside where any secrets worth keeping lay hidden.

Edward placed his forehead against hers, watching as he slid out of her entrance before slamming back to the hilt. Over and over again. When she would have turned away, he gripped her throat and forced her to meet his eyes. While his touch was feather-light, there was no denying what those eyes were telling her. No escaping the message his body was so intent on drilling into hers. He was a man at the altar, on the battlefield, laying prostrate before the last real thing he believed in. The pleasure he gave was an offering, one speaking more loudly than any words.

*I am your disciple. Your acolyte. Your past and your future both. I am your everything…and you?*

*You are mine.*

*Mine.*

*Mine.*

*Mine.*

Dusty dug her teeth into his neck, only dimly aware of the healing wound on his forearm. Something was coming to life within her, and every hoarse cry she made, every sobbed plea spoken against his skin, heralded the birth of some great, growling beast. Live wire across every nerve ending. The reality of Edward being the one there, between her legs, dragging her orgasm from her as if it owed him money, tore at her. It was *Edward* taking ownership of her body. *Edward's* teeth on her nipple, tongue laving across the sensitive peak. Dusty's eyes rolled, and her body went stiff as the beast clawed, searching for release. It was too much. The pleasure was too big for her skin, too much for her soul, too much for her heart. Her head went blank, her vision dark. Stars exploded as bliss rolled through her, emptying her of all else until ecstasy was all she had left. She seized in his arms, legs jerking as she fell over the edge with a broken, "Fuck!"

"That's my girl," he praised, husky and unrelenting. He came with her name on his lips and her legs tight around his waist, urging him on. His arm around her - her anchor as he sank back to his knees with her still in his arms.

Dusty hugged him close as she came back to herself, noting how careful he was to make sure no part of her skin touched the ground. Grief and guilt and longing were a suffocating triad.

"I love you, Adele Burdot," he said, so quiet she might have imagined it.

Shattered. At every opportunity, in every way possible, he left her shattered.

"I know," she said. It's all she had a right to say. "And I'm so, so sorry."

***

She left Edward alone in the shower, the water still pouring down over his tattered shirt, his shoulders rounded in defeat. Thinking about him made her throat tight, so she wouldn't do it anymore and would focus on getting drunk instead.

The food court held an assortment of supplies, brought in over the last two decades in addition to the original vending machines from when the bowling alley had been open. A lot of the practical stuff was expired—no bread, eggs, or milk—but there was plenty of booze to choose from, and Dusty figured if she divvied the supply up alphabetically, she should be unconscious by the time she got to H.

"We need to talk."

Dusty jumped, spilling her beer. The brown liquid ran over the side of the counter and Dusty cursed herself for her frazzled nerves. "Damnit, Ape," she spoke without heat, more interested in grabbing some napkins from the dispenser so she could dry her jeans.

She was wearing the new clothes Poppy had brought, a simple pair of dark blue jeans and a sleeveless, black, high-neck top. She didn't have a band thick enough to hold her hair back and had to content herself with weaving the front into one larger braid to frame her face on one side.

Snatching the napkins from her hand, Ape tossed them on the floor behind the counter she was straddling.

"Rude," she said, scowling.

"Shut it," he lifted a backpack and slammed it on the counter between her legs.

Suspicious, she unzipped the bag. "*O Bondye*," she gasped. "This real?"

"It ain't no monopoly money," Ape said with a grin.

"Whe—"

"Andrew," he said simply.

Dusty's excitement died. Oh. Right. "He saw the tape."

Ape slammed a fist down on the counter, as excited as she'd ever seen him. "Damn right he did, just like you said. Was even kind enough to send us some goodwill money."

Dusty's mouth went dry. For now, her dad was safe. This knowledge soothed the aching places the alcohol hadn't had the chance to touch yet. "How much goodwill are we talking?"

"Twice what we would have made off with from the bank, and then some," Ape said, doing a little dance. "Diesel and I rode in to give you the good news in person and pick up the cash."

Dusty shifted, swinging both legs around so she was facing Ape with the backpack at her side. "Did he pay you himself," she asked, brain working a mile a minute.

Ape nodded. "Not a henchman in sight, if that's what you're asking."

Dusty bit her lip. "Did he say anything else?"

Ape frowned. "Does 'Thank you' count?"

No way things had gone so smoothly. Something was up. Why be so cavalier about a man he'd tried to kill just a few days ago? If Ape and Diesel were followed, another attempt on Edward's life would have been made by now. But so far, nothing.

"Is that why you kept me around?"

For a second time, Dusty jumped. Dressed in clean clothes, that fit for once, Edward was standing beside one of the bowling lanes several feet away. Half in shadow, his blond hair was still wet from his shower. Dusty couldn't read his expression because his head was bowed. She hadn't seen his eyes since she'd pulled away from him in the shower. He was fiddling with his fingers, and her heart twisted as if someone had plunged a knife into her chest.

"Edward..." Her words fell short. What was she supposed to say? He was right, after all. "I'm—"

...*sorry.* The word died on her tongue. It didn't feel right to say it again, now, so soon after the last. And was she sorry? Truly? No. If given the chance, she'd do it again if it meant keeping her dad alive for just a bit longer.

"Dusty!"

*What now?*

Joey was sprinting toward them, dark skin ashen with nerves.

Dusty eyed him. He'd been injured during the bank robbery but was healing well, though he clutched his abdomen as he hurried over to her side. He was sleeping in a converted broom closet until he was well enough to go back to his girl. Joey wasn't homeless, but he would be if his girlfriend found out he was committing felonies again. Dusty wasn't sure how he planned on explaining the gunshot wound, but Joey's love life was none of her business. Still, she was calculating if the clubhouse had room for one more once Sheila kicked his ass to the curb, even as he slid to a stop next to Ape.

Pausing long enough to suck in a much-needed breath, Joey straightened. "We've got trouble."

"When don't we?" she asked sardonically.

Sliding off the counter, Dusty grabbed the backpack by its straps and handed it back to Ape. She didn't look at Edward as she passed, but she could feel his eyes on her. She didn't have to wonder what he must be thinking of her—she could feel the disgust in the air. The hurt. She knew what this all must look like from his perspective. As far as Edward could tell, she'd sold him out for a chance at some easy cash. Which was fair, but she wanted so badly to tell him about Rat, about what was at stake. Instead, she kept her mouth shut and prayed this would be enough to make him hate her. There was no happily ever after for people like her. Edward was meant to be someone's Prince Charming, just not hers. There was no reality in which he gave up his fortune and everything he'd worked for just for her and her felon of a father. *"Only trust yourself."* It was a lesson she'd learned well and one she planned on teaching Edward, whether he liked it or not.

"Where?"

It was time to ditch this fantasy world she'd found herself in and get back to reality. And the reality was, everyone and their fucking mother wanted her dead. Dusty didn't have time to coddle the feelings of some rich boy out of his depth. Ape's familiar presence to her right helped remind her of who, and what, she was. Reminded her of just how much she had to lose if she failed or backed down.

Joey led her to one of the boarded-up windows at the front of the building. There was a crack in the wood near the side where you could see out without being noticed. A construction worker's peephole.

Dusty peered through it, and her hands went clammy. The Brotherhood. In the light of day, she recognized the insignia on the shoulder of their leather jackets. There were hundreds of men and women outside, bikes rumbling like hounds sent straight from hell.

She pulled her gun from its holster and checked the chamber. "Joey," she said.

"What's up, D?" He was bouncing on the soles of his feet, eager to start some shit.

She grinned. Leave it to Joey to still be itching for a fight, even after getting shot. Typical Scorpio. "Go get the key to the weapons cache from Poppy."

"Fuck yes," he said, then flushed. "I mean…yes, ma'am." He loped off, still careful of his middle but moving with more speed than before.

"Where do you need me?" Ape said.

"When Joey gets back, take Edward and get the fuck out of here," she said, striving to keep her voice level.

Deadpan: "You want me to leave you here?" As if it was the dumbest thing ever to come out of her mouth. Hell, maybe it was.

"Just for a teeny bit," she said, fingers squeezing compulsively around the gun's handle as she indicated the amount of time with her free hand. An old excitement was stirring, and she was hungry for trouble. "Once you drop him off somewhere safe, get your ass back here and help me."

"Where do you want me to take him? Sally should be good to keep an eye on him 'til we get this mess sorted out."

Dusty went still, took a deep breath. "Take him back where he belongs."

Ape stared at her, his mouth opening and closing but nothing coming out.

"You're joking," Diesel said, joining them. "You're going to throw Rat under the bus over that pussy—"

Dusty's gun came up, pressed hot and close against Diesel's forehead. She angled the weapon sideways, squinted, imagined what it would be like to watch his brains explode all over the broken popcorn machine at his back.

A muscle jumped in Diesel's jaw. "Come on Dusty," he cajoled. "*Think*. Be smart about this."

When she said nothing, Ape shook his head, his scowl thunderous. "You dumbass." he snarled, eyeing Diesel as if debating whether or not he was even worth saving. Dusty stared at the redhead for a bit longer - she really couldn't afford to waste a bullet - and turned away. "Fine," she looked back out the window. "You take him then."

"What?"

In addition to the bikes, there were about half a dozen big black pick-up trucks. "You heard me," she sneered. "You want me to be smart? Truth is, I need Ape a hell of a lot more than I need you. So, take Edward and go."

Ape was already on the phone, calling in reinforcements, but there was no telling how long it would take them to get there.

"Poppy, too."

People were pouring out of the trucks, armed to the teeth. There was no point in trying to figure out how they'd found her. It was common knowledge the bowling alley was used by the Legion, so it made sense they'd swing by. Even if they weren't here for her, the Brotherhood knew damn well this was part of her territory. Like the bar, an attack here was a declaration of war, and Dusty was more than happy to respond in kind.

"Dusty—"

"Diesel-" She had another gun in the holster at her waist, along with her bowie knife and switchblade. Joey should be back soon with the key. "Hurry the fuck up."

Silence, then Diesel turned on his heel and loped away.

She had to trust him to do as he was told because she wouldn't be able to check up behind him. This was do or die. How much time did they have? People were beginning to whoop outside. She could hear their high-pitched cries as they hyped themselves up. Hootin' and hollerin' like fans on their way to a football game. They'd be inside soon if she didn't do something.

"Ape," Dusty tucked her second gun away. "Help me barricade these doors."

Grim, he followed along behind her. They wouldn't be able to hold this many off, but she could buy Edward enough time to get back home. It was all she could do, and she prayed that, for once, it would be enough.

# Chapter Nineteen

*The Crusader*

"You fucked the guy once, and suddenly he's more important than Rat? Than us?" A humorless laugh. "Hell, if I'd known she needed dick so bad, I would have volunteered years ago."

Edward groaned, the world shifting around him as he came back to consciousness. *What the hell is going on?* He pressed a hand against his aching head as he tried to get his bearings. The last thing he remembered was crouching behind the concession stand in search of a beer. He'd never confessed his love before, but liquor seemed like the perfect companion to heartbreak. And fuck was his heart broken. He was reaching for a strawberry-watermelon-flavored wine cooler when someone wrapped their arm around his neck from behind. Now, he was sitting against the brick side of a restaurant. It was late evening, and people were milling about, so many packed together until he was surrounded by a sea of legs. People were singing, and their voices grew in volume as the crowd all got on the same page, filling the street with the lyrics to some church song Edward couldn't quite place.

Getting to his feet, he glanced around, hoping to at least catch a glimpse of whoever had been muttering over him before he opened his eyes. From the corner of his eye, he caught sight of a familiar figure maneuvering through the crowd.

Jaw tight, Edward followed. Dusty would have to try a hell of a lot harder than this to get rid of him. *Leave it to me to get kidnapped from my own goddamn kidnapping,* he thought. The singing ended, replaced by a smattering of applause before the squeal of a mic signaled everyone to silence.

Distracted from the chase, Edward glanced around. His heart sank. Diesel had dropped him off at the edge of Grand Park. Even from where he stood on the grass, Edward could see the glowing fountain several feet away, streetlights reflecting like fireflies searching for purchase on the cascading surface. The fountain had three levels, each with its own shallow pool where visitors could go and splash for a bit. Everyone was gathering around a stage they'd erected up front. A stage surrounded by armed police. Standing at the mic, dressed in a somber gray suit, was a man Edward knew all too well. Ronald Edison Wilks had been the governor of LA for the last decade. A politician of some renown, he was an everyman on pace to run for congress the following year.

He was also Edward's father, and the very last person Edward expected to find hosting a vigil for his missing son. But then again, the cameras were rolling, and Governor Wilks had never shied away from the public eye despite having so many secrets to hide. Edward glanced at a group holding up a sign reading 'Gays for Willie.' He thought about his twelfth birthday when his father shaved the word Fag into his hair and kept him home from school for two weeks until it grew back in, and nausea rose to choke him.

"Thank you all for coming here today," Wilks began, expression somber. "As you know, my son Edward has been struggling with his mental health for years now. Several days ago, he found himself in crisis, and that crisis was broadcast on television for the entire world to see. Now, he's missing, and I need the help of my constituents now more than ever to bring him home safe."

Edward's knees weakened and he stumbled, a mumbled apology on his lips as a woman turned to glare at him. Her eyes widened, darting between him and the sign in her hands where an old picture of him had been plastered beneath some pithy saying. Edward didn't stick around long enough to read it. Instead, he ran, shoving past people when they didn't get out of his way fast enough. His heart was beating so hard against his chest it was as if it would crawl through his ribcage, and his vision blurred with tears. Blurry with hate. He missed Dusty. He wished she were there with him, but he was alone. Again. A terrible, yawning emptiness opened within him, and he wrapped his arms around himself and stumbled to a halt. He had to get out of there. As much as morbid curiosity urged him to linger and listen to whatever bullshit dear old Dad was spouting, he wasn't strong enough.

*Shame.*

*Shame.*

*Shame.*

Edward ducked his head and crouched. He had to get away before he lost himself. What was it again? *Five things, four things, three, two, one.* The sidewalk was cracked, with bright sprigs of green leaves fighting their way through, anxious to reach the sun. The speakers boomed so loud with his father's voice it made his stomach hurt. He wanted to cry, but he was afraid someone would call him a faggot again, and he'd have to crawl out of his skin from the shame of it.

"Hey! Dude, are you okay?"

Hands on him, and he flinched back. He didn't want to be touched. Didn't like it. But there was no point in complaining because no one ever listened to him anyway. Where was Dusty? Missing her was like an ache, something deep in his bones that made it hard to breathe right. People were cheering and there were more hands, excited hands, the pressure of a thousand bodies and a thousand eyes. They bored into his skin and left him dirty and bereft.

"No," he said, but his voice wasn't loud enough for anyone to hear but him.

He stumbled up a set of stairs, almost falling but for the hands straightening his spine and brushing the dirt from his clothes. Some kind soul smoothed his blond hair back from his brow, but he forgot to say thank you because the lights were too bright. The cameras zoomed in close and Edward shut his eyes. *Five things, four things, three, two, one.* He tried and tried, but all he knew was fear, and laughter that was more of a sob slipped through to wave hello to the ecstatic crowd.

The prodigal son! The lost lamb! Returned to his father all on his own. What a fairytale of a happy ending when so many imagined him dead somewhere, lost in the mire of his own mind.

"My boy." Arms wrapped tight around him.

Edward went very far away. Somewhere where his skin wasn't his own, and the fire of his thoughts smoldered low, waiting to consume the world just as soon as he breathed fresh life into them. The wolf was frantic, snout and snapping jaws working their way past wood shredded by relentless claws. It was almost loose. Edward hadn't been paying close enough attention to it and now there would be no holding it still.

"How much did you pay him?"

Edward went rigid; everything within him came to a grinding halt. "What?"

"The fucking biker," Ronald said with a hiss, pulling away from the hug but keeping his hands on Edward's shoulders. He was the picture of a man reunited with his son, even down to the sheen of tears in his eyes. For now, his words were hidden beneath the cheers of the spectators, beneath the politically correct smile he'd cultivated and perfected over the last twenty years.

"I thought you were dead," Ronald said for all to see.

To any onlookers watching the words take shape on their screen, Edward was sure Ronald's declaration made sense. After all, weren't they holding a vigil because of that very fear? Only Edward heard the disappointment in his voice, the displeasure waiting to be unleashed. In that heartbeat, that one delicate second of time, Edward thought back to the bank. Something had been bothering him for the last few days. On the day of the heist, Diesel had been nowhere to be found and yet he was supposed to be playing lookout. The robbery had gone to shit almost immediately, but no one was punished but Bellum. Maybe because Dusty didn't even know Diesel had been there. She'd rolled into the bar hours later, long after every person who could have told her otherwise had either been shot dead or arrested.

Well, everyone except for Bubbles. The shooter at the bank, the "fucking biker," was Diesel. Memory painted a picture of a glass dome and a window cleaner positioned just so. *Ah. So that's where you were hiding.*

The person who'd hired Diesel, the man who wanted him dead, was standing right next to him and telling an adoring crowd about his plans as their future congressman. "…the importance of comprehensive and universal mental health care. My son isn't the first or last young man to be let down by the current system. That's why it's so important we drain the swamp and fill those positions with men and women who don't just preach about change, but who are passionate about it because they know what is at stake if that change does not come to pass."

The crowd cheered their approval, and something in Edward snapped. The fear took a backseat, and something else, something dark, took its place. For once, he let it, all too happy to let go of the reins. Under the guise of another hug, he pulled Ronald Eddison Wilks close, gripping his father by the back of the neck and holding the older man still when he would have jerked away.

"Soon, Dad," he promised. "Soon."

A beat of silence while Ronald processed his words, then another boisterous laugh. Ever the politician, he turned to the crowd, raising his and Edward's joined hands into the air, he leaned back over the mic. "Do you see, Ladies and Gentlemen? Do you see the power of prayer? Do you see how much we can accomplish when we join in fellowship with one shared goal in mind? Together, we are unstoppable. Come election day, I hope to see each and every one of you at your local polls, as eager to fight for the change you wish to see as you were about the safe return of my son."

Edward turned away, making his way down the steps on the side of the stage. He didn't hear how the speech ended. Didn't need to. It was all bullshit, so what was the point. Maneuvering past the police officers guarding the parameter, he paused as a disembodied voice spoke from the radios clipped to their uniforms.

"All personnel, be advised. We have a 10-40 in progress at Sunset and Forsyth." Static crackled as the dispatcher continued, "I repeat, a 10-40 is in progress at Sunset and Forsyth. Proceed with caution."

*Sunset and Forsyth. The bowling alley.*

Edward spoke to the nearest cop, a heavyset Hispanic man with a goatee. "What's a 10-40?" he demanded. The officer glanced at his companions, and Edward remembered these people knew him as the Governor's son – not as 'Pretty Boy.' For once, his relationship with his father worked in his favor.

Goatee shrugged. "Gang activity, sir."

*Shit.*

"Don't you guys have to go?"

A woman a few feet away scoffed.

"No, sir," the first officer said, turning to glare at her. "We don't get involved at this stage."

Edward scowled, his mind reeling. "What do you mean?"

A third police officer sighed, shifting from one foot to the other as he spoke. Edward knew a lot about nervous ticks. "No point," the guy said. "The gangs around here…" He shook his head in disgust. "They're like a pack of wild dogs, always nipping at each other. If we responded every time they had a disagreement, we'd be getting shot at all damn day. We go in and make the necessary arrests once they get it out of their system."

"And how many have died by then?"

At the third officer's stunned silence, the first man reached out and patted Edward's shoulder. "Don't worry sir, it'll be taken care of. Besides, our priority right now is to get your father somewhere safe." He hesitated, then, suspecting a sympathetic ear, lowered his voice and leaned in. "His policies on gang violence have saved so many lives on the force already, sir. He's a real hero down at the precinct." He grinned as if it were a compliment instead of a nightmare. "He'll always have my vote."

Edward followed his gaze; his dad was perched on the edge of the stage, speaking earnestly with a pair of college students wearing T-shirts with WILKS

2026 emblazoned in bold white letters across the front.

"Right." There was a ringing in his ears. When he slipped away, no one stopped him. Why would they? He was a grown ass man and—as far as they could tell—in full control of his faculties. What they didn't know, what they couldn't have guessed, was that the Door was wide open. The wolf missing. Dusty was in danger and all bets were off.

Edward needed to get back to the Rinky Dink with some serious firepower. The wolf had no idea how many people were inside the bowling alley, but chances were, they were outnumbered. He didn't have a plan. Most of Edward's life had been mapped out. It gave him a much-needed sense of control. But ever since he'd met Dusty, he'd learned how freeing giving in to the uncontrollable could be. How powerful. The wolf loved the power the best. He left the park behind, walking until the sounds of the vigil-turned-rally faded.

*Diesel wouldn't hurt her, would he?*

He didn't know for sure, and it was driving them crazy. Ronald thought Edward had paid Diesel enough money to nullify the original kill order. That would make him a man motivated by money, something Edward was familiar with. So familiar, in fact, he knew there was more to Diesel than just that. The look in his eyes whenever he talked about Dusty. His muttered complaints. Had he seen them together in the shower? How long had he been watching her, and why was he lying to her about his extracurricular activities? The wolf's steps quickened until he was running. He had to get back to her. Had to…

When they asked him about it later, about why he did it, he'd say it was because the armored truck was just sitting there. The bank doors were already open in preparation for the transfer. Even from the sidewalk, he could see straight through the bank, to the doors leading to the vault. Striding toward it, he imagined the look on Bubbles' face, and the mental image was enough to bring a smile to his own. The driver's side door of the truck opened as he neared, and the officer inside stepped out, gaze darting around the parking lot in search of threats before closing the door behind him. He was already fiddling with the keys at his belt as he headed toward the back doors.

The wolf followed, stalking after him, grabbing him by the back of the head, and slamming his face into metal before he could cry out. The blow stunned the guard, and he went limp. The wolf caught him and lowered him to the ground. Undoing the security belt from around the man's waist, he put it on. The gun at his hip was heavy and unfamiliar. He gripped it anyway and retraced the guard's steps back to the front of the truck, near the driver's side door. He waited a beat, threw the door open, and pointed the gun at the second guard lounging in the passenger seat.

The woman froze, her eyes growing wide.

"To me," he motioned with the weapon. He didn't want her out of his sight or reaching for the gun he knew she had. "Slowly," he snapped when she shifted, her motions jerky. The woman nodded, climbing awkwardly over the center console to jump down.

"Your gun," he ordered, and she removed the weapon with shaking hands.

His gun trained on the back of her head, he urged her inside of the bank. At the sight of the two of them, the tellers screamed, and the smattering of patrons at the counters dropped where they stood, others in line put their arms over their heads or fell flat to the floor. The wolf ignored them, and gripping the guard by the elbow, held her still as he slipped off the safety on his stolen gun. He fired several shots into the floor and into one of the security cameras for good measure.

*There, that should do it.*

"Edward?"

He glanced over.

The woman was looking up at him, her hands up and her expression sympathetic. "Edward Hayes, right? You don't have to do this. You haven't hurt anyone yet. There's still time to..."

He frowned, confused. "What are you talking about?" he asked. "My name is Bradly Star."

He didn't expect everyone to know who he was. Still, it was always frustrating when people couldn't tell the difference. He understood it to a certain extent. He and Edward did look surprisingly similar.

He left the bank behind, sprinting back to the armored truck. The first guard was still unconscious, and Bradly breathed a sigh of relief. He shut the door and put on his seatbelt before starting up the truck. A series of tat-tat-tats against the door told him the guard was shooting at him, and he waved to her through the window. The bulletproof door was denting in places beneath the onslaught, so he drove off, leaving the bank and the guards behind.

*They should automate these things,* he thought. Keys were antiquated. Wouldn't it make more sense for the controls to be biometric? Any weirdo off the street could operate these things.

Drumming his fingers on the steering wheel, he hummed to himself. He couldn't recall the words to the song, but the refrain tasted like nostalgia. He spared his sideview mirror a glance as he blew past a red light and swiped an Audi. The car spun in a full circle and came to a violent standstill against a fire hydrant. Water erupted in a geyser behind him, and Bradly whistled long and slow. The truck wasn't as fast as the Mustang, but what it lacked in speed, it made up for in power. Time would tell if the trade-off would get him killed before he could lead the cadre of police cars where he needed them to go.

*The judge isn't going to like this,* Bradley thought, meeting his own gaze in the rearview. It was Edward who pulled their lips into a determined line and pushed the armored truck just a little faster, a little farther. For once in perfect agreement with the wolf at the door.

# Chapter Twenty

*Last Stand at the Rinky Dink*

Gunfire, rapid quick, filled the world with the acrid stench of smoke. Flashes of light in the darkened interior of the bowling alley were the only proof she wasn't trapped in hell. Dusty could scent Death on the air, could feel him whispering against her skin.

She dropped the clip in her handgun, slammed a spare one home, and filled the chamber just in time to place it neatly between the eyes of yet another member of the Brotherhood. They were everywhere, swarming the bowling alley like cockroaches. She wasn't sure how many of the Legion were currently in the Rinky Dink, let alone how many members of other gangs had been caught up in this mess. All she knew was bodies falling all around like rain, and it would only be a matter of time before she joined them.

Dusty ducked back down behind the concession stand, the quick rat-ta-tat-tat of the grappling gun Rudy was manning from inside the coat check was buying them some time, but bullets were finite. The Brotherhood had managed to break through the barricade at the front door, but the gap was only big enough for a few of them to squeeze through at a time.

"Ape!" Dusty fired off another round. "Give me an ETA!"

The bodies were all blending together. How many was it now? Fifteen? Twenty? Not even close to the number she'd seen waiting outside. Fuck.

"Where's our backup?" she bellowed.

"No one's coming."

She glanced over to find a grim Ape staring off into space. His Berretta lay in his lap, open and empty. He was bleeding from somewhere, the blood pooling beneath her shoes, and her breathing hitched.

"What the fuck are you talking about," she hissed, moving in close.

Ape shook his head. "No signal," he chuckled. "Damn, iPhone piece of shit can't find a signal."

At a loss for words, Dusty collapsed next to him.

Anyone who was able to hold a gun was manning a window or an entrance, including Eliot and Sweet Poppy, both of whom had refused to leave despite strict orders to do so. It was enough to make Dusty wonder if Edward had even put up a fight about leaving. Probably not. He was much bigger than Diesel. If he wanted to be here, he would have been.

She swallowed hard. Even though *she* was the one who'd sent him away, even though she knew it was for the best, her chest still hurt. Now, she was going to die without ever getting the chance to explain herself. He would spend the rest of his life hating her, never knowing how much she wished things could have turned out differently.

Dusty closed her eyes and imagined a world where she was anyone else but herself. What if she was a waitress? Or a flight attendant? She liked to travel. Maybe she could do it on a plane instead of a motorcycle. In her daydreams, Edward was some rich businessman on his way to do whatever the hell it was rich businessmen did. She'd bring him a drink, and then they'd fuck each other's brains out in first class. The pussy would be so good he'd propose as soon as the plane landed.

*Stewardess WAP. Yeah, that could work.*

Poppy army-crawled her way behind the concession stand, tutu dripping blood.

Dusty grabbed her hand and shifted so Poppy could settle between her and Ape.

"I'm out," Poppy whispered, voice tight and high with fear.

What would the Brotherhood—with their Harleys and obsession with White power—do with Poppy if they got their hands on her? Dusty's teeth ground together until her jaw ached, and she met Ape's eye over the top of Poppy's head. Joey was still shooting, but even she could tell the the rat-ta was no longer tat-tatting like before.

Ape was an old hand at reading her expressions, at listening to the way she moved through the world. They'd been together for a long time. He'd tutored her through getting her GED and chaperoned her first drug deal. He *knew* her. So, when she met his eyes and nodded, his expression darkened with some unfathomable emotion and he turned away, throat working.

Resolute, he wiped sweat from the side of his face and climbed to his feet. "Meet us out back in five minutes, or I'm coming back to get you."

"No," Dusty shook her head and reached under her shirt for the joint tucked between her skin and the band of her bra. "You won't."

Poppy glanced between the two of them in growing concern. "What are you talking about?"

Ape handed her a lighter and then reached down, grunting as he lifted Poppy into his arms and tossed her, kicking and screaming, over his shoulder.

Dusty waited until Ape disappeared into the bowels of the bowling alley and lit up. It was over now. Eliot was smart enough to get out while he still could. No matter how noble his intentions were, he was practical, having been raised with the same values she had been. Which meant it was just her, Joey, and a handful of others left to keep the Brotherhood at bay. She knew what they would do to her if they caught her, but she couldn't run. She wouldn't. Dusty had spent the last seventeen years clawing her way to the top, demanding respect from the very people who would have spit on her in passing if given half the chance. She'd be damned if she undermined it all by running away now. No. They'd have to kill her.

Once again, her thoughts went to Edward. Had he made it home yet? What would he do about Andrew? If being with her had given him anything, she hoped it was the confidence to stand up for himself more. The thought of anyone making him feel small again was enough to make Dusty see red.

As if *she* were one to talk.

It was funny. Dusty had spent so many days denying it, dismissing the possibility as nonsense, but it had been staring her in the face this whole time. She was in love with Edward. It was new, something fresh and small, but she could feel how large it would grow if she'd let it. Could sense how it would derail all she was and take over everything. Already, pieces of her were moving out of the way to make room for him, which was terrifying and not at all the type of love people talked about in the movies. The kind of love she used to read about. This love filled her to the brim, left her gasping and on uncertain ground. It drowned her. Dusty couldn't remember what life had been like, what *she* had been like, before him, and couldn't imagine a future without him. Objectionably insane, wasn't it? She was a human being with dreams and fears of her own, and yet inexorably, unexpectedly, she now found herself craving a man who would have never given her the time of day had they met in his world instead of hers.

*But still…*

Edward was the moon rising in the sky. All was darkness and distant stars until he'd filled the void with light, and then he was all she could see. All she wanted to see, and Dusty…she really, *really* wanted to see him.

Dusty swiped an angry hand across her face. After she emptied this clip, she'd be out of ammo. No telling how long she'd have then, but Bess was eager to come out and play – which should buy her a few extra minutes of fun. Death had always been a close friend of hers, the next name on her dance card. No point in getting cold feet now.

"I thought you would have scurried off."

Dusty glanced up, meeting Diesel's eyes upside down. She took another hit from her joint and blew a trail of smoke up toward his face. "The fuck are you doing back here?" she asked, voice tight. "I thought I told you —"

"Lover boy's fine." Diesel grinned, leaning his head into the palm of his hand. His eyes glinted in the next volley of gunfire. "I came back to see if you needed any help."

"From you?" Dusty was incredulous. "Absolutely not."

For as long as she'd known him, Diesel had been the kind of man who was content to stand on the sidelines and watch other people take all the risks. Dusty had never called him a coward to his face but couldn't hide her disdain.

Finishing off her joint, she flicked the smoldering roach to one side and dusted herself off. "Make yourself useful and go check on Joey or something," she said, waving him away as she tossed first one and then another gun onto the counter.

It was hard to see much with the lights out, but she was sure the brotherhood member she just put down had a semi-automatic. She missed her duffel bag, but whatever she'd snatched from the weapons cache would have to do. Dusty wondered if it was worth running to the other side of the building to see if there was anything left in the supply closet. Just as the idea occurred to her, she dismissed it. Chances were the others had cleared the place out. It wasn't like there was a shitload of weapons in there to begin with. It was a waystation where people could stash anything that went boom or stabby-stab while they were at the Rinky Dink. It was a lot harder to shoot someone in a fit of pique if your gun was at daycare.

"I hate when you do that."

"Do what?" She stepped past Diesel on her way to the first body.

The shooting from outside had died down, but the silence didn't mean anything. They were probably getting ready to send in the next wave. The semi-automatic fit well in her hand. In the dark, there was no way to tell how many bullets it had left, though, which could get messy expeditiously.

"Ignore me."

Dusty bent at the waist, gathering her hair into her hands so she could weave the mass into a quick bun. "What the fuck are you going on about?" she bit out.

Diesel came for her before she could rise. His hand in her hair, the pressure sudden and cruel as he yanked her off her feet. Then he was dragging her across the ground toward the darkened lanes by her braids. She twisted, legs churning against the ground in search of purchase. The deeper they went into the bowling alley, the farther away the sounds of fighting became, and ice filled Dusty's veins.

"Diesel," she snarled. "What do you think you're doing?"

"Finishing what I started," he swung her around, the floor so slick beneath her that he tossed her down the nearest lane with all the ease of a bowling ball. Dusty rolled to a stop just beyond the dark maw the pins called home and struggled back to her feet, head aching. The other lanes stretched out on either side of them, and they were far enough away from the fight to have quiet. She pulled Bess, shivering at the click as the knife came to life in her hands.

"What are you talking about?" She panted. Her body was heavy, her arms and legs like lead. She was *tired.*

Diesel stared at her in silence for a long while. Bouncing where he stood, he licked his bottom lip in anticipation. "Désirée," he said softly. So softly, as if her name were something he'd forbidden himself.

Dusty's hand spasmed around the hilt of her knife and she lowered her head, staring at him as a slow grin spread across his face.

"Don't look at me like that, Adele," he said. "I loved your sister, and she loved me." He laughed. "It was all very…wholesome." He paused for a beat. "And boring. But then, you get what I mean."

Exhaustion faded as if it had never been. Putting the switchblade between her teeth, Dusty pulled the bowie and began sawing through her braids. Wouldn't catch her slipping twice. Diesel didn't seem to notice, or if he did, he wasn't concerned. An idiot to the very end.

"The point, asshole," she interjected, and Diesel scowled, stalking toward her.

"I had a whole thing I was trying to do," he lamented, "and you're fucking it up." His voice was hateful and strange, and Dusty wondered how she'd never sensed it before, this poison in him. "You fuck up *everything*."

When he was close enough, she flipped the bowie blade over handle and launched it through the air. The knife sank into his thigh with a meaty thunk that had her grinning around Bess's cold steel.

Diesel screamed, clutching his leg as Dusty settled Bess into her palm.

"She cried," he choked out, pulling the blade free with a grunt. "That's my favorite part, when they cry. The first girl was an accident, but the rest of them?" Diesel straightened to his full height, his head falling back. He groaned, and the sound was pure sex. "The rest were because they sounded so damn sweet."

"I'm going to kill you slow," Dusty rasped, hating herself for giving him even that much. It was a struggle to keep her breathing under control, to stop herself from launching across the room.

*"He's baiting you. Fall for it, and you've already lost."*

Easier said than done when she could imagine the scene, when the memory of Desi's cries still rang in her mind just as they did in his. Even now, years later, he was still using her, still stripping her down to the bone.

"Good," Diesel said. "It'll give me time to tell you everything I did to her before I snapped that bitch's neck and tossed her in a hole." He swiped at her with the bowie knife, testing its range to see if she were close enough to gut.

Dusty moved in by slow increments. A part of her wanted to wail her grief and never, ever, stop. Instead, she forced herself to swallow past the lump in her throat.

"What do you want to hear first, huh?" he teased, knife point singing through the air. Closer this time, a little too close.

Dusty danced back, careful not to slip.

"About the first time she kissed me, all sweet and shy? She tasted like apple cider, Dusty. At first, anyway. By the time I was done with her, she tasted like my—"

With a cry, she darted in, ducking beneath the first strike in time to rise and deliver her own.

Diesel's forearm caught her by the wrist, driving her arm up and out until he switched his grip. He grabbed her by the wrist and yanked her in close so he had her elbow locked beneath his arm. She was hugging him, one-armed, when he headbutted her.

Dusty rocked back, blood in her mouth, already reeling even before Diesel backhanded her. She fell in slow motion, like a prizefighter out for the count. One too many hits to the head, thanks to Conners. Dusty hit the ground hard, cracking her skull on the alley floor.

It didn't hurt. Nothing did. In fact, as she fell back, the world bled away into a sea of green leaves so brightly lit beneath the warm weight of the sun that it hurt to look at them. The air was hot and thick against her skin, vibrating with the rhythmic call of cicadas fresh from the earth.

"What are you doing here, Adele?"

Dusty turned her head to glare at her sister. "Same thing as always," her lips formed the words from memory alone. "Looking for you."

Désirée rolled her eyes, turning on her side and laying her head in the crux of one arm.

"It's not your job to save me, Addy," Desi told her, stern mother hen in her prettiest sundress. "Never has been."

Dusty frowned. She wanted to turn away from her sister. Like the green leaves, it hurt to look at her. She hadn't aged a day. Her features, so like Dusty's but somehow not, were still rounded and vulnerable. A mirror for every thought in her head. Still, Dusty couldn't pry her eyes away, even when tears stole her vision. "You really slept with that asshole?" she demanded.

Desi groaned, flopping onto her back in embarrassment. "He was charming!" she wailed, then wistful, sighed. "And cute."

"He looks like Chuckie."

"That's 'cause he's trying to kill you," Desi said sagely. "But when you're fifteen, and the world never feels big enough?" She shrugged. "Then, a boy like him looks like freedom." Desi lifted one hand, waiting. She would wait there forever, tirelessly, infinitely, eternally fifteen.

Dusty didn't realize she was trembling until she lifted her own hand and laced their fingers together. And there he was, in a movie reel playing on repeat because there was no more life lived after him. The cutest boy Desi had ever seen had just rolled into town on the back of Daddy's bike. Rat said he was a runaway, to treat him well 'cause his mother was dead and gone.

"He can't stay at the bar, now, can he?" Rat reasoned, and Desi agreed.

He was seventeen, a whole two years older than her, and so, so quiet in the beginning. He never said much while Rat was around, but as soon as the sun went down and the Legion started knocking back drinks, Desi would sneak him in through the back door. They'd talk until morning, snacking on whatever they could find in the kitchen and watching television with the volume turned so low you couldn't hear all the bad choices being made. When they were alone, he opened right on up. She knew all sorts of things about him, though some of the stories he told her made her nervous. He liked talking about the girls he knew before her, the ones he'd met on the road while traveling with Rat and Ape. Whenever he said their names, a smile would transform his face and he would brighten in a way he never did with Desi. Each time it happened, it was another blow to her young heart.

How the hell was she supposed to compete with the memory of so many? She'd never even kissed a boy, let alone had a boyfriend. The doctors said this second round of chemo would set her right, and Desi hoped they were telling the truth this time. It was hard meeting people when you were always stuck at home alone. Addy had school, so most of the time, it was just her and Gran. Desi loved her, but the woman was always rattling on about ancestors and lwa. She said if Desi worked at it, she could learn to channel the spirits when they came. It was the lwa who would make her strong.

"But be careful, baby. These spirits," she shook her head in Cajun disapproval. "they forget what it is to be human. Some have never known. They'll break you if you let them ride you for too long."

But what did Desi care? Deisel said he loved her, and their first kiss was so sweet she wanted to love him, too. What were deities compared to a first love? Then Diesel stopped coming, and now Desi was afraid he'd found another name to add to his list and that it wasn't her. He'd begun to ask about Addy when he came to visit at night, and insecurity was a tight knot in her middle.

***

Diesel hated her so much he could taste it. He'd been waiting for this for so long, and even now, he couldn't enjoy it the way he wanted. Just one more thing to lay at her feet. It would have good company there, amongst all the other things he blamed her for. The wolves were at the door, hungry to get in, and he didn't have much time before Joey's suppression fire came to a grinding halt. Already, the silence between shots was growing longer.

He wasn't worried about himself. He was a chameleon, a shapeshifter. He became whatever he needed to, whenever he needed to. He would fit into the Brotherhood, but they would want Dusty, and he couldn't allow that. She was his, had been promised to him since she was a small, squirming thing in the dirt beneath him. He wanted her there again, but he would content himself with taking the life that had always been his to claim. He straddled her, hands wrapping possessively around her throat.

***

Diesel came for Desi in the dark and promised to take her somewhere quiet. Romantic. He'd passed the gauntlet and was wearing his Legion jacket for the first time. He was so proud, but there was a dark light in his eyes that scared her. They snuck away from the house, and he put her on the back of his bike, the one he'd been working on ever since getting into town. Soon, he'd leave with Rat and all the rest. Desi knew she would not see him again until the Legion came back home, and this scared her more than the light. So, she followed him and held on tight as they rode

farther and farther away from the bar. Away from
Rat. Away from Addy and Gran. He led her into the
woods with kisses and trailing fingertips. But his
weight was too heavy, and when she shied away, he
got angry.

So, so, angry.

And Desi ran, but she'd never been very fast, not
like Addy, and he took her down like a lion with a
gazelle. His teeth were sharp, rending her, tearing
flesh and girl apart by the seams and leaving the
pieces scattered on the forest floor. She was dead
before he offered her to the earth, dead long before
Addy joined her there, and she curled around her
sister in death much the same way she had in the
womb, clutching her close lest she drift too far away.

***

In another time and another place, Dusty seized
where she lay, back arching like a bow pulled too
tight. Her fingernails left trails through the dust on

the ground, and for a moment, just a moment, Diesel hesitated.

***

Above her, trees waved a lazy hello. Dusty stared up at them without blinking, her hand convulsing around Desi's. It was getting harder to breathe, but there was nowhere else she'd rather be than here, with her. The scent of roses engulfed them, filling Dusty to the brim until every breath was rose water on the tongue.

"You taste of dead and dying things, Adele Burdot," Desi's gentle accusation was easy to ignore. Something was coming. The trees told her so, the whisper of their leaves more of a scream, once you knew how to listen. She sat up, staring at the gathering dark. It ate the clouds, the sun, the stars. It trailed reaching fingers across the ground, a shadow with teeth biting down.

"Adele."

His footsteps rotted the earth beneath his feet. *He's wearing shoes this time,* she thought, but couldn't understand why. His boots, with their iron claps, glinted even in the darkness he carried with him everywhere he went. Here, he was stronger. Here, he was something more than bones and nightmares half-remembered. His skin, as dark as night, peeked from beneath the edge of a leather jacket, and the skin of her arm *burned*. Head tucked low, he stalked toward her—a God risen and ravenous—and Desi's world wept to host him.

"Addy!"

Dusty flinched, her gaze meeting Desi's. She needed to move but couldn't. Just like all those years ago, she was frozen in place, though it wasn't terror gripping her now, but something else. Something she had no name for.

Desi grabbed her face, forced her to stare at her and only her while Eshu strolled forth to claim his tithe. "I can help you, if you'll let me." Between one blink and the next, she was no longer the child she was but the woman she would never be.

Hadn't Dusty said something similar to Edward just days before? *As above, so below.* "You're dead," she reasoned.

"But not gone," Desi said, and there was a sharpness to her that had never been there before. "Never that." Her eyes bled to black as Eshu loomed close. "Do you trust me, Addy?"

Dusty nodded. Of course, she did. She always would.

Desi grinned as Eshu reached for Dusty, whispers trailing from the hidden places beyond his fangs. She could almost see something hidden in the darkness there, and a mad glee filled her. Then Desi was climbing within her, scrambling into her mouth like so much black smoke. She filled Dusty's skin, taking up all those empty places until they were one body, one thought, one mind. Until Dusty was back in the world of the living and clawing bloody furrows into Diesel's forearms. Her eyes rolled into the back of her head, the last coherent thing in her mind was the screaming.

*Endless.*

*Terrifying.*

***

Dusty opened her mouth, and for just a split second, Diesel could have sworn a hand, rotting and gray, nail beds dark with dirt, reached for him. He flinched back, disbelieving, eyes wide. He gasped as something heavy struck him full force in the chest, flying backward. Rolling to his feet, Deisel reached for an abandoned bowling ball and lifted it above his head. Sneering at Dusty's convulsing form as he brought it crashing down.

An armored car slammed full force through the front doors of the Rinky Dink. The wall crumbled around the front half of the truck, taking part of the roof with it. The *whomp-whomp-whomp* of helicopter blades and the scream of sirens flooded the bowling alley as searchlights, bright and inescapable, danced across the hood of the vehicle.

The driver's door flew open, and Edward stumbled out. In the movies, the cadre of police officers who followed him there would have opened fire as soon as his feet hit the ground. At the very least, someone would have issued a warning - explained that to move was to die. But as far as Diesel could tell, the police were too tied up with the Brotherhood to do much of anything at all.

Joey limped out of the coat room, laughing his ass off. "Holy fuckin' shit," he crowed.

Edward turned at the sound, but it wasn't Joey he sought. His eyes landed on Dusty first, bloody and pale, the bowling ball next to her head where its weight had cracked the wood floor. Then, inevitably, to Diesel standing over her. His expression turned murderous and he covered the distance in just a few long-legged strides.

"Pretty boy," Diesel began, trying on an affable smile. "Dusty—"

***

Edward hit him so hard the crunch of bone reached Dusty even from a foot away. He followed Diesel to the ground, fists flying mercilessly, teeth bared with effort. Head aching, Dusty sat up. Her mouth was dry, and she hurt all over. Joey helped her get to her feet, and she nodded her thanks.

"Go," she rasped, her voice practically gone.

The first time Diesel had tried to kill her, it had taken years to recover. This attack didn't feel as serious as the first, but she wouldn't know the extent of the damage until she found a hospital. One far, far, away from here.

Joey looked between her and Edward, nodded, and limped toward the back of the building. There was a hidden entrance under the desk in the office where Dusty had first woken up. Once he was in the tunnels, he could catch up with Ape and

Poppy. It was obvious by now that Eliot was long gone, and Dusty wondered if she'd ever see him again, or if she even wanted to.

The meaty thwack of Edward's fist against Diesel's face was like a heartbeat, the bass of her favorite song. Diesel begging beneath the onslaught, his face already twisted and swollen to twice its size, was the sweetest treble. If Edward kept it up, he'd kill him.

A second searchlight joined the first, the speed of the rotors kicking up dust and dirt as it circled the hole in the Rinky Dink. Dusty pushed her hair out of her face. *"Smile bitch,"* a voice chuckled from deep within her mind. *"You're on the six o'clock news."*

Limping over to Edward, she placed a hand on his shoulder. With anyone else, she might have been afraid that one touch would be enough to make him turn on her. But she knew better.

The muscles in his arms bunched as he reared back to hit Diesel one more time.

Struggling to breathe, the other man fell limp. Dusty wanted to let Edward finish the job, but she knew what it was like to kill a man, and Edward - her sweet, clumsy Edward - didn't deserve the nightmares.

She wrapped her fingers around his wrist, marveling at how small her fingers were against his skin. "Got you, Ma moitié," she rasped, voice barely a whisper. Edward turned his head, an animal scenting the air, and caught her eye. Reaching out, she brushed the hair from his forehead. "See?"

He didn't say anything. He didn't have to. He abandoned Diesel, bloody and broken on the ground, and came to her. Wrapping his arms around her waist, he lifted her off her feet.

Dusty wrapped her legs around his waist, holding him tight.

"Is that a grenade in your pants," he asked, voice muffled. "Or are you just happy to see me?"

Dusty lifted a brow. "Why not both?"

"Freeze!" a voice shouted. "Hands up! Now!"

"There's no going back after this," she warned. Her throat might never heal, but she had to get the words out; she had to give him one more chance to run away. Edward looked up at her, Icarus ready and willing to *burn*, and she pressed an open-mouthed kiss against his lips.

The clink of the pin against the ground was muffled by the sound of the helicopter. Dusty tossed the explosive toward the opening in the building, and the panicked "Oh Shit!" that followed brought a smile to her face. Edward took off with her, sliding behind the concession stand just as flames rocked the world and brought it all crashing down in a plume of acrid, gray, smoke.

# Epilogue

There was a Camero idling a few feet from the strip club, but the people inside didn't seem interested in Tuesday's discount tiddies. The valet offered to park the car for them, but the big guy in the driver's seat muttered something about it being a rental and sent him on his way. A few minutes passed, and from inside of the strip club, a commotion broke out. The doors flew open, and a blond man the size of a mountain and a curvy black girl stumbled out onto the street. They crawled into the Camero, sliding past a Korean woman in a bloody tutu, to crowd into the backseat alongside a third man. The car peeled off, and the man watching from the bar across the street sent a quick text to Papa before turning back to his drink.

He lifted a hand, smiling at the server as she came to stand by his side.

"Want another drink or something?" she asked, leaning in close.

"Nah," Eliot said with a shake of his head and a smile that was almost sad, if you knew where to look. "You can close my tab. I already got what I came for."

*THE END*

# FIND ME OUT IN THE WILD